Faery Tales, Mermaid Myths, and Other Fantastical Legends

Vol 1

Alexa Asagi Andres

Copyrighted, 2014, all rights reserved by Alexa Asagi Andres
Faery Tales, Mermaid Myths, and Other Fantastical Legends Vol. 1

Published by Yawn's Publishing
198 North Street
Canton, GA 30114
www.yawnspublishing.com

All rights reserved. No part of this book may be reproduced or transmitted in any form, electronic or mechanical, including photocopying, recording, or data storage systems without the express written permission of the publisher, except for brief quotations in reviews and articles.

The information in this book has been printed as submitted. All images used were submitted for this publication. We assume no liability for the accuracy of the information presented or any images used without permission.

Library of Congress Control Number: 2015909389

ISBN13: 978-1-943529-02-5 paperback

Printed in the United States

Special thanks to Darla Andres for the gorgeous artwork and for the heart-warming pre-tales: The Faery Queen and Dancing Tomacina,

Love you my darling!

Also special thanks to Gloria Davis for providing the lovely interior artwork!

Several of these tales were written either in honor of, or at the request of, real humans.

The following feature appearances by:
The Faery Queen -- Alexa Andres ((Written by Darla Andres))
The Bard And The Harpy -- Aarick Fariest
The Cake Elf -- Victoria McDaniels
The Costume Maker -- Sarah McSwain
The Dark Woods -- Nicole Long
The Dragon Mother -- Darla Andres
The Elf And The Bees -- Roderick Williams
The Faery Friends -- Darla Andres
The Faery Mother- Darla Andres
The Faery Pugs- Farris Yawn
The Faery Spring -- Shirley Pukett
The Flower Faery -- Branda Ondick
The Grandfather That Sings -- Harold Davis
The Grandmother Who Moved Boulders -- Gloria Davis
The Laughing Faery -- Ellie Davis
The Story Weaver -- Marie Godfry
The Troll Who Ate Dishes -- Tony Andres
The Wish Granter -- Jamie, Desiree, Rebbecca, and Emma Stewart
The Wizard's Garden -- Scott Sellers
The Wonderful Magical Stevie -- Stevie Turner
The Yorkie Who Swallowed Pixie Dust -- Isabo McKenzie Andres

On second thought, are they really fully human after all??

Contents

The Faery Queen	1
The Alpha And The Queen	3
The Bad Summer	9
The Bard And The Harpy	16
The Bears, The Ferret, And The Food	25
The Bubblegum Witch	32
The Cake Elf	42
The Chocolate Brewer	46
The Costume Maker	57
The Dancing Tiger	63
The Dark Woods	69
The Determined Mother	78
The Dragon Mother	93
The Elf And The Bees	103
The Faery Friends	108
The Faery Mother	111
The Faery Pugs	115
The Faery Spring	120
The Fire Prince	126
The Flower Faery	134
The Fox Who Became A Princess	137
The Grandfather That Sings	144
The Grandmother Who Moved Boulders	151
The Heartless Jackal	155
The Invention of Ancient Clay	167
The Jaguar And The Lady	175
The King Of Crocodiles	180
The Laughing Faery	187
The Love Of The Moon	192
The Mechanical Heart	198
The Night Children	210
The Owl And The Snowy Forest	222
The Pig's Restaurant	226

The Prince Of Mordackee	235
The Princess Dresses	242
The Queen Of Beasts	246
The Quiet Banshee	252
The Ram And The Crab	260
The Shark Spirit	274
The Skeptical Vampire	282
The Story Weaver	287
The Sun King And The Moon Queen	290
The Troll Who Ate Dishes	293
The Unicorn Queen	304
The Vampire And The Faery	311
The Vampire Who Loved The Sun	319
The Wish Granter	334
The Wizard's Garden	338
The Wonderful Magical Stevie	344
The Yorkie Who Swallowed Pixie Dust	347
The Zinnia Flowers	352

Alexa Asagi Andres

The Faery Queen

Once upon a time in a realm not so far from our own, there lived a faery named Alexa.

This faery was the most beautiful in all the land as she had long red hair, the fairest of skin and the brownest of eyes.

Alexa had the unusual color of copper wings and her head was adorned with a jeweled headband serving as her crown signifying her as the Reigning Queen of the Faery Realm.

Alexa was covered in jewelry; mounds of necklaces and arms full of bracelets.

These were gifts from those she touched; reminders of her love for them.

Having said that, Alexa had the kindest of hearts.

She was not materialistic at all as she found joy in the most simple of things like Ni-hi grape soda and ice cream; actually those two things were her passions.

Although Alexa was Queen of the land of faery creatures, she often crossed over into the human world.

Because faeries are magical, they're self-sustaining for the most part however, humans are not.

This distressed her greatly to see children in emotional pain.

She made it her mission to help free human children from this terrible bondage.

Whenever Alexa crossed over to help a child in need she took with her Isabo, her constant companion.

Isabo was a large white wolf with piercing blue eyes and served as her protector.

They were together from the beginning as they were very old souls.

When Alexa heard a child cry she spread her wings over them and fluttered copper dust on them as this is the most healing of minerals.

She then would work her magic as she whispered her message of love in their ears.

Even though some could not see her they were aware of her loving presence and could feel the warmth of her hands in theirs.

She would stay by their side as long as they needed her and would leave only when they were ready to let go.

She then would retreat back home to the faery realm to regenerate as it took so much of her spiritual energy for each healing.

Although she had more magical powers than any, it was and still is her monumental love for children that she remains Queen of all mystical, magical beings.

She is completely individual, like no other.

These things are true; I know, for I am her Mother.

Alexa Asagi Andres

The Alpha And The Queen

Once upon a time

In a land of many kingdoms

There lived a werewolf

He was a beautiful wolf with dark hair and bright eyes and who commanded respect from those around him

It was no surprise that at only age nineteen, he became the Alpha of his pack

Though this was less the werewolf's choice, and more of an obligation than anything

For many months, he did just what the old Alpha had done

And he received the same amount of respect in return

The werewolf found, however, that being a leader was rather tiring, and doing it with the same amount of toughness that his old Alpha had only made him even more exhausted

For little to anyone's knowledge, the werewolf was not actually tough or stern at all

In fact, he was rather sweet, soft, and kind

He once let a stray cat have kittens in his bedroom and had the most popular bird feeder in the neighborhood

And it didn't take long for someone to notice that either

"Please just .. stay here... I will be right back with food... please don't leave," the werewolf said in a hushed tone as he slowly backed away from the squirrel on his deck

"I really admire that you know, how you're taking care of that squirrel,"

The werewolf screamed and jumped, nearly running into the wall as he re-

Faery Tales, Mermaid Myths, And Other Fantastical Legends

entered his home

Upon recovering from his near heart attack he looked up, seeing a beautiful faery woman standing in front of him

"Who are you!?" he screamed

"Oh! I'm Meadow, the newly elected Faery Queen? I'm going around the surrounding kingdoms meeting the other leaders and introducing myself," she smiled

The faery- Meadow- had long silver hair down to her ankles, bright magenta eyes, and wings that had patterns the werewolf didn't even know existed

She was definitely unusual looking...

"And by 'meeting' you mean 'breaking into houses'?" he asked with a frown

"I didn't break in, your door was unlocked and then I heard you talking to that DARLING little squirrel- which, by the way, good for you," she smiled

"I was not talking to the squirrel," the werewolf protested

"Yes, yes you were um- Sam? Was it Sam?"

"Shawn,"

"Right, sorry, ack, Shawn, you were DEFINATELY talking to the squirrel,"

"There is no squirrel,"

"You promised him food,"

"I .. you heard nothing," he said pointedly, huffing as he looked for the sunflower seeds in his pantry

"Whatever you say Alpha Shawn," Meadow hummed

"Please don't call me that... I don't even like my own PACK calling me that," he sighed

"Then what do they call you?" she asked curiously

"In public? Alpha, in private? Shawn, never the two at the same..... you know what? I have no idea why I'm telling you this, it was nice to meet you Meadow, but I have pack things to do,"

".... Is the squirrel part of your pack?"

He dropped the sunflower seeds- which he had JUST found- in that moment

Truthfully, Shawn wished he could say with any amount of honesty that that was the last run in he had with the Faery Queen, but it was far from it

Somehow she managed to show up two days later at the grocery store too

"ALL I'm saying is that you should consider keeping four kinds of ice cream, your freezer is big enough, would it REALLY kill you?" complained one of Shawn's betas as they walked through the store

"No but it would kill YOU, don't you have a sensitivity to milk?" he pointed out

"It's a minor sensitivity, ice cream is exempt,"

"ICE CREAM is exempt but you complain about it every single time someone offers you yogurt?" he argued

Before the other werewolf even had time to defend himself a loud "HI!" was shouted from the other end of the aisle and Shawn accidentally ripped open the bag of sunflower seeds he was holding

That woman's voice could cut through glass, he swore it

"I didn't know you shopped here Shawn!" Meadow cried excitedly as she fluttered towards him, because apparently walking was a concept that faeries wanted nothing to do with

"And I didn't know you were friends with the Faery Queen," the other werewolf said with a touch of jealousy in his voice

".... This is new," and the Alpha never did clarify who he was talking to

"Oh buying more sunflower seeds? Did your squirrel friend eat all of the others already or was that the birds? That's a bigger bag than you had last time, are you going to feed them both now?" Meadow asked excitedly

Slowly, Shawn could feel himself starting to twitch

"You're feeding birds now?" his beta asked

"He's feeding a squirrel- darling little creature, I think he might have been hurt- I don't know if he's feeding birds yet," Meadow explained

"I am not feeding birds, I am not feeding squirrels, I LIKE sunflower seeds," he explained

"Then why aren't you getting the ones on the snack aisle instead of this giant bag on the pet aisle?" Meadow asked innocently

Shawn had to deal with the next pack meeting's discussion topic revolving around how popular his bird feeder was and people asking him where the feeder for the squirrels was

He was not thrilled, to say the least

As if things couldn't get any worse, the third time Meadow unexpectedly dropped in on his life was when he was leaving the bookstore....

It wasn't as simple as it sounded....

"You read to children on the weekends? That is SO darling!"

The sudden sound of another voice when the air had previously been populated only with the sounds of birds chirping and wind rushing caused Shawn to walk straight into an open door

This was really turning out to be a bang-up week

"How do you know what I was doing? I have a shopping bag in my hands, why do you assume-"

"I was watching you silly! I was picking up this book about squirrel care-"

"PLEASE don't say it's for me...."

There was a short pause

"-For this Alpha I know..."

He groaned

"And I happened to hear your very distinct voice wafting through the store so when I went to say hello I saw you reading to the children! And the way you did the voices for those imaginary friends? Just PRECIOUS, I couldn't have done it better myself!"

"I'm glad I have your approval but please, don't TELL people about this one," he said cautiously

Meadow stared at him, completely taken aback

"But... why not?"

"It's bad enough you exposed me about the birds- and the squirrels- but I can't have anything else... cutesy.... cluttering up my reputation,"

Meadow snorted a laugh, even though it looked like she was trying not to

"What reputation?"

He frowned, he thought given the way she had dropped on him that she had heard of him...

"I'm Shawn Avery? Took over for Jenna Avery? Fierce, tough, stern Alpha Werewolf from the Ausmend Coast Pack?" he added in confusion

"'Fierce, tough, and stern'? Please, you are SUCH a sweetie! How can anyone actually believe that?"

"I make sure they believe it, no one respects an Alpha who they think is too 'soft'," he replied as he opened the trunk of his car

"Oh now that is simply NOT true," Meadow protested

"Maybe it's different for faeries but for werewolves that's how it is, Alphas have to be tough but fair, stern but compassionate, it's a difficult balance to keep, but we need to be the picture of strength, not ... nursing squirrels and reading to children on the weekends," he explained

"Why can't you be both? Does it really affect your abilities as a werewolf- or as a leader for that matter that you happen to feed injured squirrels?"

"Yes, but that just isn't how it's done,"

"That may not be how your old Alpha did it, but do you really want to copy her exactly? I know you loved her and were loyal to her like the rest of your pack and I'm sure she was great... but maybe there were things that could have been improved on, maybe there are things you can do to improve it... and maybe just being yourself, softness and all, will be what the pack needs," she suggested

Shawn gave that a lot of thought, and finally decided that maybe, just maybe, Meadow was right, and he decided in that moment to ease up on the pack and run things the way HE felt they should be run

"This doesn't mean I'm not tough as nails though, when I need to be," he added, putting the books in the trunk

"You're about as tough as a chocolate chip cookie," Meadow grinned

"And those can get pretty tough if you leave the box open for days at a time!" he huffed in annoyance

"Whatever you say~" the Faery Queen laughed back

From that day the two of them became known as quite an unusual pair

The Faery Queen who occasionally helped the werewolf pack

And the Alpha Werewolf who sometimes visited with the faery kingdom

It was a strange give-and-take sort of relationship but it worked

And when they married three years later, they realized that it still worked

Being the kind, gentle person that Shawn really was actually DID improve things in the pack

There were times when he regretted not being as loud and stern as he thought he needed to be, but at the end of the day, overall, things were working better this way

And he had a very nosey Faery Queen to thank for it

Alexa Asagi Andres

The Bad Summer

Once upon a time

In a land overlapping our own

There was a girl who seemed to have very bad luck

This girl was named Felicia- an odd name, considering her luck was generally more bad than good

And one summer in particular was a VERY bad summer

It was as if every single day she woke up with a renewed purpose of being miserable

The year wasn't great to start out with, she had a horrible cavity in January

Her computer crashed beyond repair in February

Her bank account was hacked into in March

Tax season took nearly every penny in April

And then summer began

Between the months of May and June her car had broken down twice

Her dishwasher failed and her internet was out for three days

She sprained her ankle AND her dog became so sick that she nearly died

She lost her wallet in a busy mall

AND her air conditioning had gone out for THREE DAYS- the hottest three days of the year at that, as June was even hotter than usual this year it seemed

Now, mid-July, Felicia was really quite done with the world

Faery Tales, Mermaid Myths, And Other Fantastical Legends

It was at the advice of her father that she go away with him and her mother on an old-fashioned family vacation

Like the kind they had when she was a little girl

Only.... not exactly.... because the bad luck seemed to continue...

On the eight hour drive to the beach they'd be spending the week at, they had gotten horribly lost

Six hours in she realized she had left her swimsuit at home

They got stuck in a traffic jam due to road work that left them stuck in the same spot for over an hour

And by the time they finally dragged themselves into the hotel....

The hotel had lost their reservations....

Felicia, once again, was quite done

Except she wasn't quite as done as she thought she was...

That evening, long after her parents had gone to bed, Felicia found that she couldn't sleep

She didn't really know WHY she couldn't sleep

Just that she couldn't

So she resolved to go make herself some tea and hope and pray that it would help her sleep

Of course that in itself had been a disaster

She had bumped into the stove and bruised her leg, nearly dropped the cup of the boiling water (but had in fact managed to spill some on her hand) and hit her head when trying to clean the spilled water off of the counter

She was beginning to think she was cursed...

It was during the preparation of this tea, though, that something quite amazing- and really very lucky- happened

She turned back to the counter to get the tea bag to put into her water and there, standing on the counter, reaching for the bowl of fruit that was sitting out... was a troll...

It wasn't a terribly ugly troll...

But it wasn't all that attractive either...

It was a small, kind of rounded creature, with big elephant-like ears and a bulbous nose, chubby and stubby and waddling towards the fruit basket...

Or at least it had been until it caught Felicia's attention....

At that moment the troll paused, making a terrified squeaking sound and standing still, arms still raised, staring frightfully at the human

Felicia, despite her bad luck, bad day, and generally bad mood, always put kindness first, and so moved slowly and gently towards the troll, picking up an apple from the basket and handing it to the small creature

The troll made a scratched, squeaking noise again, as if uncertain that she was really giving the apple to him, before wrapping both chubby arms around the apple and running to the other end of the counter and taking a bite out of the apple, staring almost defiantly at Felicia in the process

The troll's antics were amusing, even though the lack of trust was somewhat disheartening, and she plucked some grapes from the bowl under the apples, setting them in front of the troll as well

The troll seemed rather conflicted, not wanting to let go of the apple but not wanting to pass up the grapes either

After a few tense moments the little creature reached out with one hand- keeping the other firmly on the apple- and grabbed a grape, shoving the entire thing into his mouth and chewing roughly as he tried to eat the thing hole

Felicia found it charming- so charming in fact that she began to laugh, and sat and watched the troll eat....

....And eat.....

.....And eat.........

.....And eat..............

The troll ate for three hours without stopping!

The troll ate apples, grapes, bananas, tomatoes, potatoes, carrots, even raw cloves of garlic!

Basically, anything and everything that was in easy reach and required no preparation

Finally, after three hours had passed and the kitchen was wrecked, Felicia was too exhausted to stay up any later and the troll was too stuffed to continue eating

"Well this was fun," Felicia said as she stood up

"I really have to go to bed now though,"

The troll seemed dismayed at this idea and began to squeak and squawk and try to roll over onto his feet- with no success

Felicia smiled and helped the little troll up, starting to walk away again when she heard a grunt of protest and the troll's little hands tugging on her own

"You want to come with me?" she asked in surprise

The troll grunted again in response, tugging harder on her hand

"Alright, alright, come on then," she sighed, picking up the small creature and walking towards her room again

She turned one last time and cringed at the extreme mess in the kitchen

Oh well... it was vacation after all.... she'd find some way to explain it in the morning....

Only, to her complete and utter shock, she didn't have to...

Because when she returned to the kitchen the next morning, it was completely clean, spotless, even better, in fact, than it had been when they first arrived

She could only assume it had been the troll who had done something so kind

Later that day she found a lucky penny and when they went to the amusement park down the road she won every game she played

That night the troll returned and polished off the left over pizza, breadsticks, and a gallon of yogurt

He didn't seem nearly as hungry as he had the night before and Felicia wondered how long it had been since he'd had a proper meal

That night the troll slept in her room again and when she woke in the morning she found a clean kitchen that was also stocked with donuts, pastries, and other breakfast items that her parents both swore they didn't buy

She hit a high score on her favorite video game, found a wonderful new series at the used bookstore she visited and was able to get the entire set for only $10, and when she went to the beach that afternoon it was clear skies and warm weather- but not so clear and warm that she felt overheated or got a sunburn from it

That night she expected the troll's return and had made sure to order extra room service after her parents had gone to bed

He ate a full steak dinner, a chicken appetizer, two bowls of soup, and half the giant brownie she had ordered for herself

Incidentally the troll seemed to regret at least some portion of that meal as he whined and groaned a few times in the night from what Felicia assumed to be a bellyache

"You are an expensive little creature," she mused as she stared in horror at the room service bill

The next morning she woke up to hear her parents screaming like she had never heard before

They had just won the state lottery

The troll, Felicia began to realize, was either very very lucky...... or very very magical....

That night she gave him an entire pot of spaghetti and a big salad

The next day at the zoo and aquarium she was able to hold a koala and got kissed by a dolphin

The next night she fed him pot roast and three deli sandwiches

And that day she won tickets to see her favorite musical on a radio show that she had only entered in by chance

The luck continued on and on...

The old beaten up car she had been struggling to drive was replaced with a brand new one after someone had hit the car when it was parked and in order to avoid legal action the offender left her an anonymous check for a new car

The drive home was easy, fast, and fun- which was really saying something for eight hours in the heat of early August

And when she got home her dog was better than ever

But it wasn't just the nice things and lucky luxuries that Felicia liked about the troll

She truly cared about him as a person

She gave him medicine for his bellyaches (of which there were many)

And bought him crayons and coloring books to entertain himself with while she was at work (it became apparent after her vacation ended that he was never actually going to leave again and after the incident with the lipstick and her dog... well... needless to say the creature needed some entertainment...)

She sensed when he was getting homesick and took him out to the woods behind her house to frolic and was blessed to venture into the faery realm that he came from

She understood little of what was going on in that realm as the language was so foreign to her own, but she did know she enjoyed it there

Apparently entrances to the faery realm are only in certain places and the poor little troll had gotten stuck too far away from one of them- or lost, perhaps- and was unable to get home or fend for himself

Now though, he was having such a good time with Felicia that he merely decided to stay with her

She eventually had to give him a name, being that after months of trying to communicate, the most she could get out of him was a grunt or a squeak, and due to all that had transpired over the last several months, that autumn in late October, she finally gave the troll a very appropriate name

She named him "Lucky"

The Bard And The Harpy

Once upon a time

In a land many villages from our own

There lived a bard who played beautiful music

His music, in fact, was so well beloved, that it spread far away from his own village, across to other villages, and even into the inner workings of the kingdom

Those in the kingdom who heard of his music were impressed, but also a bit skeptical

How could someone of such talent have escaped their attention?

They simply were unable to understand it

The queen, however, understood it perfectly

"Bring the bard to me," she instructed

"I have a job for him,"

The queen's men did as they were instructed and by the next days' time they had returned with the villager who played such lovely music

"Tell me your name," the queen demanded

"Aarick," he answered quickly

"What an interesting name," the queen mused, leaning forward

"I hear that your music is quite charming," she added

"I've heard the same," Aarick replied

The queen seemed to be amused at this, smirking as she leaned back in her throne

"I see, well then how would you like to put your skills to the test?" she challenged

"And how would I do that?" Aarick asked curiously

Faery Tales, Mermaid Myths, And Other Fantastical Legends

"Up north, there's a nest of harpies that have been causing quite a bit of trouble lately and you know, since harpies hate music, perhaps you can play outside their cave and... detour them," she suggested, shifting again as her long, floor-length gown moved with her

Aarick looked on at the court uncomfortably, his skills had never been tested or used for means besides joy and playing for the sake of playing, he wasn't sure how to react to this new... musical combat idea....

In fact he wasn't even sure how to feel about it...

But a queen's order was a queen's order, who was he to disobey it?

Apparently, Aarick was someone quite special, that's who

For as he arrived to the caves and cliffs that the harpies resided in he pulled the bow from his pack and then the violin, taking a breath and running the bow over the strings a few times to make sure all was in working order, before he pulled his arm back and began to play

He played whatever he could think of, both old and new

He played songs from legends and lore to songs that were just to be songs and nothing more

He played anything and everything and within less than an hour the harpies had come from their caves and were sitting around in a circle listening to him

Even the children, who were considered to be almost impossible to see by humans and tell the tale

But here was Aarick, not only witnessing just that (and still living to his knowledge) but being the reason they came out in the first place

He was so stunned that for a moment he had stopped playing, and he didn't realize it until it was too late and the leader of the harpies was walking towards him, slow and steady like a cat stalking prey

"You play beautiful music," she commented

Aarick was surprised- no... surprised wasn't the word, SHOCKED was far more like it!

"I do?" he asked in shock

"Yes you do, we like it quite a bit," she agreed

"You do!?" he repeated

"Yes," she repeated with a smile

"I thought harpies hated music," he admitted, looking a bit sheepish and quite a bit more worried as he set his violin down

"Yes, we started that rumor to detour knights and hunters from finding out our true weaknesses and harming us, clever hm? You don't look like the usual though," she mused

"That's because I'm not a knight or a hunter, I'm.. I'm just a bard, a musician, that's all," Aarick said quickly

The harpy stalked around him in circles, the feathers of her raven black wings scraping the ground as she walked

"And why would they send you here alone?"

"To detour you, to... make you move along? Queen Vianna says that you've been wrecking villages," the musician said

"WRECKING VILLAGES? HA! 'Queen Vianna' you say, lies like a rug," the harpy scoffed, turning quickly on her heel to face him

"Why would she lie?" he asked in confusion

"Because she always does things like this, she's always BEEN doing things like this ever since we were children,"

"You knew her as a child?" Aarick asked in surprise

"Yes, you could say we knew each other, we were sisters after all... well... half-sisters anyway,"

"Wait... please, what's going on here?" he frowned, placing his violin and his bow back in his pack and staring at the harpy with determination to find out what he had really gotten himself involved in

"Sit, bard, it's a long story," she instructed, quickly flying up to a high perching rock and sitting on the edge as she began to speak

"In the past, the king had a wife named Gillian, she was a harpy... as well as my mother, no one knew she was a harpy however because our clan- our nest- is very talented, we're special, able to shapeshift at will, unlike most harpies, we can bring about any feature or disguise any feature as we please... or... we used to be able to at least, my mother died when I was only five, long before she could tell me the secret to our abilities, the king knew this, but knew nothing of harpies himself, in fear of public outcry that his daughter was a harpy he remarried to someone who closely resembled my mother, Jullian, and simply had the word spread like a virus that this was the true queen and her name had merely been mispronounced all those years ago, the queen had a daughter- that would be Vianna- and the king announced that the child had been stillborn to prevent the idea that there were two children, it was all a very clever ruse and in fact, for about five years, I believed that Jullian was my mother, the maids and knights did such a good job of proclaiming she was queen and she did so well at imitating my mother that I found myself falling for it, at least... until I turned thirteen, when a harpy turns thirteen their wings start to grow in, that's when I was sent away to the mountains to live with the rest of my clan, and that's when Vianna officially took my place, when we were children we acted like sisters and we were very close, I'm not sure what happened in the ten years that I've been gone from the kingdom but whatever it is has turned Vianna against me and she's been out for my blood for the past three years, since she took the throne, she was always a bit of a spoiled child, and quick to blame others for her own misgivings, but I never thought she would be like this," the harpy foretold

"So she's faking attacks on her own village to get you banished from the area- or worse- so she doesn't ever have to worry about you contesting the crown, am I following so far?" the bard asked calmly as he leaned against the tree behind him

"That's right," the harpy confirmed

"But why would she worry about that? Even if you did contest it you can't claim anything if people know you're a harpy, didn't you hear about that terrible werewolf malfunction in the east city? Humans are too ignorant and paranoid to allow themselves to give up even a breath of control to someone other than one of their own crooked selves with a pedigree,"

"True, but they wouldn't have to know I'm a harpy if I could learn to control my features,"

"How would you do that?"

The harpy easily jumped down from her perch and strode over to him, claws tapping gently against her forearms as she stepped towards the bard

"An egg,"

"An EGG?"

"A very special egg,"

"What kind of egg?" he asked skeptically

"The egg our clan keeps our secrets in, it's a jeweled egg that was crafted many generations ago when my clan first learned to control our bird sides, the process can be modified to suit other shapeshifters or hybrids, however, like centaurs or werewolves or... lamia, I'm sure you can see why we wouldn't want it getting out to everyone in creation, so it was locked away in a jeweled egg that my mother had, to this day it's somewhere in the castle and although I have an idea of where that somewhere is I can't get in long enough to search," she said with a sad pause

The bard was quiet for a moment before standing up and holding his hand out towards her

"I'm Aarick, by the way, I think I know a way I can help you,"

The harpy stared at him for a brief moment before taking his hand in her larger, taloned one

"Viviann, I'd be pleased to hear your suggestions,"

And so Viviann and Aarick spent the next few hours discussing their plan and how to go about it before putting it into action

It would take a lot of luck for this to work, but they were hoping that luck would be on their side

Once the sun began to set a wonderful music filled the castle

The same bright, lively, and beautiful music that had been played for the harpies earlier that afternoon

"What on earth? Who is in the castle and why are they here?" The queen asked suspiciously as she sent her guards to look after the sound

However, when the guards did not return, the queen began to get rather worried

She soon decided to peel away from her throne and slinked out of the throne room and into the hall, determined to find who was playing that music and to scold them for doing so quite so suddenly and without permission

It was this that gave Viviann the chance she needed to flutter into the throne room and stride towards the throne

The only noise made were her talons, tapping against the tile of the floor and the wood of the chair

She supposed that was one advantage of slowly turning more and more into a bird as she aged....

She reached behind the throne and gave the back of it a quick tap, smirking when she realized it was hollow and opening it with ease

Sure enough, sitting there in all its glory, was the very egg she was looking for

However, she was not ever one to leave a friend in need, and so she held onto the egg tightly and took off down the hall as fast she could

Luckily she managed to arrive just in time to see the queen backing Aarick into a corner

"You know something don't you? I don't see any evidence that you were where you said you were earlier," Vianna accused him as she moved closer

"That's because he's smart enough to see through your lies," Viviann replied as she took a step closer

There was a pause as Vianna turned around slowly, leaving Aarick where he was

"Come on big sister, are we really going to do this?" Vianna scoffed

"That's really up to you now isn't it?" Viviann replied softly

"Come on, just give me the egg," she insisted

"No, you don't deserve the egg, after all you've done and the deception you've held, this egg needs to be as far away from you as possible," she replied, moving suddenly and sweeping her wing down to catch on the hem of Vianna's dress, lifting it just enough to reveal a long, slithering snake tail

Vianna gasped, moving back again as the bard jumped in shock

"I see my mother wasn't the only family secret, you never learned to control yours either but yours is easier to cover up, you knew you would eventually have to learn though and that's why you hid the egg and suddenly started acting so cruelly to me, because you didn't want to risk my exposing you due to wanting the throne, is that right?" she accused

Vianna heaved a heavy sigh and looked down

"Yes, that's right, I hid the egg hoping to use it myself but I could never open it, and when I sent the bard to try to banish you I knew it would lead to your anger and your infiltration of the castle, I hoped I would have been able to weasel the secret out of you then but this turned in your favor in the end," she confessed

"Greed, is that what all this is about? Greed to hang onto the throne?" the bard finally chimed in

"It's bad enough you're hiding something like this from your kingdom... but to bestow such misery upon your sister..."

"Vianna," Viviann spoke suddenly

"I have an idea, why don't we learn how to control our powers together? Keep the throne, I never wanted it to begin with, all I do want is what my birthright, the right to be able to control my powers, that's it,"

Vianna was surprised at the honesty but more importantly the generosity of her sister, for it was something that she had not experienced in ten years

That day the two decided to do just that, learn how to control their powers together and live in peace with one another

And so Vianna, the lamia, learned to hide her tail at will and became a great, powerful... but most importantly, kind and humble queen

And Viviann, the harpy, learned to control when and how her wings manifested at any given time, and flew far from the city to live in a quiet village where she could be at peace

And the bard?

Why he was still playing music of course, in the village with Viviann, though make no mistake, when people heard of his great talent for playing music and began asking favors, Aarick turned them down with a polite "No thank you" and went back to his village

Alexa Asagi Andres

The Bears, The Ferret, And The Food

Once upon a time

In a land just out the back door of our own

There lived a family of bears

Three bears, to be exact

A mother, a father, and a baby

And instead of a little girl coming into the bear's home foraging for food... it was the bears going into the human's home to look for something to eat

It all started when the mother bear had to go out of town, across to the next woods over, to visit her ailing sister

She reluctantly left her husband and their baby alone, given that travel may not be the best thing for a young bear in the heat of summer

She promised her return within the week and her husband promised to look after and take care of their precious baby bear as well as possible...

There was just one problem...

The father bear absolutely failed at hunting, gathering, cooking, or otherwise providing food

That had always been his wife's job, while his was to keep the family safe and teach the baby the basics of how to be a bear

The first night was easy enough, the mother bear had caught fish for them earlier that day and the two remaining bears ate it happily and without problems

....

The second night was a disaster....

Faery Tales, Mermaid Myths, And Other Fantastical Legends

The father bear had tried for HOURS to catch fish with no luck

He had tried everything from using his mouth to his paws to his cunning wit

Why, he even fetched a net from one of the human camping grounds and tried to use that

But no matter what he did, he was just too clumsy to catch any fish

He'd move too quickly or stumble or fall into the water

He'd lose his balance and flail around and sneeze and make noise

He just couldn't seem to catch fish no matter what he did

So he tried to resort to the gathering technique

He DID manage to bring back berries....

But by the time he got them back home he was covered in welts and blotches and his face was swollen.... the berries, as it were, were highly toxic.....

He tried then going to one of the oldest bear-tricks in the book and tried to raid a campsite...

Even that he failed at, he crashed into the tent (the swelling in his face had limited his eyesight) and meandered around and hit his head on the RV door

He never did find any food but the baby bear at least managed to run in and pull aside a bag of potato chips

The third night the bears came to the conclusion that the father bear would not be in charge of finding food

However, the baby bear didn't know much about finding food herself and so ended up with, again, no more spoils than a bag of chips

By the morning of the fourth day they realized that this had to stop

They tried everything they could think of to find an alternative source of food, but nothing they tried seemed to work

... Until, that is, they stumbled upon a line of human houses not far from where their woods were

"If we can get in there, we could have all the food we could want!" the father bear mused excitedly

"But Daddy, how do we get in?" asked the baby bear in confusion

The father bear thought about that for a long moment before smiling, walking towards one of the trees

"Climb up here my darling, onto the deck, then I'll follow, we can surely open the door from there,"

Not knowing any better than to follow her father's instructions, the baby bear did exactly as she was told

At first it was rather easy and simple, climbing onto the deck was no problem and even getting the door to the house open wasn't difficult

However, actually finding the FOOD... well now that WAS a bit of a problem....

The father and baby bear spent a long time searching, and although they could smell the food DEFINATELY being in this room, they couldn't pinpoint just WHERE exactly it was...

So the two bears searched and searched... and searched and searched some more for where the food was, and upon determining its location, had immediate trouble in trying to figure out how to get in the spaces

They pushed and slammed and head-butted on the pantry and refrigerator doors but to no avail

Finally, after about twenty minutes of this, a ferret bounded around the corner to greet them

"What are you two doing here making all this noise?" the ferret huffed

"We're searching for food but can't open these human storage containers," the father bear said

"And we're hungry Mr. Ferret... so so hungry," the baby bear sniffled

"Poor bears, these human contraptions can be hard," he mused, climbing over to the refrigerator with ease and clinging onto the freezer door while using all of his strength to pull the refrigerator door open and reveal unto them .... the glorious food....

He then bounded across to the pantry, climbed on the back of the kitchen chair, and easily opened that door as well

It was as if angels had begun to sing and the holy light had shown down on them....

And within an hour, nearly the entire kitchen had been devoured by the bears

The ferret- who had, make no mistake, taken part in the party- gathered some of the trash from the floor and nodded for the bears to do the same

Staring at each other in confusion, the bears each picked up some trash and followed the ferret into the next room, where they saw a human man sleeping on the couch

"He has back issues," explained the ferret with a shrug, dumping the trash at the man's feet

The bears stared at him curiously, not following

"When the humans wake up in a few hours they're going to blame SOMEONE for this mess, and I'd rather it NOT be me," the ferret explained

The bears nodded thoughtfully, thoroughly understanding that and spreading the trash around the sleeping human, the father bear even set an empty bag of potato chips on the man's chest

"Very nice touch," the ferret nodded

"Thank you,"

"Yes of course, my name is Russel by the way, call for me when you return, otherwise those pesky dogs, Brownie and Fudge, may come down here and try to stop you,"

The bears nodded immediately, smiling at him

"We will, thank you Russel," the father bear replied

And thus the process continued for another three nights

For three nights the two bears entered the human home and raided the kitchen with the help of Russel the ferret

And every morning the bears woke to the sound of a shrill, angry scream from a female human that consisted of things such as "HERMAN!!!" and "WHO EATS THREE BAGS OF CHIPS IN A NIGHT!?" and "YOU ARE GOING TO THE STORE TO REPLACE ALL OF THIS" and many many MANY words that the bears couldn't understand ... or didn't wish to repeat...

And every morning, the father bear couldn't help but snicker at what had transpired

He just couldn't help himself even though he knew it was wrong

And then, on the fourth night that the bears went into the house to steal the human food...

The mother bear returned, and found them there raiding the pantry

"ALFRED!" the mother bear cried

"What are you doing?! Stealing from the humans... you should be ASHAMED of yourself! LOOK at what you're teaching our daughter! That it's ok to steal when you have access to your own food? Oh for SHAME Alfred!"

"B-But Ellen you don't understand! I couldn't find food and the baby was hungry! What was I to do!?"

"That is to be discussed later, come Alfred, gather our daughter, we're leaving!" she huffed

The father bear thanked Russel one last time, picked up his daughter, and left, unable to help place the blame on the human this night

Though the next morning the fallout was the same

The morning after that, however, was VERY different...

"ALFRED!" the mother bear screamed, waking the father bear from his sleep stupor

He jerked up, looking around and seeing trash all around him

Empty chip bags and cookie boxes and candy wrappers and- .....

.....

He knew what was coming

"ALFRED! You stole from the humans AGAIN!? What is WRONG with you!? I'm home, I'm catching the food, and you go BACK and STEAL again!? WHAT are you teaching our child!?"

"B-But Ellen I didn't do it!"

"Oh and I suspect that it just sprouted legs and walked here on its own then? Or maybe the WIND did it, or oh I know, the baby toddled out on her own, went into the humans' house, and brought this back hm?"

It dawned on him then, as he heard the slightest, quietest giggling from the corner where the baby bear was, that yes that was EXACTLY what had happened

Although obviously his wife wasn't going to believe that and he accepted the beratement without question

There was a lesson here about "doing unto others" and "our children copy us", and if given the chance to go back in time and change things...

Who was he kidding? He'd do the exact same thing because there is REALLY nothing like that barbeque sandwich and sour cream and onion potato chips he sampled from the second night!

The Bubblegum Witch

Once upon a time

In a land quite a bit different from our own

There lived a witch who everyone called The Bubblegum Witch

For, unsurprisingly, she was the inventor of bubblegum

The Bubblegum Witch was actually associated with candy

And sugar

And pastries

And anything that tasted sweet and caused children to bounce off the walls

She was loved and adored by all, even the parents who had to deal with the energetic children later

She brought sweetness to the land in the form of candy canes and candy corn and candy apples

In the form of sugar sticks and sugar cubes and sugar balls

In the form of chocolate and lollipops and gumdrops

If it was sweet and unhealthy, there was a pretty good chance that the Bubblegum Witch had a hand in bringing it to the land

However, not all witches are as dearly beloved as the Bubblegum Witch

There is in fact another witch who many children hate without ever meeting her

This witch has no special name or title

Because no one has bothered to give her one

She merely lives by the name she had been given as a child

Which, after years of being completely alone, she had forgotten completely

Why, one may wonder, would anyone have so much detestation for someone they didn't even know?

Well that was because of the witch's power

You see while the Bubblegum Witch brought forth everything sweet and sugary

This poor unlucky witch could bring forth only healthy greens

She could only grow and create vegetables

She couldn't even make fruit (that was another witch, far into the east, who was nicknamed the Berry Witch for her many patches of berries)

No one cared for vegetables, it was true

And the few people who did never got excited over them, that was for sure

So she was never asked a favor or introduced to anyone or ever really even spoke to anyone

She lived in a cottage on the hill surrounded by her garden in complete and utter misery

....

Until the Bubblegum Witch came to visit her

It was nearing October

That meant it was the Bubblegum Witch's busiest time of year

She had to make tons and tons of candy for the children for Halloween

And that's not even to mention that she, as a witch, had a moral obligation to celebrate Halloween herself

She was working hard night and day to get all the candy ready

And as if that weren't bad enough, she had to make other confections too

Like ghost-shaped cookies or chocolate-spider-cupcakes or....

Candy apples....

Now being that the Bubblegum Witch can only make sweet things, she has to get her apples from the Berry Witch in order to decorate them with candy and caramel

There was just one problem...

The Berry Witch was laid up with a cold and couldn't conjure anything if she tried

So, the Bubblegum Witch, not really understanding the difference, went to visit the other witch

The one who created vegetables

It was ... quite a different experience

"H-Hello?" she called, pushing open the door of the witch's cottage

"Yes?" she heard, gasping and turning around to see the other witch looming over her

"O-Oh... h-hello," she said with a nervous laugh

"Do you need something?" the other witch asked quickly

She was excited, so excited to finally have a visitor!

Finally someone interested in her power!

"I-I... um.... need to borrow some apples...."

Her excitement fell immediately and she sighed, leaning against the door

"I'm afraid I'm not who you need, I-"

"Yes yes I know, but she has a cold and is QUITE unavailable as it were, Halloween is next week and I need ATLEAST two hundred more apples to sweeten! Can't you help?" she asked desperately

"I'm afraid I really can't, I have no talent for apples, those are fruit, all I can create is... this stuff..." she sighed, picking up some carrots and celery and holding it out

The Bubblegum Witch stared at it curiously and picked up a carrot, taking an experimental bite

Her nose wrinkled a few times and she chewed it like a cat who had gotten ahold of something sticky

"Well," she said, clearing her throat

"I mean it isn't BAD.... it could just use some ... sprucing up! Like with chocolate!" she said excitedly

"Miss Bubblegum I don't think that's a good idea..." the other witch warned

It was too late when the Bubblegum Witch started hacking and coughing on the bad tasting product

"Ok... chocolate is out.... maybe a nice honey glaze..."

"I don't think my food can be sweetened," the other witch warned, carefully taking the carrots away

"Oh but what about peanut butter? I remember once about fifty years ago I put some on one of those green sticks for someone!" she grinned

The other witch stared at her for a moment

She clearly had never seen vegetables before....

"How are you even alive...?" she asked suspiciously

"Oho you silly goose! Witches who conjure food can live on what they make of course!" she laughed

That explained EVERYTHING much more clearly than the other witch had ever wanted it to be explained....

"Well I'm sorry but unless you want to caramelize celery- and really, you shouldn't- I just can't help you,"

"Oh but there must be SOMETHING you can do! Advice? A map to the nearest other fruity witch?" she begged

"Advice? Stop giving children things that will ruin their health,"

The Bubblegum Witch just giggled and snorted at her

"Oh dearie that's not- .. oh... what... what is your name?" she asked

The other witch looked down, fiddling with some lettuce

"I... I don't have a name...." she confessed quietly

"Oh why that's silly, everybody has a name!" the Bubblegum Witch insisted

"Not me... I... I forgot my name so long ago... because no one has asked for it in so many years..."

The Bubblegum Witch pitied the other witch, her heart aching for her

"I'll give you a new name then!" she resolved

"I-... I don't know... I'm really not talented at anything like you are,"

"Oh that's silly! You're very talented! You grow things out of the ground instead of making them pop out of thin air! That's talented!"

".... I think you're a bit backwards Miss...." she muttered

"Um, Sally... my.. my real name is Sally," she said shyly

"Your name is SALLY?" the other witch asked in shock

Of all the names the Bubblegum Witch could have had, she did not expect SALLY to be on the list....

"Yes, my parents were the hippies of their generation," she sighed

The other witch laughed softly and swayed on her feet

"NOW for a name for YOU! How about.... Victoria?"

The witch shook her head- that name was too strong and powerful for someone quiet and shy like her

"Scarlet?"

Another head shake, that name was too unique and special for a very ordinary and untalented girl like her

"How about... Gabrielle?"

The witch blinked at that, the name was soft and spoken of fondly and sweetly, it was gentle and graceful... it... felt suiting....

"I rather like that name," she said quietly

"Then your name shall be Gabrielle," she offered

The other witch- now named Gabrielle- nodded softly

"Miss Bub-"

"Just call me Sally,"

"...Sally, I might have a way to help you," she said

"Oh you can conjure apples after all!?" she asked excitedly

"Um... no, still can't do that... but I have an alternative," she said, walking towards her bedroom and rifling through the chest in the corner

"Gabby- if I can call you that- if you're about to pull out more of those orange sticks for me to chocolate-cover, I don't think that's gonna work..."

"Not at all, I'm pretty sure vegetables aren't meant to become candy," she insisted, pulling out a thin, old looking scroll and smiling

"What's that? A spell?"

"Sally not everything in the world is done by magic," she chuckled, untying the string on the scroll and laying it out on the table in the kitchen

"What's this?"

"A map, to a world where food isn't created by magic, I hear that apples there grow out of trees,"

"Out of TREES? How do you eat them? Do the people in this world have really long necks?"

"I believe you have to cut them loose from the branches my dear,"

There was a pause of silence

"Well that's violent," Sally commented

Gabrielle shrugged, walking out to the garden and moving over some spinach plants to reveal a rather large hole in the ground

"I have rabbits and other animals always digging around here, one of these is BOUND to lead to another land,"

"Well, I have nothing better to do today... do you?" Sally offered

"Nothing better to do all year, let's go," she confirmed

They did in fact find the land in which apples grew on trees, and once there they spent all day picking apples from a nearby orchard (despite Sally's constant concerns that they were hurting the trees)

By the time they left, in fact, they had gathered more fruit than should be humanly possible

Of course they ARE witches so that means what's "humanly possible" probably doesn't actually matter

They had gathered apples and berries and grapes

And melons and pineapples and bananas and just about everything they could find!

"I have GOT to use this.... 'candylope' in a pastry sometime!" Sally laughed excitedly as she took another bite of cantaloupe

"It isn't CANDYlope, its CANTELOUPE," Gabrielle corrected

Sally took another bite and shrugged

"It tastes like candy,"

There was another pause

"You're going to call it that and take credit for inventing it, aren't you?" Gabrielle accused

"Nah, I wouldn't do anything dishonest, and besides I already created bubblegum! That caused SUCH a fad... I didn't sleep for MONTHS!"

"Did you though? Did you REALLY create bubblegum?" Gabrielle asked skeptically

"Well of course I did! It was an accident actually, when I was a teenager I was trying to make gummy candies but the spell went all wrong and they were inedible... that's how bubblegum came about~"

"I see," Gabrielle mused

Sally smiled and snapped her fingers, handing Gabrielle an orange piece of gum

"Here, it tastes like that orange stick you gave me earlier, I bet you'll like it," she smiled

Gabrielle wasn't about to deny it

"Made especially for me? Why thank you," she smiled, popping the gum in her mouth

Sally hummed, getting a piece of gum for herself as she sat at the kitchen table and started caramelizing and candying apples

"What flavor is yours?" Gabrielle asked

"Pure sugar," Sally hummed

".... I really should have seen that coming...."

"Gabrielle?" Sally asked suddenly

The other witch looked up from where she had been making two salads (she was going to find a way for Sally to eat this thing, even if she had to cover it in some sort of dressing, she would just never believe that a person could live eternally healthy on nothing but sugar and colored dye)

"Yes Sally?" she asked

The other witch stood up suddenly and walked over to her, tugging on her hand

"You know... next month the BIG holiday season starts..."

"Yes I know,"

"We're all gonna be REALLY busy because of all the food people eat around that time of year..."

"Y-Yes I know..."

"Do you... will you help us?"

"Me? But what could I do?"

"Well you could use up some pumpkins- I've used those before- and some ... um... whatever it is you're making there... and I'm sure we can find a way to make those orange things edible! But.. I think we need your help, will you help us?" she asked softly

"It would be my greatest pleasure," Gabrielle smiled

"Oh lovely! You simply must teach me how to make food out of these things you grow Gabby!"

"I'll put it on my to-do list," Gabrielle smiled, turning back to the salads and seeing that Sally had taken a few leaves of spinach

Before she could warn her, the kitchen was filled with terrible hacking and sputtering sounds, like a cat trying to cough up a hairball

Gabrielle shook her head slowly

"Mark my words Bubblegum Witch, I'm going to force you to be at least 10% healthy even if it kills me,"

"I think, dear, it's much more liable to kill ME!"

And so from that day on the witch who made vegetables, Gabrielle, began helping to make food for the rest of the land again

With the Bubblegum Witch's endorsement people tried and surprisingly came to like it

Gabrielle even started getting visitors from time to time and had to move her cottage into the main witch's circle so people would know where to go

There, she and Sally spent their days together, each trying to convince each other of the merits of their own foods and coming up with different and new recipes to combine them

Sally never did try to market cantaloupe as candy (Thankfully...) but once she introduced the concept to the Berry Witch her own business skyrocketed too

Finally, after so many years, Gabrielle had a name and a place to belong, a real place to call her home

And she lived there, side by side, with the Bubblegum Witch

Faery Tales, Mermaid Myths, And Other Fantastical Legends

The Cake Elf

Once upon a time

In a land filled with sweets

There lived an elf

She was a very beautiful elf, with chocolate brown hair and a radiantly charming smile

And also, she was a baker

Specifically, she was a cake maker

She absolutely loved making cakes, every kind of cake she could

Big, small, short, tall

Of every color and shape and with every filling and frosting and flavor

She was a very talented baker and in fact became quite famous around the land for being able to make any request come to life

It started with small things, like putting strawberries on cookie cakes or forming a cake out of cupcakes

And slowly, the requests became bigger and more lavish, baking a cake with whole cherries on the inside or one that had a big pit of chocolate directly in the center

... Or a cake with real flowers on it or one that looked like a dog and barked when people came near it

These, she supposed, were easy enough, after all, the REALLY challenging ones were yet to come

And it all started.... with fireworks

"Miss Victoria! Miss Victoria!" shouted a little pink-haired pixie as she fluttered towards the elf

"I need a very special cake for my sister's anniversary!"

"Well of course, what can I get for you?" Victoria smiled brightly

"I need a strawberry cake with chocolate frosting and pink flowers on it,"

"I can do that," she smiled

"And I need it to shoot fireworks,"

There was a pause

"Um.... shoot fireworks?" she asked in slight confusion

"Yes, my sister had fireworks at her wedding, fireworks and pink flowers, so the cake needs fireworks and pink flowers," she explained

"Can we draw fireworks on the sides and have pink flowers in the center?" Victoria asked hopefully

"Hm.... no it has to shoot fireworks," the pixie replied with determination

The elf leaned back, thinking about that for a moment, before nodding slowly in confirmation

"Ok, I can do that, it'll be ready in three hours!" she smiled brightly

And just as promised, when the pixie returned to pick up the cake, Victoria had a beautiful pink floral cake waiting on her that shot fireworks whenever it was sliced into

This was the single action that lead to a chain of events that brought Victoria the title of the Cake Elf, because after the pixie took the cake home to her sister- who was equally as overjoyed- the word began to spread about the magnificent and unique cakes.... and the elf that made them

The next customer to request something as difficult as the firework cake was a mother who came in one day in the late afternoon looking for a cake for her daughter

"You want it to have goldfish in it?" Victoria asked in surprise

"No no, A goldfish, a REAL goldfish, in a bowl, swimming around, it's her first pet and I want to surprise her with it," the mother said enthusiastically

"Do you have a color scheme in mind?" the Cake Elf asked

"Mmm... would blue and orange work?"

"Blue and orange should work," she agreed with a smile

And sure enough, by the next day when the customer came to pick up the cake, it was done

A beautiful blue and orange vanilla cake with the fishbowl discreetly hidden in the center so that when the little girl sliced into it she would see her new goldfish swimming about in the bowl

"I need a cake made entirely out of steak," requested one customer

"STEAK?" Victoria asked

"Yes, my brother is having his first shift this full moon, it's a sacred thing in werewolf culture,"

"Do you want frosting..?" she asked, a little disgusted at the idea but she figured elves and werewolves probably had different diets

"Fudge if you please, with buttercream filling,"

She wasn't sure how but her gag reflex managed to stay unperturbed throughout the process

"And would you like that cooked or raw?"

"Cooked of course, medium well,"

And when she came back for the cake, Victoria had fulfilled the order with a steak-cake waiting on her

There was even a little wolf figurine to top it all off

"I need a cake that won't fall apart underwater for my mermaid girlfriend," requested one faery

"I need a cake that floats," requested another

"I need a cake that will flick you if you take more than your fair share,"

"I need a cake in the shape of a mouse that can run, for my cat's birthday,"

It took a lot of work and a lot of elven magic but without fail Victoria completed every order- and she did so with a happy smile on her face, no matter how difficult she found the work- or the customer- to be

And thus, she became known around the land as the Cake Elf, the maker of any pastry- especially cakes- that one could imagine

And when the end of the day came and Victoria was cleaning up the bakery, she found one, single cake left

A small vanilla one with buttercream frosting and a single flower drawn into the center

A smile crossed her face as she picked it up and opened the box, grabbing a fork and a plate

This happened to be her favorite

Faery Tales, Mermaid Myths, And Other Fantastical Legends

The Chocolate Brewer

Once upon a time

In a land a great distance from our own

There lived a werewolf

This werewolf was a very kind and gentle soul

He only wanted to make people happy

People around him that he didn't know

People around him that he did know

And honestly, he sort of wanted to make himself happy too

But unfortunately, some people just don't like the idea of people being happy

For the werewolf, who was so gentle that blue birds landed on the tips of his claws, was chased out of the village

And the next village

And the next

And the next

Until there were no villages left in the area and he was too tired and too sad to try any further

And so the werewolf left and he went further and further away from the humans who seemed to hate him so

He considered living in the woods, but that was too close to the humans, and it could get uncomfortable out there at times anyway...

And so the werewolf continued on until he found a tall, tall cliff with a cave just beneath its tip

He decided that this would be his new home and so he climbed up all the way to the cave and started to make it more to his liking

For a few months the werewolf lived there entirely alone

He had no company and no purpose

Until one day he decided that his boredom must be resolved and decided to leave the cave

He went back to the ground where he used to live and wandered into the forest, starting to gather herbs

The werewolf, you see, loved to cook- but more than that, he loved to bake

Cakes, cookies, doughnuts, turnovers, pies, anything that came out of an oven tasting sweet

He absolutely adored it

And so he stood in the forest, gathering some mint and cinnamon and other such spices for some baked goods, when he heard shouting near him

Lifting his head, the werewolf heard quite the commotion coming about and saw a group of angry people stomping his way

"There he is! There's the werewolf!" one shouted as he pointed at him

The werewolf fled from the woods, his basket of herbs and spices laying on the forest floor as he scurried back to his home to stay away from the fighting and anger that humans always carried towards him

He went back to his cave and stayed there, vowing never to return to the humans who hated him so deeply

It was a few hours later that he heard the fluttering of wings and poked his head out from his hiding spot in the very back of the cave to see if a bird had come to speak with him, which wasn't all that uncommon

Surely enough, a beautiful and sleek raven stood at the entrance to the cave with the werewolf's basket of herbs and spices in his beak

"You seem to have dropped this in your hurry to leave the forest," said the raven

"I'm sorry about that my dear friend, I was afraid and had to rush away in a hurry," the werewolf explained as he cautiously approached

"Do not worry dear werewolf, the humans are not the end of the world, there are others who will gladly be your friends," the raven said

"Thank you my friend... but I'm still afraid to leave again," he admitted shyly

The raven nudged the basket closer and nodded to him

"I understand, then in that case at least allow me to bring you things from the outside world so that you may retain some form of happiness," he offered

The werewolf thought about that for a moment before nodding his agreement

He wasn't sure if the raven would really bring him much of anything from outside his cave

After all his luck in the past was not ... great... when it came to friends

But to his surprise (and delight) the raven did not abandon him

And in fact, he and the raven became quite good friends

The raven often brought him new ingredients to work with and before long even started staying to help him bake

... Or supervise, at least

In fact, it was through this very thing, that the two discovered something that would change the world forever...

It was through experimentation in the kitchen that the werewolf and the raven discovered...

Chocolate

And what a brilliant discovery indeed!

The two became so enthralled by the taste that soon they were making it more than anything else

The raven loved it so much that he asked the werewolf if he may take some to his friends

And of course how could the werewolf possibly say no?

It didn't take long before the entire forest knew of this wonderful new thing called chocolate

From the birds to the foxes to the squirrels, the word- and food- was really getting around!

And of course, as humans are prone to do, the humans of nearby villages came looking for the thing that they had heard so many murmurings about

And when they found it, they became just as enamored with the mysterious chocolate as the rest of the animals

Of course they didn't know who was responsible for discovering and creating this sweet treat, as the werewolf's identity had been lost long ago in the chain of gossip

But that didn't make the chocolate taste any less delicious

And it was shortly thereafter that the werewolf realized something, something very important

In a way, he was doing exactly wat he had always wanted to do

He was making people happy...

And so for a long time the werewolf made more and more and more chocolate

He made more and more of his other sweets too

And he'd package it all up- save for a few of the misshapen but still good tasting confections that he and the raven kept for themselves- and called forth the raven and his friends to deliver them to the forest dwellers and the villagers alike

And so for a long time this worked

For a long time it did really make him feel happy

But sadly, that long time wasn't forever

As time passed on the request for chocolate grew more and more and more frequent, until the werewolf could barely keep up with it anymore

He worked night and day, often sacrificing sleep to finish the last box

It was due to this lack of sleep, in fact, that things once again changed forever

He was in the middle of making chocolate when he realized that he had run out of sugar, and being that all of the birds had already flown off to make deliveries for the day he knew he would have to either stop for a break or get it himself

The werewolf, despite his gentle, calm nature, was a very stubborn man who refused to take breaks (as his lack of sleep will tell you)

And so for the first time in many, many, MANY months, he climbed down from the mountain and entered the woods

It was there that he began to gather the sugar he needed, and there that his lack of sleep was most apparent

For his restlessness had dulled his senses, and the humans in the area took the opportunity to sneak up on him

He didn't have a clue, as he stood, innocently gathering sugar to make more treats, that one of the humans had drawn their gun and pointed it at him

And had it not been for the raven, he wouldn't have noticed until he had a bullet in his heart

But thanks to the raven, who screamed out an angry, fearful message, he managed to dodge just in time for the man to fire his gun into the tree instead of him

Still tired and with slower reflexes the werewolf stumbled to his feet, backing into the tree behind him fearfully

And the raven landed in front of him, the anger that fueled the bird was so immense, that it rolled off of him in waves and could be felt all through the forest

The anger was so immense, that for the first time, the raven shifted into a man, because as a bird, he could do little, as a man, he could do quite a bit

"How dare you," bellowed the raven

"How dare you point your instrument of death at this innocent creature, how dare you try to take his innocence from the world!" the raven shouted in fury

"You people have spent months doing nothing but consuming chocolate and baked goods and destroying the nature around you, killing plants to create needless buildings and shooting animals for no reason other than to hang them in your homes like bloody trophies! And you just couldn't live with yourselves until you tried to take away the last remaining joy in this forest!" he screamed

The humans, not quite knowing what to do, stood in stunned silence as they listened to the raven and watched the werewolf behind him sink to the ground and shake in fright and exhaustion

Faery Tales, Mermaid Myths, And Other Fantastical Legends

"You have no idea... the chocolate and sweets you've all been so happily consuming, so happily ordering and demanding more about, has been the creation of the very person you just tried to shoot, had you succeeded, there would never be chocolate in this world again, he's the only one who knows how to make it, even I can't do it correctly,"

The crowd of people seemed to understand all at once the gravity of their actions and murmured and whispered about how horrible it would have been to lose their precious chocolate

The raven heard this, heard their concern for a sweet food, but heard not one single person speak of concern for a lost life

And the anger boiled deeper in him until he began to grow wings again

Maintaining his human form, a set of massive black wings jutted out from between his shoulder blades, his fingernails turned into claws and his eyes seeped into pools of black

The raven, a creature who embodied the very principal of magic, had become so angry that he bent the rules of his own power, he no longer could only shift between a bird and a man

He now had developed the power to do both

However, as he would learn later that day, this power came with a price

For shifting between a bird and a man was now a painful process, where as it had been flawless and clean before

The damage he had done to himself by allowing the anger to overtake him and merge the two halves of his soul into one had been immense

But, as the raven will gladly tell anyone who will listen, he would pay the price a thousand times over again and again before he would let the humans tear down his werewolf

The humans were now afraid of the raven, who walked towards them with anger sunk into his bones like chocolate in a cake

"You only care about yourselves, you only care about what you can get, what you can have, you do not care about anything... or anyone else," his voice, despite his emotion, was not one pounding of anger

It was instead, dripping in grief

Greif, for his own ignorance

Greif, for having allowed himself for so very long to believe that there could be good in the humans of these villages

Greif, for not taking action sooner

"There will be no more chocolate, and no more sweets from the mountains, there will be no more magic in this forest and no more joy in this village, I'm not placing a curse... I'm making a prediction,"

And his words were true

Ravens cannot cast curses, they don't hold that type of magic

But they are brilliantly intuitive and stunningly accurate in their predictions

And this was no exception

The raven turned his back to the humans, escorted the werewolf back to the cave under the edge of the cliff, and helped him sort and pack up his few belongings

"Where will I go if not here?" the werewolf asked sadly as he looked at the unfinished bowl of chocolate sitting on the table

"We will find another place, just as not all werewolves are rough and dominant, not all humans are hateful and selfish, or at least... I hope not,"

The raven left that evening with his werewolf companion and insisted they travel as far away as they could go, taking their secret chocolate recipe with them

As the raven predicted, the other animals soon began to follow

They had always thanked the werewolf (indirectly, through speaking to the raven) and kindly complimented his skills when accepting chocolate

And they had never asked for more than they thought reasonably possible for him to make

They too had been hurt and scorned by the surrounding villages

And when the animals left, the magic soon followed

It followed on the heels of the ravens and foxes and rabbits the way leaves follow the wind

And when the magic left, so did the joy

The forest died, having no bees to pollenate plants and keep them growing and no magic to help it stay alive in the heat of summer or freezing of winter

And when the forest died, the last remaining magic died with it

The people of the surrounding villages never had chocolate again, and never told any of their descendants about what life was like once, for they were bitter about how it had become and too cold-hearted to take responsibility for it

For this is not a story about people seeing the superficial good in someone else and "changing their ways"

Nor is it a story about forgiving people who have done you wrong and continue to do you wrong because they now see a self-serving value in you and have decided to become more well-mannered to your face

This is a story about protecting one's self from those who seek to harm them

About knowing when it's time to give up before one is hurt any further

About knowing that it's much better to walk away from someone who has hurt you into a place of uncertainty, rather than stay where you are, continue hurting, and always question if their smile is genuine or if it's just because they want something from you

And this is why the people of the villages became bitter

Because things didn't work out in their favor and not all people suddenly change for the good because they see value in something- not someone- that they hadn't seen value in before

The werewolf and the raven however, and their animal friends, settled down many, many, many villages over

In a large town, in fact, populated with faeries and witches and vampires, and other werewolves and ravens of course....

... And yes

Even populated with humans

And not a single soul there ever spoke badly to the werewolf, much less try to hurt him

They truly appreciated his gift and not long after moving into the town the werewolf and the raven opened a sweet shop where they made chocolate and baked cookies and filled the town and the surrounding woods and forests with so many tasty delights that people countries over heard of them and visited the town just for a single taste

The people here- from faery to vampire to human- eventually learned how to make chocolate as well and their descendants did too

But no one, of course, ever made it as well as the werewolf did

It was no wonder that as time moved on he even started a chocolate factory with the raven, but at the end of the day they still spent the vast majority of their time in the small sweet shop in the town

The shop where they were thanked and complimented for their gifts and where they could close down at the end of the day and go home to a warm house and a happy family

Faery Tales, Mermaid Myths, And Other Fantastical Legends

Where the werewolf no longer closed himself off for fear of the other people and where the raven no longer felt angry and upset

And of course, where there was not such a demand for chocolate that the werewolf worked himself sick trying to produce it

It was a good life

It was a happy life

And in the end the kind and gentle werewolf got what he wanted most

He was able to make the people around him- people he knew and people he didn't know- happy

And he was able to be happy too

Alexa Asagi Andres

The Costume Maker

Once upon a time

In a land not too far away from our own

There lived a beautiful Dragon Fae who was a master at her craft

What, you may ask, is this craft?

Making the most beautiful of costumes, that is the craft

Everything from the most astounding masquerade ball gowns to the most unique and outstanding of suits

Though unlike most costume makers, her specialty was not alone in the clothing

This particular Dragon Fae, who they called Sarah, was capable of making anything for any disguise

Be it shoes, or masks, or even weapons

She had once crafted a scythe for one costume that was so believable that knights continuously rushed after her to examine it

She was adored for her talent, but more so for her personality

Energetic and cheerful and always up for an adventure

She was known for making more use of her wings than any other Dragon Fae in the land, for Sarah found that flying was the most exhilarating and freeing experience in the world

In fact, she sometimes shifted into her dragon form purely so she could see how high into the sky she could fly

But that's another story for another day

This story specifically is about how the Dragon Fae Sarah met a Vampire Princess

Faery Tales, Mermaid Myths, And Other Fantastical Legends

It was long ago, when Sarah was still quite young, that she first saw the Vampire Princess

While working on a ball gown for a friend, she happened to look out the window of her cottage and see the princess in the distance, and for that moment, she felt nearly certain that she and the princess had locked eyes...

But she let go of the thought, for she had heard nothing from the princess in many months after

It wasn't until the Vampire Princess held her grand Annual Ball that she and Sarah met again

Sarah had been commissioned by all the grand attendants to the ball to design their masquerade costumes and she was swarmed with work for many months

Up until the very night before the ball she was still attaching chiffon, adjusting bow ties, glittering masks, and polishing fake weaponry

But such was life as most costume makers would attest

It was not until she had already dressed and said goodbye to the animals who lived in her cottage with her- three dogs, ten cats, an countless other frequent visitors- that she met the Vampire Princess again

She left the cottage, shifting into her dragon form and flying eagerly into the sky, savoring the feeling of being in the air for a while before finally seeing the Vampire Princess's balcony up ahead

She had been asked specifically to specially deliver this dress to the princess and so she supposed that a balcony entrance was as good as any other

The Princess, however, didn't seem to be expecting it, for as soon as the Dragon Fae landed on the balcony and began to shift back into her Fae form, she found the Vampire Princess directly in front of her, baring her fangs menacingly

"Rawr to you too, did you want your dress?" Sarah asked plainly

She wasn't quite sure if the princess was embarrassed about attacking her dress maker... or stunned that someone had spoken to her so plainly

But she seemed shocked either way and quickly straightened herself out, combing her short black hair behind her ears and clearing her throat

"My apologies, I wasn't expecting you to come in through the balcony," she noted as the Dragon Fae handed her the beautiful ball gown and masquerade mask she had crafted

"Its fine, I should have remembered- vampires are jumpy," she smiled

The Vampire Princess smiled back and held her hand out politely

"My name is Mika, please .. address me plainly,"

The Dragon Fae smiled and shook her hand gently

"Sarah, you can address me as your queen if you want," she teased

Mika chuckled slightly, breaking her usually stern facade and staring at the dress for another moment

"Thank you," she said quietly, rushing back into her room before the ball began

The Dragon Fae decided to go ahead and join the forming party, and didn't see the Vampire Princess- Mika- for several more hours

It wasn't until the masquerade ball was almost over, in fact that they met again

"Mika, why are you out here all alone?" Sarah asked with concern as she spotted the nocturnal princess and approached her

"I'm ... not needed there," she replied with a heavy sigh

"Why do you say that?" Sarah asked in confusion, going to sit beside her

"This... fanciful, formal, dressy .. occasion really is not for me, I don't want to stay trapped like a porcelain bird inside a cage like this, not for another year, another day, another moment..."

"So where do you want to go?" Sarah asked curiously

Mika thought about that for a moment, considering it

"I... think I would like to be a knight," she replied firmly, staring up at the night stars

"Then why don't you?" the Dragon Fae asked curiously

"A vampire princess acting as a knight? Surely you're joking," she sighed

Sarah smirked, standing up and holding her hand out for her

"Mika, come with me," she insisted

Mika stared at her with uncertainty, but Sarah never withdrew her hand, so after a few moments of hesitation the Vampire Princess placed her hand in that of the Dragon Fae's and within moments found herself holding tightly onto the scales of a large, beautiful dragon

"Are you sure you know what you're doing?" she asked skeptically

As if to answer her, Sarah took off into the sky, abandoning the ground below and flying higher than she had ever been before

Although initially frightened of the experience, Mika got used to flying fairly quickly, and after only a few moments had passed by, she could no longer stomach the idea of returning to the ground below, and to the life it had in store for her

They flew for a long, long while, until the Vampire Kingdom was a mere thought in the backs of their heads, before finally landing in an open, clear field and going to stargaze once again

"You should suggest becoming a knight," Sarah said with an affirmative nod

"No one will agree to it," Mika said softly

"You'll never know until you try, besides, you're an adult, and your brother is the one in line for the throne, why are you letting aristocrats rule your life?" she asked quite seriously

Mika thought about that for several moments

Several hours

Several nights

And by the time a week had gone by Sarah received a knock on her cottage door late one night

The dogs barking woke her up and she stumbled tiredly out of bed, flanked by the gaggle of cats who were as eager to see who was at the door as the dogs seemed to be

Sarah leaned close, cracking the door open and staring in surprise at the red eyes that stared back at her

"Mika?" she asked in surprise, opening the door wider

The Vampire Princess, in riding pants, a blouse, and a vest and gloves, looked a far cry from the elegant beauty she had seen nights ago outside of the ballroom

This Mika looked stronger and more determined, hair pulled back and clutching a small bag over her shoulder as she stepped forward and pulled the Dragon Fae into a tight hug

"I'm going to do it, I'm going to become a knight," she smiled brightly

"That... that's wonderful," Sarah smiled as she hugged the vampire back

"Come with me," Mika proposed, pausing for a moment

"Just for tonight, I ... I want to fly again,"

Sarah smiled and stepped outside, shutting the door behind her and letting her dark blue wings stretch out

She never did miss a good opportunity for flying...

From that night forward every kingdom and every land had heard the story

Heard of the valiant knight who rode upon a dark and lovely dragon

Heard of the first time in history that a knight was partners with a dragon and they helped to rescue princesses and slay human monsters together

Heard of the Vampire Princess who became a knight

... And who found herself on the doorstep of a certain Dragon Fae more than her own, whether it be to request assistance or to offer it, or simply to indulge in the animal company that was so abundant in the house

But although all of these things were frequently heard throughout the kingdoms, there was one thing that everyone heard more than all of the rest

They heard of a Vampire knight who flew high, high, high into the night sky on the back of a dragon

It didn't matter if they were working or relaxing or something in between

Mika and Sarah would fly as much as they could

For flying was the truest form of freedom there was

And that was what started their relationship to begin with after all:

The promise of freedom

Alexa Asagi Andres

The Dancing Tiger

Once upon a time

In a land very near and dear to our own

There lived a tiger who longed to do something that tigers were not specifically known for doing

He wanted to dance

Now, this may sound like a silly wish for a tiger

But it really wasn't!

Tigers are graceful and swift and light on their feet

But more importantly than that, it wasn't silly for a tiger to dream of becoming a dancer

Because no dream is silly, no matter how far reaching it is

The tiger, Ajit, wished to dance more than anything in the world ever since he was a cub

"Put such silly hopes aside Ajit, learn to hunt like tigers are meant to do" his mother would instruct

Ajit never listened, and whenever he wasn't training to hunt with his mother, he practiced dancing

He listened to the music in the world around him to help guide him

From the chirping birds and rush of the wind

To the instruments and voices in the villages around him

To the indescribable faery music around him

There was music all around him and he used that magic to dance, even if it was only for himself

He wished that one day he would be able to dance for others

But even he knew that as a tiger, no matter how skilled he was, his skills were truly limited

For he had two too many legs and a cumbersome, long body that wasn't designed for pretty motions

It was all very disappointing, but he kept up trying

And then one day, not long after he became an adult, Ajit encountered the solution to his problems

Laying in the grass, staring up with disdain at the tree above her, was a Wood Nymph

She began to curse and shout in anger as she tried to loosen her braid from the roots of the tree

Ajit cleared his throat, stepping closer and easily slashing the root with a claw

The nymph stared up at him with her mouth ajar and her body still

"... If I had wanted the tree to be injured I could have done that myself," she finally said as she made it back to her feet

"It seemed you were struggling," the tiger pointed out as he stalked before her

The nymph swallowed and tensed as he neared closer

"I ... was only struggling to find a more peaceful solution than injuring the tree,"

"You called the tree a name that my mother would never let me repeat, I do not think you really intended for it to be peaceful," he pointed out, circling around her

"You don't know WHAT I was thinking or intending," she argued

Although the curse she had uttered was true....

"Perhaps not, but I can read people fairly well," he mused

She opened her mouth to argue but paused when she heard music begin in the village near to them

Ajit heard it as well and gave them both a small smile, starting to sway their hips and move their bodies in graceless and joyful dance

"You like to dance?" the nymph asked in surprise

"I see you do as well," Ajit confirmed with a nod of his head

"I've always wanted to be a dancer," they both said in a longing sigh at once

They paused, slowly staring over at each other and starting to grin

"Are you thinking... what I'm thinking?" the Wood Nymph smirked slowly

"I believe I am," he agreed

It took no time at all for the Wood Nymph to gather information from some of the elves in the area about how to use Pixie Dust and spells

"Are you SURE you know what you're doing Wood Nymph?" the tiger asked with a worried frown

"Mostly, and my name is Asha," she pointed out

Ajit didn't feel comforted in the "mostly" part of her statement and watched as the purple dust fell over him

"Ajit," he said finally

"Mm.. that's a strong name," she confirmed, her long black braid swaying behind her as she moved around him

"As is yours," he replied

Asha didn't comment further, just took a step back and studied her work

"Alright, let's see if this works," she said, taking a deep breath and snapping her fingers

Ajit coughed and blinked and twitched his paws....

Only to find that he no longer HAD paws at all....

He had fingers....

.... And toes....

And it was all a very strange sensation

"You're suited for being a human," she mused as she took a step back and nodded

Ajit grunted in response, apparently you can't take the tiger out of the man...

He studied over his features- long hair, dark skin, no tail....

"Why do I still have my stripes?" he asked

"I'm a Wood Nymph, not a witch or a faery, you're lucky you got out of it with everything intact," she pointed out

He frowned deeply but she had a point, the fact that he was still breathing, he supposed, was a miracle all on its own

"So, how do we go about this?" Asha asked as she stared up at him

For yet another time, Ajit was at a loss for words, truly not sure how to reply to that

"I'm..... I have no idea," he finally admitted

"... So I see who the planning master is going to be in this relationship..." she mused, shaking her head as she started to walk deeper into the forest

"I can catch us food," Ajit offered helpfully as he followed after her

"I'm pretty sure that Wood Nymphs don't eat.... carcasses.... and if they do, I do not, unless you can chase down some apples or something... I don't think you'll be very useful for that either,"

There was a pause

"What if I put the catch inside of one of those big heat-boxes the humans have? It would.... cook.... could you eat it then?" he asked curiously

After all, anyone who didn't enjoy the divine flavor of raw meat was crazy

Anyone who tried to live on grass and leaves like the Wood Nymph was obviously even worse than crazy

She never did answer him about the heat-box

But a few months later Asha and Ajit began to make a bit of a name for themselves

The two were quickly becoming a success as dancers in the Fae community

And even Ajit's mother seemed impressed

Why, they were even tempted to go show the humans

Of course with all the laws and restrictions that took it would be ages before they could even try....

There was only one problem in gaining their success

Ajit didn't really do it as a human

They learned during- tragically- their first show for some local forest animals that Asha's spell failed in more ways than just leaving Ajit's stripes

It also failed to transform him all the way

For every several hours, seemingly randomly, Ajit would become a tiger again

At first it was confusing and odd and concerning

Ajit couldn't dance as a tiger and he had made a deal with Asha to be her partner and pursue this together with her

But over the course of a few shows, two things became increasingly clear

First, the transformations were not random at all, they happened when too much energy was expended and sadly there was no way to get rid of and redo the spell, it was already in place to work this way

And as for the second thing....

People absolutely LOVED it when he shapeshifted

They were impressed and awed and encouraged him even more to dance in his tiger form than they did in his human form

It was really the most confusing thing

But over the course of several weeks Ajit began learning to control the transformation so that he could become a tiger or a human as he pleased

He and Asha worked into their routine a large window for the tiger to take center stage and dance only as a tiger could

And much to their surprise

It was a complete success

Before long the entire Fae world was talking about Asha and Ajit, as was much of the animal kingdom

And there were even rumors fluttering about of getting an advance on going to see the humans

Everyone wanted to see the two fabulous dancers they had heard of

The weretiger and the Wood Nymph, doing everything from classic dances that the humans prided themselves on inventing (even though it was usually one of the Fae Folk responsible) to truly original and modern dances... well... modern for the time...

And most wonderfully of all, besides the talking and the people and the job, there was one thing that was very important that this turn of events proved

It seems that, after all, a tiger really CAN dance

Alexa Asagi Andres

The Dark Woods

Once upon a time

In a land almost near to our own

There was a place that they called The Dark Woods

Within these woods existed things that most people would find belonging in their nightmares

From the natural, such as tall and scary looking trees or an almost eerie fog rolling over a deep dark lake

To the supernatural, such as ghosts, talking pumpkins, moving scarecrows, and the monsters that live under the bed

Of course, not all of these creatures are bad, or even scary

Some of them are just misunderstood

Like the werewolves, for example, who had found a part of the Dark Woods to call their own

There was one werewolf, in particular, who was often called upon to do the more stressful, bothersome work for the woods

For she was one of the only beings in the woods who was strong enough to handle it, even if she didn't like to

But then, no one liked to it seemed, however it had to be done

This werewolf was named Nykol, and she was special indeed

For although she often was stuck with the most frustrating and difficult tasks that the Dark Woods had to offer, she was also very gifted

Nykol was no ordinary werewolf

Nykol possessed a very special power, the power to create and travel in between worlds

This was no average witch's magic, nothing as fancy as being able to open portals or dimensions

But it was something even more special

Nykol had been blessed by a Moon Witch when she was a child

Nearly all witches carry the same magic and it's up to them to learn how to use it correctly

Nearly all.... except for the Talent Witches

Talent Witches possess something that usually only Fae Folk such as faeries and merpeople possess

Talent Witches possess a specialty, in addition to normal magic, that separates them from the rest

Some Talent Witches are rather self-explanatory in their names, such as Fire Witches or Water Witches

Or Nature Witches and Potion Witches

But then there was the select few who had a hidden, secret power that their name did not reveal

Moon Witches and Sun Witches are part of that category

No one, not even other Talent Witches, are sure what they can do

Thus, being blessed by a Moon Witch, meant that Nykol could mature to have nearly any power imaginable, no one was sure until she developed said power exactly what it would result in

But no one expected this

Werewolves are usually not magically inclined, so to pair the powers of a werewolf with the World Jumping and World Building powers of a witch was a power that only the strongest, most special of beings could possess

It was possibly due to this power that she seemed to always be stuck doing the worst work around the Dark Woods

But at the end of the day, when she wanted to escape the frustrations of the world around her, all she had to do was open a book and use her magic to jump into the world there

Or, in some cases, even create her own, just by writing down what she wished for

It was an adventure that only the bravest of hearts could handle and Nykol, who spent as much time in these other worlds as she did her own, was definitely one of these brave hearts

It was on an adventure such as this, in a world that she had created a few nights before, that her life changed forever

After arriving back to her cabin in the Dark Woods from checking the perimeter for Wolfsbane, making sure that the human hunters who lived nearby hadn't tried (Again) to trap or poison her kind, she trekked towards the door, and was surprised to trip.... over a book....

Supposing it was one of her own, she picked it up without much care to look and see what it was

It wasn't until she had already begun the spell to take her to another world that she realized the book didn't belong to her

It was too late, however, to change her mind, for before she could interrupt it the book opened and pages began to swarm around her and abduct her, taking her to another land, one that she didn't even know the name of

When Nykol woke up in the new land she found that it was far brighter than her own

It seemed to be mid-day now and she found herself standing on the edge of a tall cliff

Taking a quick step back to get away from the imminent danger, she looked around further than just the sky and tried to get a bearing for her surroundings

The ground beneath her was not much unlike the ground she was used to in her own world and when she looked behind her she found that there were woods, much like her own, behind her

She didn't have enough time to contemplate it however, as she heard the shouting of human voices behind her

Quickly, she sprinted into a run and turned to her wolf form, a beautiful black wolf that landed gracefully on her feet without problems, she ran to the edge of the woods and took a few steps to hide behind the woods

Perhaps it was better to hide and keep attention away from her until she at least figured out where she was...

She watched curiously as the humans shouted and screamed at each other, often handing out orders and instructions as they passed around everything from burnt out torches to swords and pistols and pitchforks, the usual things one would see in an angry mob formation

She stretched her head up a bit more, watching in surprise and horror as the humans dragged a large, beautiful dragon behind them

The metal chains yanked and pulled against the being but the creature's emerald green and black-edged wings fought and struggled desperately against them as the being tried to get away, snorting smoke through its nostrils as chains were still wrapped and clasped around the creature's mouth, preventing fire breathing of any kind

Nykol, being a brave and defensive creature, didn't have to think twice before leaping out to save the dragon

She didn't know where she was, she didn't know who these people were, she didn't know anything about this world that she had landed in

But she did know a creature in distress when she saw one and she refused to just let this poor creature be hurt or worse killed for her self-preservation

She put her skills as a werewolf to work and easily tore apart the mob, leaving them all stunned and many of them clutching to life as she neared the dragon

The reptile stared at her with warm brown eyes, watching as she shifted from a wolf to a woman with ease

The dragon stayed still, allowing her to remove the chains without any struggle and watching as the long, wickedly beautiful black dress swayed around her with every movement

"You are free now," Nykol said as she took a step back

The dragon paused, staring at her before seeming to perk and snatching her in one clawed foot and taking off into the sky

A strong, brave soul she was....

But dangling from a dragon's foot impossibly high in the sky was less of an adventure and more of a death wish and it was no surprise that she screamed in surprise at the action

Luckily the flight was not long before the dragon landed in a large cave many, many skies away from the cliff and set her down, walking towards the back of the cave before smoke surrounded the beast

And slowly, the dragon shrunk... and shrunk.... and shrunk....

Until the smoke cleared and Nykol saw that it was not a dragon any longer at all

But a man

A man sporting the same warm eyes and a smile so bright that sun should be ashamed of its self

"Thank you for saving me," he said, reaching out to shake her hand

"It ... was no problem, but you could have stood to leave me where I was," Nykol replied, setting her hand in his only to be surprised as he tugged her into a tight hug

"No, I really couldn't, I heard hunters coming,"

Nykol frowned, squirming slightly as he let her go

"I didn't,"

"I'm not surprised, dragons have mildly better hearing than werewolves,"

She wasn't quite sure how she felt about that but it wasn't pleasant...

"Oh..." she mumbled

"Oh I'm sorry, I forgot to introduce myself... I'm Allistair, hi," he chuckled

The werewolf nodded politely

"I'm Nykol,"

"Nykol.. that's a pretty name," he commented, walking further into the back of the cave and pulling a torch off of the wall, coughing up a fireball and lighting it for her

She couldn't help but be reminded of what a cat looks like coughing up a hairball...

"You've never been around dragons before have you?" Allistair commented as Nykol took the torch from him

"How could you tell?" she countered simply, continuing to follow and wondering how far back this cave went

Allistair laughed joyfully, the sound resembling the brightness of ringing bells

"Sarcasm, I like it,"

"No, I was being serious, how could you tell?" she replied with a small frown

"Ah... most people who know dragons know about the hearing, and don't look so disturbed when they spit fire in their human form," he shrugged

"I know OF dragons... I just haven't MET a dragon before..." she explained

"You're a werewolf and yet you haven't met a dragon even once?" he asked in surprise, pausing mid-step

"You must be from the Dark Woods then,"

"How do you know that?

"Because the only werewolves in this land who don't know dragons are from the Dark Woods,"

Nykol was greatly confused, in all of this time she had never before entered into a land where the Dark Woods existed other than her own...

"I'm not from this land, the Dark Woods I'm from is in a different land,"

Allistair began walking again, looking at her curiously

"Are you sure about that?"

"Pretty sure," she nodded slowly

"How did you get here?"

"I... traveled," she replied vaguely

Allistair paused, turning and smiling excitedly at her

"You ... you can World Jump can't you?" he breathed

"How-"

"I knew it! I knew there was another World Jumper somewhere in this land! You must have found the book I left for you in the Dark Woods!" he insisted happily

"YOU left that book there? Where are we? Where did it lead to?" she asked urgently

"Don't worry about it, I just created that book so it would send someone who lives IN the Dark Woods OUT of the Dark Woods, sorry if that's deceptive, but I just... really wanted to meet someone like me," he explained

"You can World Jump too?" she breathed

"Yeah, absolutely," he nodded, taking the torch from her and setting it in place along one of the walls

"Were you blessed by a Moon Witch too?"

"Sun Witch," he replied with a small chuckle, moving back so that she could see into a room that was so full of books that one probably couldn't even move in it

"This is amazing," she said quietly

"No, this is a hoard, I am a dragon- I hoard, this is my hoard, I hoard books,"

"Gee you don't say," she said with a small smile

"You can go in, I trust you," he smiled

"Already?"

"Well you DID save my life...." he pointed out

That was true she supposed....

"I wish there was room in my cabin for a library like this," she mused as she stared along the stacks and stacks and stacks of books

"Then why don't you stay here? I did call you out here because I was lonely, I want someone to go with me when I World Jump, why go alone when we could go together?" he proposed

Nykol stared at him with uncertainty for a brief moment

"We could at least try right?"

Although she had just met Allistair, she found herself feeling pulled towards him

She wasn't exactly sure why, she had always heard werewolves have a natural instinct for things like this, but it still surprised her

She took a step forward, taking Allistair's hand and staring at all of the books- all of the worlds- that she could travel to, and this time not alone, this time with someone else by her side, adventuring, exploring with her....

"We can try," she agreed

Allistair smiled brightly and held his hand out for her, squeezing when she accepted it

"Then I guess there's only one question left," he mused

Nykol stared up at him curiously

"And what would that be?"

"Where do you want to go first?"

Nykol began to smirk as well, taking a step towards the books with him

"Let's take a leap of faith and see where we end up," she suggested

And just like that, the two took a step forward, and walked into the pages of another book, stepping into the land of an entirely other world

The Determined Mother

Once upon a time

In a land full of wrong-doings

There lived a mother

This mother had only one person in her entire life, her daughter, but her daughter was enough

She named her daughter Neveah, for she believed that the baby girl was a gift from Heaven

The mother, Cheyenne, and her daughter were inseparable

They were closer than any other

They lived a very simple existence in a small village where Cheyenne worked as a baker

And for five years, they were happy

That happiness, however, was not meant to last

For one day, seemingly out of nowhere, the King sent his men to destroy the village and take Neveah away

The King found that no matter how he tried, he could not produce an heir for the throne

And after his wife died a year before, he gave up trying

Deciding that it would be better for the country for him to have a daughter, who he could marry to the prince of another, wealthier kingdom, than a son, he sent his men out searching for a village small enough that it wouldn't do much harm to tear it down

For a girl young enough that she would eventually adapt to her new situation

And for a family weak enough that they could not fight back

When the King's men found Cheyenne's tiny village, found a five-year-old girl and found that her only family was her baker mother, they decided that this was surely the one

And a day later, they set the village aflame

In the fire Cheyenne searched desperately for her daughter

She coughed through the smoke and fought against the heat of the flames as she scrambled through her bakery

When she finally managed to get to the backroom where Neveah was, she only barely was able to reach her hand out and touch her daughter's

"Mommy!!" Neveah shouted as she reached out desperately for her mother

Cheyenne coughed and stared up at the soldier holding her daughter away

"Give her back.... give me my daughter!" she shouted

"You should be grateful, your daughter is going to a better place now," the soldier said coldly

Cheyenne gritted her teeth and launched forward, reaching out for Neveah's hand and not noticing when the General gave his soldier the signal he needed

And before their hands could touch again, the soldier buried his sword deep into Cheyenne's stomach

Tears rolled down the mother's face, not out of pain, and not out of fear, but out of desperation

Desperation as she fell forward and tried one last time to grasp her daughter's hand

"MOMMY!!!" Neveah shouted again

But the soldier and the rest of the guard took her away before she could reach out to her mother

It was by much more than sheer luck that the blacksmith next door found Cheyenne in the flames and pulled her out

It was fate

"You can't go against the King, I know you want your daughter back, but it's probably for the best, Neveah will grow up a princess, she'll have a privileged life- a GOOD life, isn't that what you want for her?" the doctor asked as he tended to Cheyenne's wound

"You don't understand, politics aren't for my daughter, she's too tender-hearted and strong-headed, she'll never survive it,"

"Are you sure that it's HER who won't survive this? You're lucky to be alive, and your daughter is living in the lap of luxury, to try to get her back is not only foolish, it's selfish," the doctor reprimanded as he finished placing the bandages over Cheyenne's stomach

"You're mistaken," she replied, standing up and struggling to stay on her feet

"I'm not going to get my daughter back because I deserve to have a daughter- I'm going to get my daughter back because she deserves to have a MOTHER," she explained, grabbing the nearest walking stick and limping towards the door

"You are making a GRAVE mistake Madame," he warned

"Then you can put on my grave that I died without giving up on my child, I will NEVER give up on my child, I will come back from the dead if I have to," she said seriously

"Are you sure you don't want to at least wait until your wound has healed?"

"No, if I don't go now I'll never be able to follow them," she replied, pausing and staring across at the blacksmith who had saved her

"Are you going to tell me I'm acting like a fool too?"

"No, I'm going to tell you that you're doing exactly what I would do, I'm going to tell you that you're acting like a MOTHER," she smiled, offering her hand to Cheyenne

"I don't understand," she said bluntly

"Is it that hard to believe that I'm a mother too, just because I work with instruments of death and fire? Come with me, let me lend you a horse," she offered

Cheyenne paused, but nodded and accepted her hand, allowing the blacksmith to lead her out of the half-burnt cottage the doctor was practicing in

"You know you can't come back here once you've got her, you have to go far, far away, to a place that they'll never find you," the blacksmith warned as she helped Cheyenne towards the stables- or at least, what was left of them

"I know, I'm not sure where we'll go but... I know we have to go somewhere," she replied quietly

The blacksmith was quiet for a moment, helping her to lean against one of the stable doors before starting to unlock the other door

"Yeah, I was thinking it's about time I get out of this place too, there's a quieter place down south of here, larger, but better, there are all kinds of possibilities there, actually, my mother lives there, my kids and I were thinking of leaving soon," she paused, taking a small pouch from her pocket and placing it securely in Cheyenne's hand

"Maybe you could go ahead of me and check it out?"

"You don't have to-"

"I'm a mother, if I don't, who will?"

Those words sent a chill through Cheyenne's body and she hung her head, waiting for the blacksmith to ready the horse

In these five years that she had been a mother- and even in some time before that- she was faced with nothing but criticism

From men, from women, from parents and from those who never had children, from old and young, from everyone around her

She was always told she was doing something wrong

And now, in a time of tragedy, in a time when she's about to do terrible things, she's earned the approval of a complete stranger

"Here, take Buttercup, she's the fastest," the blacksmith said as she handed Cheyenne the reins of a beautiful black horse

Cheyenne paused, wrapping her arms around the blacksmith and hugging her tightly

"Thank you," she said quietly

"Don't spend too long on gratitude, you've got something you have to do don't you?" the other woman smiled as she hugged her back

"I do.... but if anyone ever tells you something horrible... just remember that the world needs more people like you," she said sincerely, placing the pouch in her pocket and quickly mounting the horse

"WHEN someone tells me something horrible, I will... you remember that too," she said with a smile, stepping back to allow the horse room to move

"Wait... what's your name?" Cheyenne asked as the horse began to trot

"Faelynn, we'll see each other again Cheyenne, and I look forward to meeting your daughter," she replied with a wave as the horse picked up into a gallop

Cheyenne watched her curiously and wondered how she knew her name, but put it out of her head, she had other things she needed to concentrate on

She rode as fast as she could down the roads, trying to recall and recount where the inner kingdom was so that she could at least make good time getting there, even if she didn't catch up with the soldiers

Over the course of the next day she only stopped when Buttercup needed a rest or to eat or drink

She barely drank water or ate the small amount of food that she found in one of the bags the horse was carrying

And she never slept

By the third day of riding she could see the wall of the inner city and snapped the reins to move faster

She knew she was close and she was overwhelmed with the urgency to get there, to find her daughter and take her away

She saw the gates in front of her and took a deep breath as she rode forward, staring down the two guards in front of her

"Who goes there?" one shouted

"Just a simple baker, I'm here to make a delivery upon request for the new princess," she said as she dismounted the horse and reached into one of the bags

She could feel the outline of several sheathed blades against her glove-covered fingers and made a mental note to bake a pie for that blacksmith later

The guards exchanged looks, apparently letting their guard down a bit at the realization that someone knew about the princess when her arrival had not yet been widely announced

"Alright, just show us what you have there in your bags and you can go," the other guard said

"Thank you," she smiled, grabbing one of the blades before reaching into the other bag and pulling out a loaf of bread

"Nothing much, I have some other pastries if you wouldn't mind just holding this? It's awfully hard to navigate around," she said with a soft look

The first guard shrugged, stepping forward and taking it

And as soon as the bread left her hands she quickly unsheathed the dagger she had been holding and slashed at the only open skin she could see

The other guard went for his sword quickly, but not quickly enough as Cheyenne twisted around and kicked him in the head, grabbing the bag of weapons from the horse and running to the gate

She could see the guards stumbling back to their feet from behind her and flipped the bag open, finding some sort of smoke bomb and tossing it at them as she scaled up the gates

She could hear the guards shouting all sorts of commands and warnings from all around her but she kept going, successfully making it to the top of the massive gates and looking around for any sort of escape

She couldn't jump from this height without the risk of breaking her neck... but she could jump into the haystack a few yards over if she could just make it closer....

She looked around, desperate for any sort of escape as she felt the gates start to move, opening for the other two guards to come inside as the rest of the guards began their focus on catching her

When the gates opened inwardly she smirked to herself, for that was all she needed

She jumped from the edge of the gate and landed in the stack of hay with only little difficulty

And when she emerged she began running, she grabbed the first horse she spotted by the mane and mounted quickly as she tugged on the horse's hair

The horse reared up with a loud screech of protest, thus effectively forcing the guards back and even knocking several of them on their rears before finally settling back on all fours and stampeding forward

Cheyenne could see the castle only a few dozen yards away and she knew she could make it

If she could just get to the castle, she could pull this off

When the guards started to ride up beside her, however, she realized that she was going to have to resort to something else

Looking inside the bag she had taken earlier, she found a slingshot with several small, metal balls

She wasn't exactly sure why it was in there but it would have to do

And so she strengthened her legs around the horse's sides and began shooting the little balls at anyone who came too near

Luckily, just as she was running out, she saw the castle and quickly jumped down from the horse, managing to stun the remaining guards long enough to roll onto her feet again and run behind the main entrance of the palace

It was somewhat lucky that royalty always seemed to keep towers on their buildings, it made for easy climbing access

She reached hopefully into her bag again and felt a wave of relief when she found a grappling hook

Winding it up, she tossed it towards the edge of the nearest tower- not very far up, thankfully- and breathed again when it landed and hooked right in

"There she is! Get her!" the guards shouted as they rushed towards her

She reached into the magic bag and found that she was starting to run low on weapons

Pulling out another dagger, she looked around for the best place to launch it and smirked when she saw a young man, probably a servant from the castle, behind them stacking some barrels

Hoping the barrels were what she thought they were, she tossed the dagger and the boy barely moved out of its way, in the process easily knocking the barrels over

When they landed, chaos erupted

The first barrel crashed and wine exploded everywhere

And the others started rolling downhill, right towards the guards

She used this as the distraction she needed to climb up to the tower and took a few steps back, leaping towards the window and kicking with all of her might

Luckily the glass shattered with ease and she fell in

She groaned as her wound throbbed from all the exertion but she ignored it, forcing herself onto her feet and shaking her head to rid her hair of any larger shards of glass

She scrambled up and started for the stairs before the interior guards could start her way

She knew her daughter had to be in one of these towers, it was just a matter of finding which one

Luck- or perhaps fate- truly seemed to be on her side as she found a maid half-way up the stairs and easily cornered her with her last remaining dagger

"Where is the princess?" she growled, pressing the blade to the maid's throat

"F-Fourth tower," she squeaked back

Cheyenne nodded and pocketed the dagger, tossing the empty bag away to keep from slowing her down as she raced up the staircase

This was the first tower, so she had three to go

Arriving at the second tower, she didn't even bother stopping

But when she came to the third, she was seen by the guards and was forced to quicken her pace as they began chasing after her

They were shouting up to the guards on the fourth floor and Cheyenne panted as she felt her wound starting to open up again

But she pressed on

She was too close now to just give up

And so she fought

She kept going until she was at the top of the steps and found herself with a sword drawn in front of her face

"We have you now," chuckled the guard behind her

He was right

They had her

But that didn't mean she had to give up

She took a breath, thinking about her choices as the guards started rambling on about surrendering

And then she made her move

She elbowed the guard behind her in the face hard enough to send him tumbling backwards and when the one in front of her aimed she ducked with ease, giving her time to pop back up as he tried to readjust his footing and plunge her dagger into his shoulder

She then took his sword and listened with a smirk as the other half of the guards began their descent down the stairs

She swung the sword with no skill and no aim and that seemed to keep the guards at bay, at least at first

It was all she needed, just long enough to get past the guards and run to the door at the end of the hall

As soon as the door was in sight she broke into a run, slamming against it and turning the knob, taking a breath when it turned and she managed to push it open

"Neveah?" she breathed

The little girl turned and smiled brighter than the sun as she stood and rushed towards her

"Mommy!!" she cried

"Neveah..." Cheyenne breathed, bending down and picking her up easily

The two embraced tightly and Cheyenne took a breath, turning to find not only a group of guards in front of her, but the King himself as well

"This was all very touching, but it's time for your little reunion to end," the King said simply as he stepped forward

"Mommy..." Neveah whimpered

As if it were a command, Cheyenne clutched her harder in her arms

The mother was just a normal human

She had never even thought about using magic before because she merely COULDN'T

It just wasn't part of her DNA

But as the king came closer and Neveah started to scream, she found herself moving one hand off of her draught's back and aiming it outwards

"What is this now?" the king laughed as he started to draw his sword

"Your worst nightmare," Cheyenne breathed out

And much to the surprise of everyone there, a bolt of lightning suddenly shot from Cheyenne's hand and struck the king

She rushed out, glad everyone was too busy trying to tend to the king and running past them

"Get them you fools! Don't let them get away!" she heard

She clutched her daughter tighter and started to rush down the stairs

And every guard that came in her way she used magic on

At first it was just lightning bolts, but then it grew, it became fire, ice, even things like tree vines

She soon found that if she needed it badly enough, she had access to more magic than she could have fathomed

She held Neveah closer as she burst out of the palace and ran to the nearest horse, mounting with ease and taking off towards the gates again

"Mommy..." Neveah sniffled

"It's ok, I'm here... I'm not ever letting you go again, I swear it," she promised, clutching her daughter closer as they rode

As soon as the gates were near she pressed her daughter against her and jumped from the horse, running to the edge of the gates and taking a breath as she fanned her fingers out and the gates burst open

Breathing a sigh of relief that the horse was still there, she placed her foot in the stirrup and hoisted the two of them upwards

It only took the motion of her grabbing the reins for Buttercup to race down the hill from the inner kingdom

And from there, the journey was easy

Well, easy in comparison to what it had been

It took quite a while for enough soldiers to ready their horses and chase after them and that gave them a great head start

But Cheyenne knew that if they stopped for too long, they would be faced with the King's Guard again

Stopping close to sunset so that Buttercup could drink some water from the nearby river, Cheyenne took the opportunity to finally open the bag that Faelynn had given her

She expected to find coins or metal or some other sort of trinket that could be used as currency or as a sign that she was sent by the blacksmith

And she definitely expected to find a map or at least some sort of directions

But all she found instead were a key and another, smaller bag

The key was beautiful, wooden with intricate details of vines and leaves carved into it, and inside the smaller pouch was some sort of strange pink powder

Swallowing nervously, Cheyenne held the items in one hand and raised the other, biting the fingertip of her leather glove and yanking it off so she could reach into the bag with her bare hand

As soon as she did and that strange pink powder graced her fingertips she could feel a surge of energy burst through her and she instantly knew what the powder was

"Pixie Dust..."

It all made sense now, every single thing...

"Neveah, come here," she called

The little girl turned away from the horse and walked towards her instantly, wrapping her arms around her mother's legs in a hug

Cheyenne smiled, reaching down and petting her daughter's head adoringly

"We're going to go somewhere new... ok?" she said softly

"Ok," she said quietly

Taking a breath, Cheyenne poured some Pixie Dust over the key and pointed the key into thin air, turning it in an unlocking motion and gasping as a beautiful door came out of nowhere and opened for them

The door looked identical to the key, so she knew it was the right place

"Come on," she said softly as she stared at the bright, but warm light

Neveah looked pensive but Cheyenne leaned down and gave her a tight hug, picking her up again

"I promise its ok, do you trust me?"

"Of course I trust you Mommy,"

Those words meant the world to the mother and she nodded, reaching out and taking Buttercup's reins, pulling the horse away from the water despite her protests and taking a step forward

"Trust me...." she said quietly as she stepped through the door

At first, it was just the light

But when the door closed behind them, a beautiful land was revealed to them

The sky was the bluest of blue and the grass was the richest of green

Fae Folk walked all around with their wings and ears and other features displayed proudly about them

The energy was light and happy and music played around, the air smelled of sweet scents and it was a comfortably warm feeling in this new world

Not hot like the heat of summer, but warm, like a home's comfort

"Where are we Mommy?" Neveah asked innocently as Cheyenne slowly put her down

"We're in the Faery Realm," she said quietly

"The Faery Realm?"

"Yes..."

There was a pause as she surveyed the area, clutching Neveah's hand tightly and suddenly relaxing, smiling brightly when she looked ahead and saw Faelynn staring up at her and waving calmly

"Are we going to be ok here Mommy?"

Cheyenne nodded, looking down at her daughter and smiling warmly

"Yes, my princess, we're going to be wonderful here, as long as I have you... everything is going to be wonderful,"

Alexa Asagi Andres

The Dragon Mother

Once upon a time

In a land far luckier than our own

There were dragons of all kinds and sorts that roamed freely

Big and small

Loud and quiet

Strong and gentle

This was a land where all dragons could feel truly free and at ease

A land that was not far from the bigger lands of the faery realm, but was still enough of a distance that the dragons basically had it to themselves

It wasn't a terribly large piece of land

Much like an island

And although every dragon of every shape, size, and color lived there- and was more than welcome to live there-

The dragons who were most commonly found, were in fact, baby dragons

More specifically, orphan dragons

For it is on this island, that the Dragon Mother lived

The Dragon Mother's name suits her well, for she was one of the first dragons ever created

Her kind, maternal nature has kept her away from any ensuing battles or problems that most of the other older dragons have encountered over the course of centuries

Because the Dragon Mother did not care to be involved

True, she loved her people, she wanted what was best for them, but her duties were not on the battlefield, they were at home ensuring that the hatchlings had the best chance of survival for the next generation

And she did her job well

Despite having many children of her own, the Dragon Mother quickly became known as a foster mother for the orphaned or lonely hatchlings

Even those who had families sometimes came to her when they were feeling especially downtrodden and alone

And the Dragon Mother was always waiting for them with something that would make them happy

Something unique to each and every individual hatchling that assured them that they were special

One hatchling had an affinity for crystals, and so when she came to the Dragon Mother one day after feeling lonely she found a basket of the brightest, sparkiest crystals she had ever seen waiting for her

Another had a special liking for freshly baked bread and when he went to the Dragon Mother to get advice for his misery he found three full loaves- still steaming!- waiting for him

It was the Dragon Mother's intuition and natural gift for nurturing and mothering that made her so good at her job

And in the Dragon Mother's centuries of life she could not recall a single thing that she hadn't dealt with at some point

Every kind of heart aches and breaks, and broken bones and sore bruises

Mourning and grieving and loss and tragedy

Depression and anxiety and loneliness and worthlessness

She took in orphans from every age and mothered dragons who were even parents themselves

And in all that time, in all those ways, the Mother Dragon had been able to remain calm and peaceful and uninvolved in any kind of battle

But of course, there's always a first time for everything...

The times change in every world, even if it seems like the Island Of Dragons has stayed frozen for the past few thousand years with nothing too interesting going on

Even though time in the faery realms moves much differently than it does in the human worlds, it does still move

And lately, there's been a bit of a trend going on in the faery realms that has slowly but surely reached the Island Of Dragons

That trend was visiting humans

Everyone wanted to try it and test their luck and see if they'd be found or seen or discovered

From faeries to merfolk to werewolves to vampires

If you weren't human, you sure as the moon wanted to see one in person!

The dragons were no exception of course

But up until now, interaction with humans has been sorely limited

Up until now, most sightings are just that- sightings

Fleeting glances, sparkles of Pixie Dust on the wind, a few fingers in someone's hair

Spectacular sure, but short lived

Up until now, that is....

Because up until now, no one had the thought (or the spell) to disguise themselves as a human for much longer than a few minutes

That was, up until now...

Now that a spell had been discovered and curiosities about the human world had risen anew, it was becoming a quickly growing trend to disguise one's self as a human for a day or two or sometimes even longer at a time and see what human life was all about

Even the hatchlings were eager to explore it

However, this brought forth problems that the Dragon Mother had never dealt with before

The hatchlings, of course, were disguised as human children when they went off to explore, which meant that many of them attended school for a time or two

It was easy to do with a few altered memory spells from the witches they knew

But that ease was very short lived

The hatchlings began flying home in great despair

And the Dragon Mother had never seen such a flock of dread hit her hatchlings all at once

The hatchlings were now dealing with things that dragons simply do not have

Bullying, pressuring, teasing and taunting, placing blame and just being mean

The hatchlings had never experienced so much raw hatred in their entire lives

And although it wasn't uncommon for dragons to have dealt with human hunters before (the faery realms were hidden now for a reason...) that had been so long ago that they hadn't warned the hatchlings of how cruel humans could be

That, and there was definitely a discernable difference between an adult dragon dealing with an ignorant human hunter who merely saw them as an animal..

...And an innocent baby dragon who didn't know the world had anything cruel in it at all suddenly being tossed into the thrush of name calling and hair pulling and guilt tripping

And the Dragon Mother, for her part, had never experienced anything like it either

She had first tried to calm the hatchlings the classic ways- "Ignore them", "Don't let them bother you", "Tell one of the human adults" et cetera....

But none of this seemed to help

The hatchlings just continued to fly to her and weep

The Dragon Mother was at a loss for what to do, she didn't know how far she could even allow herself to get into this involvement

That is... until one day, one of the hatchlings came to her with a hurt claw...

"What happened my darling child?" cooed the Dragon Mother as a little pink and violet hatchling glided into the cave in tears

"One of the humans said I looked funny- even though I was wearing my human disguise- and.. and..." she paused to sniffle

The Dragon Mother frowned, pushing the plate of donuts and glass of chocolate milk closer as she pulled the hatchling into a hug (human culture wasn't ENTIRELY cruel after all if they had made these delights... of course... now many of the hatchlings were becoming ADDICTED to the man-made sugar highs... but that was another problem for another day....)

"And? What else happened my dear?"

"And... he..... he slammed a big book down on my finger..." she sniffled, holding her small, trembling front paw up

There was, indeed, one claw that was slightly crooked in comparison to the others that the Dragon Mother swore with absolute certainty wasn't that way the morning before

It was at that moment that she realized things had gone MUCH too far, and she would have to intervene

And so the next day she went with the three little hatchlings that had planned to journey into the human world that day, a plan in mind to get this problem fixed once and for all

The moment she entered the door with the three hatchlings at her side, she immediately felt the heavy, suffocatingly negative air surround her

Why it nearly choked the life out of her!

The first step she had to take was going to the leader of this "School" to confront them about what had happened to her hatchling the day before

What she expected was a sincere apology that something like that had happened on their grounds and the promise to pull the offending child aside and at the very least force him to apologize

.... What she got was far, far less than that

"I'm afraid it's her word against his, Mrs. Dragone`, your daughter should have gone to the teacher straight away," the leader- "principal"- admonished

"I did!" the hatchling protested

"Well unfortunately there's no evidence of anything having happened and like I said, it's your word against your classmate's, with no proof I'm afraid there's nothing we can do,"

This was the first of three strikes that had the Dragon Mother ticking in anger

The second was when she was escorting her hatchlings to the lunchroom after classes (which she had not been allowed to attend for some backwards reason)

She was never more proud of herself for the forethought of bringing food with them from home after seeing what the place DARED to call "food"- and to tack a colorful "healthy" sign right above it too, somehow, that had to be breaking some sort of law....-

Regardless and for reasons still a mystery to her she and the hatchlings had to stand in line anyway before being allowed to sit down.... and that was when it started...

"It" being one of the other children continuously and literally stepping on the toes of one of her hatchlings

"Ouch!" the hatchling cried, taking a step back

The human child seemed to snicker and the Dragon Mother cleared her throat

"Excuse me, please watch where you're going, you just stepped on her foot," she said politely

After all, the Dragon Mother was a mother to all and a fighter to none, she could never even fathom being rude to a child

This child, however, ignored her warning and stepped on the hatchling again

This time the Dragon Mother repeated herself a bit more curtly

The third time she gently pushed the child up in line to keep him away from her hatchling

And the fourth time...

Well....

The fourth time she decided there was nothing else she could do.....

Except to take a step forward in line and "accidentally" step on the human child's foot in retaliation

The child reared back, staring at her with a slack jaw and stunned eyes as she glanced down at him

She said nothing, simply put an arm around her hatchlings and herded them forward

She didn't want to say she was proud of herself

....

But her hatchling had suffered more than enough bruised toes by now and the child was far more stunned than he was hurt

Of course, this is a dragon for you, it's ill-advised to try such a thing at home

The third and finally incident that struck a tally off of the patience line of the Dragon Mother dealt with something that, once again, the Dragon Mother had never expected to witness

An adult being cruel to a child

More specifically, one of the humans deciding it was suddenly ok to push around one of the hatchlings

It was just after lunch and although technically the Dragon Mother was supposed to leave by now she didn't, she was a dragon, really, what were they going to do about it?

Instead she stood outside the classroom door and listened, waiting for signs that the hatchlings were ok

What she got however was quite the opposite

"You're late," she heard the teacher accuse

"No I'm not, class starts at 1:45, it's exactly 1:45," one of the hatchlings protested

"That clock is two minutes slow," the teacher replied briskly

"But.. it's the only clock down this hall.... how was I supposed to know?"

"That's something you should have been aware of beforehand,"

"But no one told me-"

"Are you this argumentative with your parents? You need to learn some manners,"

The Dragon Mother tensed, waiting to hear the hatchling's reply

"My parents are dead," he said slowly

There was a brief pause

"Then your guardian, whoever it is that looks after you, this is no excuse for being late,"

The complete disregard for the hatchling's well-being- not to MENTION the complete idiocy of the argument to begin with- finally struck the third tally in the Dragon Mother's book of patience and without hesitation she swung the classroom door open and marched straight in

"You can't be in here, if you're waiting for your child you have to wait at the office," the teacher said briskly

"I can and I will be in here, how dare you treat a child with such disregard and hold them to something so insanely and idiotically malfunctioned? How dare you condone other children being harmed because you don't want to get your hands dirty? How dare you refuse to actually WATCH the children who have been left in your care!?" the Dragon Mother shouted

"Ma'am, you are going to HAVE to leave," the woman insisted

The Dragon Mother's eyes flickered gold and she took a deep breath, exhaling smoke out her nose

"Oh.... am I?" she asked slowly as she began to shift from her human form into her true self- her dragon form, which was far too big for the low-ceiling of the classroom and busted through it with ease

"Tell me again what I'm going to have to do?" the Dragon Mother snarled

From then on the experimentation of disguising one's self as human just for fun ended

If there was actually a reason behind it then that was up to be discussed

But no more random humanizing- and CERTAINLY no more children attending human schools

However, during the interim when these rules were still yet to be decided on, the Dragon Mother had had to come forth again on multiple other occasions to defend her hatchlings....

And during the wake of that, had even taken some human children under her wings

Even still there are slews of supernaturals out there that live among us, some may not even know they're anything but human

So, it may be best advised, that before you hurt someone's feelings, or do something that you wouldn't appreciate being done to you in return, watch out

You never know when the Dragon Mother is watching...

Alexa Asagi Andres

The Elf And The Bees

Once upon a time

In a land not so distant from our own

There lived an elf

Elves are not always the small creatures with big hats that live in tree trunks like many believe them to be

These elves exist too of course, but much more commonly are the Woodland Elves

The elves that resemble, upon first glance, a human

But once one takes a closer look and sees the sparkle in their eyes (or the pointed ears)

One can quickly come to the conclusion that these are not humans at all, but elves

And one elf in particular lives in the middle of the woods to tend to the herbs

He's one of the lucky few who travels all across the woods every day to take care of the herbs and spices and other natural foods that grow there

Unlike most elves who stay mostly to one region to keep from being detected by the humans in the towns nearby, this elf is one of those who travels all through the woods, collecting nuts, tending to herbs, caring for the natural life of the forest

This very lucky elf is named Roderick, and he sends much of the herbs he picks to a wizard who lives in a nearby cottage

He sends some off to the villages and towns as well, but most of the herbs that grow deep within the forest are of less interest to humans

This, however, is where his job gets interesting

Roderick is one of the only elves who can not only travel the entire expanse of the woods, but also can go to the edge of the woods

That thin line where the forest meets the towns and villages

It is here that some of the most important woodland work takes place

For it is only on the edge of the woods that humans are capable of gathering herbs and spices (being that many are too frightened to go into the woods themselves)

So in order to ensure that the humans get the foods they need and don't die off quite so quickly, Roderick and other Herb Elves must plant and tend to the herbs and spices at the edges of the woods

It can often become a game of seeing how close one can get to the humans without being seen

However, it's one afternoon, during one of those very such games, that the Herb Elf heard a sound

A sound that was really quite a bothersome sound

It was the sound of trees collapsing

And it sent vibrations of sadness and mourning for the lives of the trees all throughout the forest

Hoping it was just a one-off problem, Roderick tried to ignore it and go back to his herb planting

.... Unfortunately it was much more than just a one-off incident

And when Roderick went to investigate why the trees were collapsing, he spied something quite terrible

A gang of humans were brutally and ruthlessly tearing the trees down as if they were mere objects....

The birds fluttered and flew around, chirping and wailing in distress as the trees were taken away from them

The squirrels and chipmunks ran around on the forest floor, seeking shelter now that their homes were gone

And the distress of the birds, squirrels, and chipmunks were sending other animals into distress as well

Deer ran in fright and rabbits hopped away anxiously

It was a tragedy and a wreck to watch and Roderick found his heart aching for the trees and his forest friends

But what finally shocked him out of his moment of mourning was when one of the greatest, fullest honeycombs in the entire forest was attacked and the bees were sent away, forced to flee from a home that was about to be destroyed

The bees were Roderick's best friends, in the entire forest...

Not only were they the most helpful when it came to planting herbs, but they were also some of the best conversationalists

Seeing them forced to flee made up his mind once and for all and the Herb Elf waited for the humans to leave before heading over to the destroyed land before him

Frowning, he gathered as many acorns as he could find and planted them, the trees weren't herbs, but he had enough talent to raise the trees anyway

And by the next morning, everything seemed back to normal, the trees that were once there were replaced with new trees and the distress was gone from the forest....

Until the humans came back, and they didn't seem all that pleased with the new development....

Roderick was forced to watch once again as the beautiful trees that he loved were cut down and destroyed for no reason but to expand land

And that night, he repeated the process of planting the trees again

And the next morning the humans returned to take them down again....

It was a bitter battle that neither side seemed to be winning and he wasn't quite sure at all where to go from here

"Why don't you seek help from others?" suggested one of the rabbits who came to watch the destruction with him one day

"I think everyone in this forest has done all they can do... we're made up mostly of the smaller creatures, there isn't very much that rabbits and squirrels can do against humans.... in quantity,"

"Not from this forest, from neighboring forests, from far away forests, from forests all across everywhere," the rabbit replied with a smile

Roderick stared down at the rabbit and smiled brightly, rushing towards the bees, who were currently trying to figure out where to place their new home

"Bees! My friends! I may have a way to save our home!" the Herb Elf said with a bright smile

The bees looked up at him a bit skeptically but he nodded his assurance to them regardless

"I'll need your help though,"

After discussing his plans with the bees, Roderick did what he had done every late afternoon for a week now, he gathered the acorns that had been left strewn about the woods and planted them

And just as every night had gone for the past week, the trees grew back

The humans, to their one credit, seemed to have been expecting this when they came back and weren't at all surprised with the development

What they WERE surprised with, however, was the sudden growling that came from the woods

And before they could set foot too close to the trees, forest friends from many lands away began to emerge

Wolves, foxes, coyotes, bears, snakes, elk and moose...

These animals were not nearly so easy to scare away like the birds and squirrels were, and luckily for everyone involved, the humans seemed to notice that pretty quickly...

All it took was for one of the wolves to step closer and let out a low, menacing growl, for the humans to promptly drop everything and go running

"Impressive," Roderick said with a smile, reaching down to high-five the wolf

"We wouldn't have been here to help if it weren't for you, thank you for alerting us to the trouble our neighbors were having, if it were me, I would be willing to say that YOU are far more impressive," the wolf reasoned

"Not at all, it's really the bees that we owe our thanks to, without them I never could have gotten my message to so many of you,"

The wolf stared back at the other animals who had gathered there and nodded to them, all turning at once towards the bees and bowing to them in respect

It was from that day forward that the bees had their own holiday, humans didn't know about it, of course, but those who dwelled in the forest sure did, and they celebrated every year

And for his help and kindness in the matters, the Herb Elf Roderick was awarded with honorary Bee Status, which in the forest was quite an honor

The humans continued to try, of course, humans never give up on anything

But it was alright, because now they had a plan, they had bees...

And most importantly of all, they have Roderick there to keep an eye out and protect those who are unprotected

Faery Tales, Mermaid Myths, And Other Fantastical Legends

The Faery Friends

Once upon a time

In a land full of wonder

There lived two faeries

Well, to be more specific

There lived a mother faery and a daughter faery

And these faeries were the best of friends

Some people found that odd, they believed that parents and children shouldn't be friends

But to these people, the faeries merely scoffed and brushed them off

The faery mother, Darla, was stunningly beautiful

She was kind, caring, smart, funny, and surprisingly strong

Not physically perhaps, she hadn't inherited her mother's super-strength

But emotionally, she was the strongest person her daughter had ever met

The two of them had a bond like no other, stronger than just mere parent and child

They had the bond of twins, of friends, of two souls connected past any earthly tether

And sometimes, people envied them for that

Envy is a funny thing, because sometimes it can stay dormant and simply be expressed as envy, as wanting what someone else has

But other times it can do just the opposite

Other times envy turns to anger and far worse expresses its self as degrading or insulting the very thing they're envious of

The faeries did everything in their power to ignore the voices around them, who would shout that they were too close or that friendships between parents and children were wrong because then there would be no authority

They ignored these people sometimes.... but other times, when these people got too loud and disruptive, Darla had to speak up

"You know, I pity the fact that you have no friendship with your child, what a lonely existence," she would say to them

This of course only incited more of their anger, but they couldn't deny that she was right

The hateful words of those who had no good relationship with their children or parents weren't the only ones who crawled beneath their skin

The younger faery often faced upset when she was a child for other things

She faced children and even adults who were cruel to her just for being different

And she came home many days in tears for this

Her mother, ever the strong one, ever the warrior, stood and defended her

"You have to let children face these things alone, you can't protect them all the time" would say the teachers and other adults

"That's a load of malarkey, I'm not leaving my child to be tortured, as a mother it's my job to PROTECT her from these things, and I will never understand anyone who leaves their children to fend for themselves," Darla would say

And this was perhaps Darla's most pronounced quality

She was a mother, first and foremost

She was by nature, a nurturer

And once her daughter got older- though never too old to stop being her child, of course- she found another creature to lend her nurturing hand to

A little dog, who tested her patience and her very sanity

At first the dog, Isabo, was nothing but trouble

And she put Darla's skills in motherhood to the absolute test

But, because her mothering skills were so astounding, she eventually tamed the wild beast

And turned said beast into an adoring, loving, happy child of the dog variety

And thus Isabo became strong friends with the faeries too

They were a rather peculiar bunch

Spending their time reading, writing, talking- even if Isabo could only speak Yorkie language and relied on improper translations- and enjoying each other's company

People thought it was strange, how could anyone be happy with such a simple life?

The answer was somewhat evasive

Few people ever understood and in fact, the faeries barely understood it themselves

Darla, of course, eventually knew how to answer them though

When someone asked how they could enjoy such a simple life, her answer was this:

"Because I have a best friend to enjoy it with,"

Alexa Asagi Andres

The Faery Mother

Once upon a time

Very long ago, there was a great sadness that fell over the faery land

For the goddess, Morgana, had to leave for another land

The faeries cried for many days and many nights, for they had come to honor Morgana like their own mother

Morgana's heart ached for her faery children, she couldn't stand to see such sadness in such a beautiful kingdom

So Morgana came up with a plan

"My children, gather around me," she said one day

"I know you will miss me, and I will miss you, you are my life and soul, but I must go on, I am needed elsewhere,"

The faeries continued their silent sobs as they stared up at her, but Morgana smiled down sweetly at them

"I am needed elsewhere... yet I cannot bear to leave you here alone, so I have found someone to take my place in this land," she said, stepping aside

From behind her emerged a beautiful, very small faery woman, with long sweeping blonde hair and swirling blue-green eyes

She was small and appeared to be almost fragile, but exuded such a kindness and gentleness that the faeries were taken by her

They were so taken by her, in fact, that they stopped crying to stare at her

"My darling children, this is the goddess Darla, she will take my place as your guide here, I will always be with you, but for now, please allow this woman to guide you as I once did,"

The faeries were hesitant but they said their goodbyes to Morgana anyway, knowing she was needed elsewhere

Over the coming days the faeries began to gather around Darla, a few at first, but then many more

They spoke with her, asked her for advice in dealing with their missing of Morgana

The Goddess Darla sat with them each and spoke to them softly

She spent as many hours as it took to make each and every faery smile again

And in only a year, she had been granted the grand title of Faery Mother

And this was how she was known forever more

The Faery Mother was such a legend that beings came from other lands to meet her

She took them each under her wings with the same gentleness and kindness that she gave to the faeries

It mattered not to her who or what they were, be they goblins or mermaids or moles or birds

Each was as precious to her as the last

She was not nearly as fragile as she appeared, beneath her soft skin and gentle eyes she was full of strength and power

And any who were unkind to one of her children would pay dearly

For despite her kindness and loving, the Faery Mother had no tolerance for any who hurt her children, and the beings of darkness that had once pained them came to fear her, and soon began to leave the faery children alone

The Faery Mother was treasured by all and even the humans who had heard of her

The humans told a legend of a beautiful faery maiden, the most beautiful they had ever seen

They said that if any were to ever see this faery maiden in the woods all would know immediately who she was

For children would flock to her

And music would play

It was a grand ritual and a true honor to witness

But over time the Faery Mother began to see the suffering of human children

She noticed the orphaned or the injured

She saw the pain in the human children and reflected back to the pain her faery children had once suffered and it made her so sad that for the first time in many, many, many years, she began to cry

The faeries, so shocked and saddened by their mother's tears, decided to construct a gift, so that their mother would never again shed tears

They worked for many days and many nights constructing this gift and when it was finished, they sent the youngest of the children to find her

The Faery Mother smiled, although sadly, when the young children came to her, and allowed them to pull her away

When they arrived at the gift the Faery Mother stared at it in confusion, for it was a bit of an odd gift to receive

It was a door

Nothing special, nothing ornate or grand

Just a small door in the middle of the woods

"Faery Mother," said one of the faeries

"We've made this door for you, so that human children can travel into our world at will, so that you can bring the children who are alone and hurting to our world, so that you will never cry again, Faery Mother,"

And the Faery Mother, so touched by her children's gift, began to cry again "Why do you cry Faery Mother? Have we done something wrong?" the faeries asked

"No, my beautiful children," she said softly

"I am just so happy that you have come to treasure me so,"

The faeries smiled back and they never again saw their Faery Mother cry after that day

For from then on, when she found children alone and hurting, she would bring them with her to the faery world

And she would treasure them and care for them the way she treasured and cared for her own children

For that was the gift of the Faery Mother

Mother to all

The Faery Pugs

Once upon a time

In a land mere pages away from our own

There lived a wizard..

But there also lived pugs

These, however, were not just any ordinary pugs (although, no pug is actually anything like any other pug, they have a tendency to all be very unique)

These were faery pugs

Because long ago, in a land far, far away from this one, there lived a faery

This faery had only one interest, only one love in life: Animals

Every animal

Big and small

Gentle and rough

Loud and quiet

She loved every last one of them

But there was a problem, for you see, earth animals cannot stay in the faery lands

They were meant for here, and although there is nothing wrong with them being in the faery world, if they were to get a taste for it, just like humans, they would never want to leave

Animals were created as companions

To each other, to humans, to Fae folk, to all living beings

Faery Tales, Mermaid Myths, And Other Fantastical Legends

If they were to all stay in the faery world, there would be no animal companions left for the world that humans live in

And without companions, human lives would grow dull and grey, anger would mount, violence would occur, the world would quite likely just simmer over and explode

For humans are naturally very prickly creatures, it's the animal companions that give them a softer touch and make them wish to do better and BE better than they are

The faery realized this, and knew she had to let go of the idea of keeping the animals with her

That is.... until she realized she was missing a pug....

Pugs, you see, are very small animals when you compare them to, say, lions or horses or even bigger dogs

It's very easy to lose track of one if you aren't careful

And the faery was a lot of things, but careful was certainly not one of them

For hours she spent looking for that pug, and eventually she did find her....

... Sitting in a bag of Pixie Dust.....

It's a common tale that Pixie Dust can make people fly

This is true, it's only one of many, many, many things that Pixie Dust can do

But that's the effect it has on HUMANS....

The effect on animals is really quite different, for animals do not just pick up from the ground and fly...

When animals are blessed by Pixie Dust, they grow wings and become part of the faery bloodline themselves

Animals are much purer, simpler, lighter souls to carry than humans', so while Pixie Dust eventually runs its course and drains out of a human's system, it sticks with an animal for life

And that is how the faery got an idea

Seeing the pug sitting there, wings already grown and staring cheerfully up at her, the faery got a very, very mischievous idea

She took aside her animals, flew into the air, and sprinkled bag after bag after bag of Pixie Dust over top of them

And that's when it began, the creation of faery-animals!

Why there were faery dogs and faery cats

Faery horses and faery rats

There were faery cheetahs and faery dolphins

Faery elephants and faery lizards

Faery pandas and faery ocelots

Every animal, mark her count, was blessed with Pixie Dust

Of course, the faery reminded herself, these were only HER animals

The animals that had wandered into the faery realm

There were only a few of each species there, the vast, VAST majority of the animals were still in the human world

This was alright, she knew, because unlike simply wandering into the faery world and never returning, these animals had evolved, become something entirely different, and thus, the other animals would have no reason to look for them

After all, dogs evolved from wolves, do you see wolves tapping on your neighbor's door asking where the poodle is?

And this is where our pugs come in

As you can see, they are not ordinary pugs at all

They are descendants of the very first faery pugs

And they hold the title well

But, back to the wizard

The wizard you see is quite an extraordinary man

His job is to organize and record stories and turn them into books and scrolls and other readable instruments

It's a very difficult job, trying to organize so many thoughts and ideas

And when he saw two faery pugs fluttering down the sidewalk, tiny as they were, he realized that there they were- his partners in publishing, his assistants!

This was quite alright with the faery pugs, for they had no place else to go

And so they were quickly deemed Pugslee and Wednesday, for it happened to be a Wednesday and some parts of the faery world were celebrating the Festival Of Pugslee

Now THAT is a long story.......

Pugslee and Wednesday and the wizard, Farris, became the fastest of friends

And the pugs happily helped him with his work

They were given a comfy spot in the office with toys and food and a nice fluffy bed, everything they could have wanted

And their primary job was to alert the wizard to arriving guests

Every time the door would open the pugs would scramble to their feet and stare down the visitor, letting out a GRUFF and a RUFF and a guttural cross between a huff and a growl

"Now girls, I see them, stand down," the wizard said gently, patting them on their heads and going to greet the visitors

Surely, the girls decided, if they could have balanced on three legs, they would have given him a firm salute

It was a daily process- more than daily in fact- that the pugs stood on guard and alerted the wizard to trouble (or, you know, the mailman)

And no matter how tired they became after people here and people there would wander into their place of business, they never failed to stumble along and greet the visitors

It was all a very demanding job and the pugs were always the most glad when the day was over and they all went home to have snacks and watch TV

That was truly the most enjoyable part of the day

After all, nothing was better after a long day of pointing out intruders than popcorn and watching whatever those pesky zombies were getting up to on cable

Faery Tales, Mermaid Myths, And Other Fantastical Legends

The Faery Spring

Once upon a time

In a land that was bridged across to our own

There was a little girl named Shirley who lived in a house on the edge of a town

This house on the edge of a town was very close to the woods

The woods that lead into the faery world

The little girl would frequently ask her parents how she could interact with the faery world

For she so badly wanted to be in touch with it

"Find a spring, and when you do, the faeries will leave coins underneath," her parents told her

Shirley made it her mission from then on to find a spring in the woods so that she could receive coins from the faeries

Perhaps, she thought, she would then be able to meet them

So she wandered into the woods every day after that

For as long as she was capable, she wandered each day and searched high and low for a spring

She searched behind trees and under rocks and in puddles

She searched on the dirt path and to the west woods and to the east woods

She traveled forwards and backwards and in circles

And finally, after a grand 35 days, she found one

It was old and small and rusted

But it was a spring nonetheless

And so Shirley picked it up with care and carried it back to her house happily

She told her mother what she had done and left the spring on the kitchen counter that night

Hardly able to wake, she jumped eagerly out of bed the next morning and raced down to the kitchen table, lifting the spring up and looking beneath it

And there it lay

A penny

It wasn't much

It was a single and quite plain, even a bit dirty, penny

But it was a penny none the less

And this penny was proof that the faeries had come

She took the penny and for many years refused to spend it

She took the penny and for many years she treasured it

However, the human world is a cruel one, and by the time Shirley had become an adult, the wonder and hope for faeries had disappeared from her life

She still loved them and she still wondered about them

But she had long since realized that it had been her mother who left the penny beneath the spring

Not a faery at all

And so she gave up believing in faeries, no matter how much she loved them

It was when she was still young, only a year into adulthood that the faeries entered her life again

She had been wandering through the woods, looking for some berries to bake a pie with, when she saw it

Straight ahead was a beautiful, crystal clear pool of water...

No.... not a pool....

A spring...

It was a spring

And it was stunning, breathtaking

It glistened in the sunlight and beckoned forth life from all corners of the forest

From the rabbits and deer to the bears and foxes

They all gathered near the brilliant spring and drank or swam or simply breathed in the nice scent of the spring water

And Shirley was drawn to it as well

Just as well as any of the other forest dwellers did, she walked forward and felt a sensation in the forest that she had never felt before

It was simply impossible to describe

But it was warm and inviting

It was peaceful and relaxing

It was everything good about the world

She bent down at the spring and cautiously, almost hesitantly, dipped her hands in and brought them back

When she withdrew the water was so clear and sparkling that she could see a reflection of herself as well as everything around her in it, as if it were a mirror

She took a breath and raised her hands, closing her eyes as she drank the spring water

And suddenly, just like that, everything changed

Colors brightened and sounds heightened

Everything became more musical, more magical, more brilliant

The colors were more vibrant and the sensations she felt were all so much softer and warmer

It was like everything was at once brightened and toned down

It was the most astounding experience she had ever felt

And when she inhaled, she felt something odd on her back

Turning her head, she was shocked to find a beautiful pair of faery wings having attached themselves to the space between her shoulder blades

She spun on the ball of her foot and turned her head as she tried to see every inch of her beautiful wings

She stepped closer to stare into the spring and saw with wonder and amazement that beneath the water.... were coins...

Layers and layers and layers of faery coins

Gasping, she realized then what her parents had meant all those years ago

It wasn't that faeries would leave money underneath a spring

It was that they would leave money underwater in a spring!

Smiling, she fluttered her wings and lifted off of the ground

The sensation of flying was unlike anything she had ever felt before and it was so amazing that she never wanted to land

She realized then what drinking the water in the spring had done

It had not just turned her into a faery

It had brought her into the faery realm

It was the spring all this time that was the portal between realms but no one seemed to realize it

Or perhaps, the spring just wasn't always there

After all, in all her life, Shirley had been traveling these woods day after day and yet had never once before stumbled upon the spring

It wasn't even a question that she was going to stay there in the faery world

She made a life for herself there

A happy life, far more happy than the mundane one she had started to live in the world of humans

She spent her days visiting the spring and leaving coins for any who visited it from the human side and when she wasn't visiting the spring she was at home in her cottage

It was a simple existence, she liked to craft things, making everything she could for decorations or tools or anything really that she was capable of crafting

She liked to cook and garden on occasion, but making things was really where it stood

Well that... and caring for the cats that wandered in and out of the faery world

It had all started with one little kitten

A small Himalayan that saw her wandering into the human world from the spring to leave coins and who became enamored with her wings

The kitten was so impressed by them, in fact, that she ran up and jumped onto Shirley's back in an attempt to get a better look

The jump surprised her and she gasped as she turned to retrieve the cat from her back, but she was left relatively unharmed

Ever since then she realized that she was a bit of a cat magnet and in a way began to collect them, keeping them safe on her grounds away from loneliness or human cruelty

It was a simple life, but that was what she always wanted

It was a simple life, but that was what made her the happiest

And every day she paid her respects by leaving what little coin she had by the Faery Spring

For without the spring

She never would have been given this beautiful life

The Fire Prince

Once upon a time

In a land filled with snow

There lived a prince, destined to save his kingdom

The prince's name was Ramsey, and he had beautiful wavy black hair, soft, gentle features, and dark brown skin

And he was the most gentle and kind ruler the land had ever seen

However, with kindness, came criticism

Many questioned Ramsey and believed that he would never- could never- be a good king due to his gentle heart

Others argued that it was because of his gentle heart that he would be the finest king there ever was

The land was divided on this and each side grew evermore certain that their beliefs were correct

The argument was escalating in the worst of ways over how King Ramsey would rule

If he would become the greatest failure.... or the greatest success

But it was Ramsey himself who was most undecided

As much as he wanted to be a good king, even he saw the flaws in his kindness

What good was a king who was too gentle to slap the wrists of criminals or use an army to defend his lands?

But, he decided, there was no use worrying about it

He prayed for his father to have a long life

Perhaps so long, in fact, that Ramsey would never have to rule at all

But this was another tale entirely

What changed everything- not only Ramsey, but the people too- was what happened one cold November day

The land had always been a chilly one and snow made its place there at least six months out of the year

But this year it was unnaturally heavy and had started to fall even in early October

The people were beginning to worry, as the snow only seemed to increase, that it wasn't going to stop

There were stories about a time many decades ago when it snowed year-round and destroyed all the crops

That the snow lasted without stopping for three years and the people nearly died out

There was always something, depending on what version you listened to, that melted the snow and brought back the sun and crops

And although Ramsey had always adored the story, he couldn't afford to occupy his thoughts with it now

For now, he was in a very questionable situation

He had been on his way to a neighboring kingdom to deliver some information when suddenly he spotted something rather odd

There was a bird lying in the snow

It was a somewhat large bird with shocking red and orange and gold feathers, and the bird wasn't moving at all

Quickly, the prince hopped down from his horse and stumbled through the snow to get to the bird

Upon picking up the fallen creature, he found with despair that the poor dear's heart had nearly stopped beating

"At the very least, I can take you somewhere so that you will not die alone or in the cold," Ramsey said with determination, taking off his own cloak to wrap the bird in

He rode with great speed to the next kingdom over and wandered into the palace, asking the guards not to tell of his arrival just yet so that he may make the bird's final moments comfortable

He took the bird to a fine room, wrapped it in lavish and expensive fabrics and made sure there was a roaring fire in the fireplace to heat the room enough so that snow was but a distant memory

He even managed to smuggle some hot soup away from the kitchen before anyone noticed him

He was fairly certain birds didn't actually eat soup but he had limited knowledge and even more limited resources and so he did the best he could

And to his surprise, the bird leaned down and lapped at the soup like a dog

And to his even greater surprise, a full hour passed, and the bird had not died

"I really have to be going now to deliver these scrolls, but I swear on my life, I will come back for you," Ramsey said with a gentle smile as he left the bird alone in the room

He rushed through his meeting with as much kindness and politeness as he could before hurrying back to the room a full two hours later

And to his surprise, the bird was now walking across the floor, clearly having improved in health

Ramsey felt his heart fill with so much joy, so much rapture, that the anxieties and fears he had of one day becoming king melted away, just as the snow had melted off of his feathered friend

"I'm not sure what kind of bird you are," he began as he offered his arm out to the bird

"I'm not even sure how much you can understand me... but I'd rather like to keep you with me at the palace if you don't mind,"

The bird thrilled lowly in its throat and carefully walked forward, stepping onto Ramsey's arm and holding there tightly as he rose to his feet again

"I think you can understand me just fine," he mused as he gathered his cloak and began to tidy up the room

"I just need something to call you now..." he mused, looking at the bird intensely and smiling more

"I'm reminded of the sun when I look at your feathers my friend, it reminds me of a time when the sun shone more often, and I pray to the God and Goddess that it will soon shine again,"

Ramsey paused suddenly at that, smiling widely

"Goddess... that's it! You must surely be a gift from the Goddess herself to assure us that warmer days are on the way! I should give you a fitting name then, Batari, truly fit for a Goddess," he exclaimed

The bird, Batari, thrilled with excitement and chirped happily, nuzzling against Ramsey's cheek

As promised, Ramsey took Batari back to the palace with him, and although many were weary of his new "pet" (Ramsey insisted she wasn't a pet, but a friend), they didn't dare to upset the already fragile-hearted prince

For many weeks Ramsey and Batari spent their days together, becoming nearly inseparable in fact

Ramsey cared for her as he would care for a member of his family, for when he looked at Batari and stared at the vibrant fire in her feathers, he felt his heart alight with hope that warmer days would approach

For weeks, this practice held, and it was the happiest Ramsey had ever been

But then, that happiness came to a screeching halt

Ramsey was about to set off again to go to the neighboring kingdom, this time to discuss a new trade agreement, and was torn on if he should take Batari with him or not

On the one hand, he could hardly imagine spending so much time away from his friend and he worried that the others at the palace wouldn't care for her as he did

But on the other, he worried- perhaps more- that being outside for so much of the journey would inspire Batari to fly away and she wouldn't come back, or worse, that the cold would sink into her frail bones and cause her ill again

Just as he was deciding to leave Batari behind, he heard the sound of an arrow being let loose from one of the practicing archers nearby, and when he turned, Batari fluttered in front of him and fell suddenly to the ground, the arrow having struck her chest

"BATARI!" Ramsey shouted in horror as he dropped to the ground

Healing from the cold was one thing, but an arrow to the chest- especially for such a small and fragile creature as a bird, even the bigger sorts- was not nearly so easy

And as he stared down into Batari's eyes, he found that he couldn't even call out for help before the light was gone

The screams and shouts of panic around him died into murmurs and whispers as the prince openly sobbed and mourned for his lost friend, thoughts of selfishness berating him the entire time as he wondered what the outcome would have been if he had been more decisive earlier and kept Batari safe inside the palace

But then, just as his heart felt such a throb of ache that he realized he would never recover from it, something shocking happened

Batari's body suddenly burst into flames, shocking the prince as he moved backwards to escape being burnt

And from the ashes, rose a girl

With hair as black as night and glorious feathers the same color as Batari's attached to her back

The girl had fire licking at her dark skin, but it didn't seem to bother her at all

Her feathers curved around her body and soon a dress made from said feathers fell onto her like a custom gown, and she rose to her feet

And when Ramsey looked into her eyes, he gasped at the realization that it was the coal black eyes of Batari staring back at him

"Batari?" he asked breathlessly

"Yes," she confirmed with a gentle smile

"But... how? I don't understand..." he said softly

"I am a Phoenix, Prince Ramsey, every thousand years phoenix will die and burst into flames, and from their ashes, will rise a new Phoenix, it is the cycle of rebirth, however, every ten thousand years, something different happens, instead of being reborn into merely a bird, a ten-thousand-year-old Phoenix may become a shapeshifter, with the capabilities to become human, IF, their death is stunted for a time, no matter how short or long, when you found me in the snow many weeks ago, it had been my time to become new again, but your kindness saved me, and granted me the ability to become more than I once was, you may not have been able to stop my death this time, but I assure you Prince Ramsey, it would have struck me soon enough even without the arrow's help, now I am renewed, and with it, comes new power," she explained, taking a step closer and extending her hand

"Prince Ramsey, take my hand, and allow me to thank you for all that you've done for me,"

With heavy caution, Ramsey slowly placed his hand in her's, and felt her gently wrap her fingers around him as flames began to snake up his arm

The guards and other onlookers screamed and shouted and rushed towards him, but stopped when they realized that the flames weren't burning him at all

The fire, as hot as it would be to anyone else, was nothing but a soft graze of warmth as it encased Ramsey's body

And just as suddenly as it had begun, it ended, and Batari let him go

"I've given you some of my power- some of my FIRE- and you are free to use it as you will, with that fire, you will always be reborn, no matter how mortal your wound or how high your age,"

Ramsey stared at Batari in shock in amazement and snapped his fingers, surely enough, a flame leapt from his fingertips and onto the ground, melting the snow around it

"Batari, is there a way to channel the flames to cool down and spread? Is there a way I can melt this blasted snow?"

Batari smiled and nodded in confirmation

"It will take practice, but I can show you a way," she promised

"Batari?" he asked again

"Yes?"

"I ... I know you're much more than just a bird now but.... would you consider remaining my friend?"

Batari smiled, laughing joyfully and turning as her wings tucked against her back

"Ramsey, it isn't even anything I have to consider,"

Weeks later, after the bizarre incident had long ended, Ramsey emerged from his studying with a beautiful gold and red staff, an orb atop it that looked as if fire itself had been crystalized

And when he struck the ground with the staff, the snow suddenly began to melt and warmth spread in waves and waves throughout the land

He thus became known as the Fire Prince, for he took warmth with him wherever he went

And thanks to melting the snow, the Fire Prince had gained the respect of ALL of his people, and they no longer felt that his kindness was weakness at all

Ramsey ruled for many years, as did his future wife, Batari

And when the time came that Ramsey was slain in battle, Batari's words held true, and he- like a Phoenix- burst into flames and rose again from his ashes, now sporting the same beautiful wings that his wife and children had

Eventually he allowed his oldest daughter, Indah, to take the throne in his place, and he and Batari settled down to live a more peaceful life

But, no matter how old he gets, or how long he's been retired, three things remain true of the Fire Prince that had been true all those years ago

The first, that he would always melt the snow when he needed to

The second that he loved Batari with all his heart and soul

And the third, that he took kindness with him, no matter how far away he went, or what circumstances he was under

That was the truest warmth that the Fire Prince had to offer

The Flower Faery

Once upon a time

In a land within close proximity of our own

There lived a faery

A very special faery

Oh at first glance she seemed like every other faery

She fluttered in the flower beds and danced amongst the leaves

Any regular old garden faery it seemed

But this faery, Branda, was much more than that

Branda was not a garden faery at all

She was a flower faery

What, one may wonder, is the difference?

Well, much like a common garden gecko is different than a chameleon

A garden faery tends to the flowers and plants

They water them and make sure the sun shines upon them and gives them a little pixie dust when they start to wilt and take the seeds of the dead plants to plant anew

They ensure that animals like bees and hummingbirds all get their fair share of nectar and try to detour pollen from creating discomfort for the larger animals like humans (with only little success, pollen is a very stubborn substance)

They plant plants and help them grow and make sure that nature blooms everywhere they land

This is not what Branda does

Alexa Asagi Andres

What Branda does is much more special

She, the Flower Faery, does not plant flowers or merely care for them

She CREATES flowers

It's a rare talent born only in every several generations

But Branda was lucky and blessed with the ability

The ability was not just to grow flowers wherever she went, it was to create new types of flowers all together

Have you ever wondered why it seems like there are always the average, roses, violets, sunflowers et cetera, and then all of a sudden a rare and rather new flower will bloom, seemingly out of nowhere?

That is Branda's power

She flutters about when no one is around and lands in the nearest garden or flowerbed and begins to sprinkle her very special pixie dust

And from the roots of the other flowers grows an entirely new species

Have you ever heard of the Silverarum Orchid?

That was Branda's doing

So obviously she doesn't JUST plant new flowers in gardens

She travels all over the world, to the forests and woods and jungles and anywhere that plants often grow

She creates new flowers, and even new colors for old flowers

She's been working on developing a natural blue rose for a while now and it seems that it's nearly ready

She's so proud of her work, in fact, that she sometimes leaves little messages in pixie dust for people to discover the new flowers she's created

Of course she's careful to make sure that the humans don't find out she's the one creating them, otherwise they'd never leave her alone!

Besides, it was fun to let them think that nature just sporadically spits up randomly new flowers

However, every now and then, a fellow Fae Friend would make a request of her

"Branda! Branda!" shouted a Spring Elf as he rushed towards her

"I want to give my wife something truly special for our anniversary, but I'm at a loss, I was wondering if you could create a new flower just for her? Her favorite colors are blue and pink," he explained hurriedly

"Why of course!" Branda said with a bright smile, fluttering over to her garden and sprinkling some faery dust into the ground

Being that she only had to grow a single bouquet and not an entire species worth, it only took a few minutes for a bush full of beautiful blue and pink-splotched flowers to grow, she plucked them off of the bush with ease and wrapped them in some tissue paper, even tying a ribbon around the stems

"I hope she likes them," she smiled

"Oh I'm sure she will, thank you, thank you!" the elf said excitedly, rushing off to show to his wife

This, by far, had to be Branda's favorite part of the job

Sure she liked to create new flowers and it was always nice to come up with new ideas and see her creations

But seeing people happy

MAKING people happy

That was her favorite part of being a Flower Faery

Alexa Asagi Andres

The Fox Who Became A Princess

Once upon a time

In a land not so different from our own

There lived a fox who wished to become a princess

The foxed lived most of his life believing that this was not possible

He was everything a princess was not He was not royalty

He was not prim or proper

He was not human

He was not even a girl

How, then, could the fox ever hope to become a princess?

But destiny had a great plan in mind for the fox

Fate had a funny way of intervening in the fox's life of sadness and wishful thinking

For one day, when the fox was roaming the forest just outside the palace, he heard a rather magnificent announcement

"Come one, come all! We are searching for a princess!" shouted the announcer at the edge of the gate

The fox paused in stunned silence and stared in disbelief

"We have lost our queen this morning, and there is no heiress to follow in her footsteps, the king will be holding a tournament to determine who will become a princess to take the place of the queen once the king has died," the announcer shouted

The fox stepped forward, into the crowd of human women and girls, and sat patiently waiting

"ALL are welcome to participate in the tournament, no matter how rich or poor she may be, so long as she is unwed and under the age of thirty,"

The fox nearly began to dance in happiness, why, he was under the age of thirty, surely he could enter

The announcer gestured to where the signups were to take place and the flock of women and girls rushed like the fox had never seen

Using his flexibility and speed the fox easily maneuvered onto the wall separating the town from the forest and leaped down, taking the quill to sign his own name

"Why, fox, whatever are you doing?" one of the women asked

"I am signing up so that I may become a princess!" the fox replied happily

There was silence for a moment before one of the women cleared her throat

"You, fox, cannot participate in the tournament,"

The fox's face fell, heart skipping a beat

"But... why? They said any who wished to enter... I am under thirty!"

"But you cannot BE a princess, you are neither a human nor a lady, a male fox as a princess? Why it simply won't do! What would people SAY? What would people THINK?"

"But... that doesn't matter... I would be a good princess I swear," the fox said gently

"You cannot become a princess fox, go back to the forest where you belong and forget these silly ideas,"

Before the fox could protest further the announcer picked him up by the scruff of his neck and tossed him back into the forest

The fox, devastated by the turn of events, ran away

He ran and ran and ran and ran and ran some more until he was so tired that he collapsed in the middle of the forest, surrounded by nothing but trees, and began to sob

He sobbed for he was not just disappointed, but because he was miserable

The fox had always dreamed of being a princess

But even more than that, the fox dreamed of being a lady

He dreamed of no longer living in the forest where he had to hunt for his own food

He dreamed of no longer hunting for shelter when the rain came

He dreamed of no longer being taunted or laughed at by the other foxes for his dreams

He dreamed of belonging

And so the fox sobbed

He sobbed and wailed until the very heavens heard him

And Heaven ALWAYS answers a call

"Why my beautiful fox, what's wrong?" asked a gentle elf from behind the biggest and oldest oak tree in the forest

"I... I cannot live this way anymore," the fox replied between tears

"I cannot live in this skin in which I do not belong, I cannot live lying to myself and to others about who I really am, I cannot... I cannot live being trapped in a body that doesn't suit me, it has brought me nothing but harm,"

"I see," said the elf as she walked closer

"I see that you wish to change yourself is that right?"

"Yes, I wish more than anything in the world to become a princess, and now a chance has risen... but I cannot even ask to take it, because I am in a body that I do not belong in,"

"Darling fox, if I change your body, will you become happy?" the elf asked as she bent down to look at the fox closer

"Happier than any creature in the forest, in the village, in the land, in the world, I will become happier than I've ever been," the fox promised

"Then, I shall change your form for you, but promise me my dear fox, that you will find happiness, and you will not let the hateful looks of others tarnish my hard work," the elf bargained

"I promise," the fox swore

"Then, let you become a maiden," the elf smiled, raising her hands to the sky and humming a low, soft tune

The skies began to grow dark as if the tree branches themselves were covering them for shelter and a beautiful, almost angelic glow enveloped the fox

And when the fox's eyes opened again, the fox had gotten what he'd always dreamed of, for the fox ... had become a lady

"Oh thank you! Thank you Maiden Elf!" the fox-now-a-lady cried in happiness

"Do not thank me yet, you still must have a name more suited to this form, for your fox name cannot be pronounced by the human tongue," the elf chuckled

"What do you think my name should be?" the fox-now-a-lady asked

"Hm... well.... how about Sabrina? For in some lands, it means 'legendary princess', and you, my darling lady, will become just that- a princess of legend,"

"Sabrina..." the fox-now-a-lady tested out

"I like it," she confirmed

"Then you shall be Sabrina from here until your last day, and even then some," the elf promised

Sabrina smiled and took a deep breath, for the first time in her life... she felt she was in the right skin

After the elf went back to tending to other duties, Sabrina ran happily through the forest and celebrated in being happy

She celebrated in being who she really was

She celebrated just for the reason of celebrating

And so when the next day came, she tidied herself up, bargained with a merchant for a slightly nicer dress and painted her lips with berry juice and her cheeks with flower dustings

And she walked barefoot through the village once again and signed her name to enter the tournament

Once she was signed in she went back to the forest for a time, spending the remaining days she had to wait practicing how to be a princess

She practiced how to curtsey

She practiced how to speak and how to sit with her hands folded perfectly in her lap

She practiced everything that a princess would need to be a real princess

And when the day came for the tournament, she really, truly, felt ready

Sabrina entered into the palace with the rest of the women and waited her turn patiently

But when it was time for her to show her abilities- penmanship, manners, and other princessy things- she was called out by one of the other participants

"Wait your highness!" shouted one of the other women

"This is no lady! This is certainly no princess! This is the fox from the forest who tried to get into this tournament before!"

Sabrina took a step back and held her hands against her chest

Fear spreading through her as if she were a fox once again facing down one of the hunters who so often took the lives of foxes

"No..." she said quietly, shaking her head

"Yes you are! Your hair is the same shade of ginger that the fox's was! Your stance is just the same as the fox's was! And those eyes.... eyes that shade of amber can only belong to a fox! Just look at them!"

It was true

Although she looked mostly like a human woman now, her eyes still belonged to a fox

And nothing, not even the greatest of magic, could change that

For eyes are the window to the soul

And those windows, no matter how poorly decorated, can never be destroyed and rebuilt the way a body can

"Is this true Lady Sabrina? Are you truly a fox?" challenged the king

Sabrina had always been raised an honest soul

She knew not to lie

"Yes," she contested, hearing the shocked gasps and mummers from the crowd

"I just... wanted to become a princess.... but more than that, I wanted to become a lady, I was given this new body- given what I've always wanted, and ... even if you do not accept me as a princess, even if you toss cruel words at me or shoot me with malice in your heart, I will not stop being happy, for once I am happy, I have had my wish granted, I am on the outside who I've always been on the inside, and I will not let you take that away from me," she said with gentle determination

The king rose to his feet and began to walk forward and Sabrina bowed her head, waiting for the inevitable

"Everyone, bow to the new princess- bow to Princess Sabrina," the king ordered

If there were shocked gasps before, they were nearly breathless now

Sabrina looked up in complete surprise and saw the king smile at her

"My dear girl, it does not matter to me what you once were or what you look or looked like, what matters is that you have the soul of a princess, your heart is strong and steadfast but also kind and gentle, you know how to rule but you know how to do so without cruelty or judgement, that is what a princess is, and you my dear, are the most royal princess of them all,"

Sabrina could hardly believe her eyes as one by one, the crowd began to bow to her

"I promise you, Princess Sabrina, no more pain shall accompany you, your strength and kindness will become legend- YOU, will become a legend," the king added

Sabrina felt herself begin to cry again, but this time not from pain, but from joy

And so Sabrina lived the rest of her years- many years at that- as the princess that she had always hoped to be

She never forgot being a fox and often visited the forest to speak with the friends she had once had there

But now she was able to be what she always believed she was deep in her soul- a princess

Faery Tales, Mermaid Myths, And Other Fantastical Legends

The Grandfather That Sings

Once upon a time

In a land not so far away from our own

Lived a wise-cracking old man who sang everything he spoke

Children from all around came to view him as their own grandfather, for he so treasured the children of the land

The old man spoke many languages and so could communicate with anyone in the world

But most of all, what drew the children to the old man, was his singing

Long, long, VERY long ago, the old man was, in fact, a YOUNG man

When he was young he was told by his mother to go into the woods and pick berries for the pie she was baking

The young man gladly did so, for he so treasured pies

But as he bent down next to the berry bush, deep into the woods, he heard the chirping of a bird

And then the squawking of another

He heard the way twigs and leaves crunched beneath the feet of the foxes

He heard the way squirrels chirped and chattered to each other

He heard the buzzing of the bees and the swaying of the trees

He heard the beauty of the nature around him and was unable to resist humming along

His hands worked to pick the berries but his mind was elsewhere

Concentrated on the songs around him

His voice rising slowly from a hum to a song

And he began to sing with the other natural songsters around him

"Nature, what beauty, such beautiful nature, how I love to nurture the songs of your people," he would sing

The animals in the land started to listen in curiosity, for they had never heard a human try to sing in tandem with them

"Birds, such lovely songs you sing, what beauty to the world you bring," he sang as he picked the berries

"And foxes, so fast and sleek, yet it seems to be music that you seek,"

"The squirrels and chipmunks as you chipper and chatter, as if nothing in this world or any other could be an upsetting matter,"

The animals began to gather closer and closer, listening to him with intent

But before he could sing much further he found his basket full and had to head home

The animals watched him with such curiosity that they decided to wait until the next time that he would venture into their woods

They didn't have to wait long

For the next day the young man's mother instructed him to go into the woods to collect apples for pies

And he did, for he so loved pies

And as he stood on the tips of his toes, using a branch to knock apples down from the branches, he listened

The birds were singing louder, in a wider chorus

The foxes had gathered the coyotes to help them crunch the leaves and twigs beneath their paws

The chipmunks and squirrels were speaking in balance now rather than shouting over each other

Even the bears had joined in the fun with their deep, baritone roars

The young man couldn't help but to smile with joy as he picked the apples

And so he began to sing again

"Bears singing so loud and so deep, after a long winter you've woken from your sleep," he sang

"Coyotes crunching leaves beneath their paws, won't you allow your beautiful voices to slip from your maws?"

"Ravens, though you screech and squawk, I've found so much more music in you than most people can mock,"

The animals gathered closer and began to dance, enjoying not only their own music for once, but also the music of the singing man

But his apples were picked far too soon and he had to leave again

The animals waited for him to return as they had done the day before

And he returned the next day once again

The young man's mother had prompted him to pick peaches for a pie

And he did, for he so loved pie

So he entered into the woods and began his journey towards the peach tree

And as he did he listened

And as he did the animals began to sing

The birds had gathered in gaggles in the forest to sing their songs

The foxes and coyotes had brought their friends the wolves from lands over to rejoice in their beautiful howls

The chipmunks and squirrels were on the ground today to keep their shy friends the rabbits company

The bears had spoken with the fish in the streams and the fish splashed and splished to create more sounds within the forest

The songs were loud, boisterous, and beautiful

And so the man began to sing again

"Rabbits so quiet yet you are, I'm glad to see you so near and not quite so far,"

"Wolves how I enjoy your magnificence of your voice, it makes me want to dance around and rejoice,"

"Fish in the stream, you are so much more musical than you seem,"

The animals had such a wonderful time with their new human friend and found so much pleasure in his songs that they realized how sad they always became when he had to leave

And they decided that they didn't want to ever hear his songs end

The young man had finished picking his peaches and turned to leave

But instead of leaving to return to his mother, the animals gathered closer and began to hum a low song all together, with every voice in their wooded chorus present

The wind picked up around them, leaves began to spin in a whirlwind, the animals' voices grew louder and louder and color began to rise from the earth and descend down from the sky

There was magic forming in the air and the animals were propelling it forward

Just as quickly as it had begun it all stopped and the young man was left quite surprised

"What was that beautiful display?" he sang

Although, this surprised him, for he had not meant to sing it at all

"The animals have blessed you with the gift of song, so that you may create joy and happiness wherever you go," came a deep, soft voice

The young man turned around and gasped in surprise when the Spirit Of The Forest stepped towards him

The Spirit Of The Forest was almost never seen by human eyes

She was elusive and only appeared among humans who were the most gifted and treasured by the woodlands

To see her was much more than just a mere honor, it was a treasure, it was a gift

"You are a gift to the lands, your songs are so beautiful and cheerful that even the birds and wolves are impressed, I haven't seen this much joy and dancing in these woods in many years,"

She smiled softly, bending down to pick up a rabbit and pet the small animal

"I treasure the happiness of my woodland friends, and you bring it to them, so I responded to their call and blessed you with the gift of song, you will never speak again- but sing, you will sing everything you say and you will make the people in this land and any others you travel to happy and bright with your songs,"

The young man was at first not sure what to do with his new gift

Admittedly, he was a bit scared of it

The people in the towns and villages at first thought him strange for always speaking in song

But these were the adults, who had lost the gifts of magic and joy as they grew older

The children, he soon came to find out, adored his songs

The children gathered everywhere he went to listen to him recite strange stories in his beautiful songs

"Now gather around and listen here, come over and lend me your ear, I'm about to tell you a story that only children can hear," he sang with joy

"Listen as I tell you the story of a rabbit who traveled west and east, he traveled far and long and was quiet tired after his journey, so the rabbit stopped at my house without my permission and snuck into my ice chest, I was cooking with Mother when she asked that I retrieve for her some ice, so I went to the chest and opened it up and saw the rabbit sitting there, 'Rabbit!' I exclaimed with shock as he looked up at me, and I saw that he had gathered many, many foods from around my house and set them in the chest with him, 'What are you doing in my ice chest?' 'I traveled long and I traveled far- I traveled out of a tavern and into a bar, I traveled slow and I traveled quick, I traveled in the sun-burned sand and when the roads were rain-slick, I traveled north and south and had not even water to wet my mouth,' 'Yeah but rabbit,' I started again, 'What are you doing in my ice chest?' 'Can't you tell?' the rabbit asked me, 'I've traveled west-end and I've traveled east-end, and now I'm in your house and I'm sittin' and feastin',' this rabbit made about as much since as hot stew on a summer day, so I shut the ice chest and told Mother we would need a new one,"

The children delighted in his stories and songs for years and years and years

And they delighted in them for so very long that they even came to delight in them as adults

This man had brought joy to the villages and towns once again, even to the previously stiff and sour adults

But time stops for no one and as the years passed the man grew older and older

He still sang his songs and told his stories to the children

He sang about everything, from the woods to the gardens, the skies and the seas

He sang about animals and food and people and the earth

He sang of things that the people had never even heard of, like telling-you-phones and Phillip's cheese stakes

(The people wanted to find this Phillip but the old man only laughed joyfully at their efforts, reluctant to admit that there was no such person)

The old man sings with as much joy and delight as he had so many years ago in the forest, when he first received his gift

And even centuries later, long, LONG after that day, the old man still sings

He has become as much a legend as the Spirit Of The Forest, and still recites his magical songs as he travels the villages and towns as a spirit

All in the land, even those who cannot see him anymore, hear his songs

They hear his songs in the wind and in the trees, in the rain and in the water in the streams

He appears to children as much as he can to continue his songs and on his travels he often joins the Spirit Of The Forest, to help restore peace and happiness to the lands

Alexa Asagi Andres

The Grandmother Who Moved Boulders

Once upon a time

In a land very near to our own

Lived a wise old woman

The woman was a legend in her village, and the village next to her village, and every village who had ever heard of her

For she was the strongest woman any had ever met

She was so strong that she was able to move boulders without any effort, lifting even the biggest and heaviest of rocks in a single hand

She was so fast that she was able to build entire houses in a single day and barely break a sweat

But these were not her only gifts

She was also so wise that everyone, even from the villages expanding across the sea, sought her advice

She was so kind that even if it took many, many days, people would travel for a single moment to meet her

The old woman was treasured by all and many wished to pay her for her many good deeds

But she never accepted payment

In fact, it was one of the things that frustrated her more than any about people, they could never take a kind deed lying down

"If one more person offers me money I'm going to bury them," she would say with a frustrated huff

People tried to be clever by leaving money on her windowsill or in her garden but whenever they did she would saddle the nearest horse and ride to the poorest village in the area, leaving the money with them instead

The old woman was talented too

Her cooking was almost as legendary as she was

Just a simple bowl of rice had people from seventeen villages over lining up in wait for a taste

"Every single one of you has lost your mind," she would say absently as she cooked

She would give out all of the food she made, leaving only a small portion for herself for that was all she needed, and give her leftovers to the cats

Leaving a bowl by her doorstep, cats from lands anywhere and everywhere would flock over

Eventually, it got so bad, that the old woman simply built a house for all of the cats to live in

There was one cat in particular that she had a fondness for

For he was different than all of the others

While most cats would flock to the food and meow insistently for more, this cat stayed back, lying in wait, and approached the bowl after every other cat had left to get a single grain of rice

The old woman respected this cat, he had patience and kindness in him as well

But most of all he just didn't care to deal with the crowds and she felt a kinship in that, she wasn't fond of crowds either

After many months of this same routine the old woman did something that she had never done before

She invited the cat into her house, for he seemed so very unhappy with the other cats

Although hesitant at first, the cat who avoided crowds walked into her house and made himself at home

He and the old woman had a lot in common, he didn't need or ask much of the world and he avoided things like compliments

He merely had a small bundle of blankets by the heater that he decided to make into a bed and two bowls beside him, one for water and one for food

The old woman appreciated the cat's lifestyle for it much resembled her own, and so she did something else that she had never done before

She bestowed the cat with a name- for she felt that he needed one

"Butterball," she dubbed the cat

For his fur was as yellow as butter and he liked to sleep in a ball

The old woman and the cat became quite the pair for Butterball enjoyed working for his dinner as well

He often helped to make the food, gathering ingredients and bringing them to the old woman or turning on the water with his tail

He often helped her by carrying supplies to build houses or meowing when some more rocks needed moving

He helped dig holes in the ground for her to plant her garden and nicked the thread on spools with his claws so it would separate without the woman needing to exert too much energy to it

The cat slowly began getting recognition as well around the village, but much like the old woman, he refused to accept any thanks or compliments

He and the old woman were really two peas in a pod and they enjoyed each other's company

And just as she had drawn a crowd with her many, many talents, so soon did the cat

Now twice as many people came to see them as they had before, half interested in the old woman and half in the cat

On one particularly full day she turned to the cat, shaking her head slowly and sighing as she started to lift up some wood to make a house for the local rabbits

"I just don't understand it," the old woman said with slight frustration

"Why on earth do all of these people keep flocking to my house?"

The cat, like the old woman, was at a complete loss

Alexa Asagi Andres

The Heartless Jackal

Once upon a time

In a time long, long, long, long, LONG ago

There lived a Jackal

Well more correctly, there lived several Jackals

You see when the world was first beginning and those who could shapeshift came into being they all had purpose

They all had order and different positions to take in nature

From hunting to healing to child bearing and everything else, each shapeshifter had a special quality about them to reside over

And for Jackals, that quality was death

The first Jackal was Anubis, the Egyptian God of the dead

It stood to reason that after Anubis' success the guardians of the dead from then on would be Jackals

This, however, was not the case

The dead came to have many guardians and the Jackals were only one of a few

There were banshees and Guardian Angels and Hellhounds and spirits...

There was an immeasurable amount of representatives of the dead

Some were good, some were bad, some were in both and some were neither, and some were not any of these things at all

But by far still one of the most unique guides to the dead were the Jackals, those who were descended from Anubis himself

Jackals were capable of weighing the hearts of the dead to decipher where to guide the spirits

But far more amazingly, Jackals were capable of resurrection

They were one of the very few Death Dealers who could take life and bring life with the same hands

But the cost for resurrection through a Jackal is higher than nearly any other, and nearly impossible to perfect

People who seek to bring back the dead however rarely think about or care about these consequences and so the Jackals have gone into hiding to protect themselves as well as the greater good

However, before one can understand why the Jackals have been cursed with such a difficult position in life, it is important to understand what happened to the first Jackal

Namely, how he disappeared

Long ago, when the population of souls on earth started to become too difficult for only a few Death Dealers to handle, the Gods and Goddesses bestowed ounces of their power onto descendants- modern day shapeshifters, angels, dullahan, Valkyrie, Black Shuck, to name a few- in order to help keep the balance

These days those spirits such as Anubis, Osiris, Hades, Hel, and many others who rule over death and the afterlife are mostly overseers, leaving the leg-work to the descendants they had created

These descendants you see, are not the children of these Gods and Goddesses, but merely spirits who have had the blessings of these great beings passed to them

And in the case of the Jackals, there were originally four- two females, and two males

The oldest Jackal, Asim, was by far the most curious and the least respectful of his own self-preservation

Jackals, like many Death Bringers, cannot die the way most creatures can

They do not age once they have developed to maturity and almost never are struck by illness, and any injuries they sustain heal immediately

Should a wound be fatal, however, a Jackal merely discards the flesh and bones they're using and move to another one, an identical copy of themselves

And it was due to this immortality that Asim let go of his boundaries and ignored the caution of his well-meaning younger siblings

He did as he should do by rule of being a Jackal, but he did so recklessly, with little care to the people in this world who wished to harness the power of a Jackal and bring back their lost loved one

Or even their lost foe

He had no care, it seemed, for his self-preservation

And because of that, he walked into a trap

Despite the warnings of his sister Bahiti, Asim left their tomb to take the spirit of a thief many miles out of their usual range

She had warned him to leave it for one of the others, something didn't feel right, but Asim, with his love for the job and his delight in the feeling of freedom and fresh air, ignored Bahiti's warnings and left anyway

Asim never returned

He found all too soon that his sister had been right and the thief was not truly dead, but that he had managed to find a type of poison that would merely simulate death for a predetermined amount of time, and when Asim came to take his soul to the next realm, he found there was no soul available for him to take

And when he turned to leave, he found the walls and floor lined in Sage, warding him away from the exits

Faery Tales, Mermaid Myths, And Other Fantastical Legends

No one knows exactly what happened to Asim that day

But there are legends

Rumors that his very heart was ripped out of his chest as Jackals so often did to the dead

But instead of being weighed on a scale, Asim's heart was turned to stone, and chipped into pieces to be used for immortality

These stones were given many names, but they all did the same thing

Blood red stones that promised eternal life and the power of resurrection

And so it was left to wonder, if Asim could not die, and he had no heart to bring him into another form in life, what happened to him?

For thousands of years, no one knew, and no one dared to find out

Bahiti tried, despite the advice of her younger siblings, she searched for answers on what had happened to her brother, but she never came away with anything more than desert sand

Now, thousands of years later, another Jackal is ready to try again

Akila, at the age of only 24, is one of the youngest Jackals alive

Bested only by her younger brother- at the age of 16- and a Jackal born countries away at the age of only seven

Akila had only recently stepped into her skin as a Jackal when she heard the tale of what happened to Asim many centuries ago, taught to young Jackals as a warning to be cautious

"But why don't we still look for him?" Akila asked in confusion

"Darling, it's only a legend, we don't even know if Asim was real," Akila's mother explained

"But ... there has to be proof that he was, what about Bahiti? Or their siblings? Wouldn't they know?"

"It's been too long dear, no one can keep track of someone for that long, not even Jackals," her mother explained gently

She ultimately detoured Akila from the conversation, but Akila did not forget it

She was determined to find out the truth for herself of what happened to Asim, and of what exactly Jackals must do to resurrect the dead

It was a secret practice that stopped being taught long ago due to the great risk it posed

But Akila, much like Asim, was impulsive and careless

For all of her passion and curiosity, she had little care for her own being or for the consequences of her actions

Her mother had enrolled her early in life in ballet to teach her discipline, to ease the edge of her impulsivity

But it backfired, now, if anything, Akila was only more impulsive as a professional ballerina

Despite this, she had never been drawn to being a Jackal as Asim had been

The concept of death was still one that frightened her, and she didn't wish to be close to it

Unfortunately, fate has a way of evening these things out

And one day, on the way to their next show, the tour bus containing herself and her fellow dancers was run off the road and flipped over

When Akila came to consciousness she was met with blood and broken bones littering the bus

And her eyes glowed gold with the Sight of souls leaving their bodies

It was Akila's first time escorting souls across the border of life and death, and it was made all the more painful by the fact that so many of them were her friends

None of these deaths had been easy, and many of the spirits begged Akila to allow them another chance at life, even though it was not up to Akila to decide that

"My dear, by the time I can see your soul, it is already far too late," she sobbed to one of her fellow dancers as the ballerina tried fruitlessly to return to her body

Akila sent them on their ways across the border, and when she returned, she found that the few remaining lives on the bus were unconscious, and so she fell to the floor and sobbed

She grieved

She mourned

But not for the souls she had sent away

She mourned for herself

Because although those souls would eventually be reunited with their loved ones- one day, it was certain- she would not be

Such was the fate of a Jackal, immortality

She mourned for herself and for her life as a ballerina, she knew if she stayed here too many questions would be asked

This would be only the first of countless times of running away and starting over

Standing slowly, she wiped the tears from her eyes and clutched at the bottom of her hair tie, letting out one final scream of agony as she tore it from her hair and allowed her thick black locks to tussle loose

Akila decided from that moment that she would pursue the legend of Asim, no matter how long it took

Her first love had been dancing for as long as she knew, and now it was gone from her, at least it was gone for quite some time

What better use was there for her time and abilities?

And so, without telling anyone, Akila left, completely alone, to pursue the legend of the heartless Jackal

When the desert air grew too thick she shapeshifted into her animal form so that she could tolerate it more easily

This was the start of a journey that took many years

Years of searching libraries and pouring over books, of speaking to other Jackals and anyone else who would listen to her questions

It took so much time and effort that her life eventually became consumed with the single mission to find Asim

And finally, seven years after beginning the journey, she had a lead

A Jackal who was of a grand three thousand years of age tipped her off to someone who was suspected of being the long lost Bahiti

And so Akila chased this lead

And she finally tracked the lead down in London, six months later

"Hello?" Akila called out as she entered the used bookstore in front of her

A few moments later, a woman who appeared no older than Akila herself with long black hair and dark brown skin came towards her, smiling gently and tying her hair back into a ponytail

"Yes? How may I help you?" she asked innocently

Akila swallowed, but willed herself not to break

"Are you Bahiti?"

The woman shrank back, clutching a hand to her chest

"Who are you? What do you want?" She asked accusingly

"My name is Akila... I'm like you," she said, pausing as her eyes flashed gold

"Many creatures have gold eyes, how do I know you're a Jackal?" she asked cautiously

"I can shapeshift right here and now if you want, or kill someone and I'll take them over the border... I'm not here... for you exactly, I'm here about your brother,"

"What has that bumbling buffoon done now?" she sighed as she started to arrange some books by the counter

"I'm here about Asim,"

Bahiti stopped, her shoulders tense as she turned around and straightened her glasses

"Asim? Do you have any idea... how many CENTURIES it's been... since I've heard that name? I had nearly forgotten how to say it,"

"Please Bahiti, I believe that Asim is out there, somewhere, and I want to find him," Akila said with determination

Bahiti smiled sadly, adjusting the business card holder on the counter

"I don't know who you are, but you remind me so much of myself when I was young and naive... IF Asim is anywhere to be found, he does not WANT to be found, I learned that after my third century looking for him,"

"You only gave it three hundred years?" Akila teased

Bahiti didn't seem to find it funny, however

"You don't understand.... things weren't this way back then... in three hundred years, I WOULD have picked up a lead, if there was any lead to pick up," she insisted

"What about the stones? The immortality stones?" she asked

Bahiti narrowed her eyes and Akila sighed, closing her eyes and shifting into her Jackal form, strutting around proudly for a few moments before shifting back into her human form

"I'm afraid I know nothing of the Immortality Stones, I don't even know if they really exist," Bahiti admitted

"What do you know?" Akila asked gently

"Not much, I know that when we went to search for my older brother, we found a tomb with Sage lining the entrance, but that's all, we searched for Asim for a long time before we gave up, I longer than the others by far, but even I lost my faith along the way," she admitted

Akila nodded slowly, biting her lower lip

"Bahiti, can you do me a favor?"

"What is it?" Bahiti asked curiously

"Can you tell me where the last tomb Asim went to is exactly?"

With reluctance, Bahiti told her, and within moments, Akila was gone

It took a full year to find the tomb, even with Bahiti's directions

Akila knew far better than to enter someone else's tomb, even if it had already been desecrated by another, she still respected that, but she felt that being in the same area might give her some sort of clue

She shifted into her Jackal form so she could attempt to pick up traces of the last people who were there through scent

But as soon as she started to inhale the scents around her, she felt a very strangely... nostalgic feeling...

She fell to the ground, eyes fluttering as the visions started to play out before her eyes

Visions of Asim cornered by humans in the tomb

The humans demanding that they resurrect a woman from the dead

Asim tried to tell them that it wouldn't work, he tried to tell them that it wouldn't be any good to try

But they wouldn't listen

And in the end, not knowing what else to do in his panicked state, Asim did what he was told to do

He brought a woman back to life

He cut out the heart of someone who he believed had a heart the same weight as the mystery woman's and compared them on the scale

Surely enough, their hearts weighed the same and Asim was able to exchange the man's soul for the woman's, and thus he brought her back to life

However.... as Asim had tried to warn them before, the woman was not the same as she had once been

Her soul was not the same and what was left was an empty shell of who she had once been

A shell... filled with vengeance and willing to take out her revenge on anyone who came too close, the human bandits who had originally kidnapped Asim included....

Before she did this, however, the bandits realized that there would be little time before they would be needing Asim's services again, and so they cut out his heart, the way Asim so often cut out the hearts of the dead

But instead of weighing it, they crystalized it and smashed it into stones

The woman only took hours to kill the bandits, and once she was done she wiped the sage from the entryway to the tomb and allowed Asim to escape

Without his heart, he was incapable of guiding souls

Without his heart, he was incapable of feeling anything except longing and emptiness

Without his heart, he too was an empty shell of the person he once was and feared going home to his family

And so Asim set out on a journey to regain his heart

A way to turn back the hands of time perhaps, or to get a new heart altogether, or even just to piece back the old one

He no longer possessed the ability to care

And so for many centuries Asim searched for answers

He searched for magic

Asim even searched for faith

But nothing seemed to work

The more the days passed on, the more he grew restless without his heart

It was just over a thousand years into his searching that he finally found something

Legends told by a wise old dragon on how to heal heart breaks

Asim visited her, desperate for answers, desperate for a solution, desperate for anything

The dragon assured Asim that he would one day have his heart back, but that to do so, he must first gather the Immortality Stones and piece them back himself

Until then, wondered Asim, what would he do?

He was only getting worse as time went by, he admitted

"Do not worry, until you can find your heart and return it to your body, your soul- the purest form of you there is- will simply coincide with another," the dragon explained

Within moments Asim found his soul removed to his body and placed inside the body of a young a child

"You will move your soul wherever you see best, for now, until you can track down the stones, you can share the body of another Jackal," the dragon explained

Asim agreed, and ever since he has found a temporary home in other Jackals

Akila realized now, as she moved away from the tomb buried beneath the sand

That the reason she was so drawn to the story of Asim and to finding out what happened to him... was because in a way, she WAS Asim...

Or at least, he was a PART of her.. a much stronger, bigger part of her than she ever would have anticipated before....

She remembered everything suddenly

From what Asim looked like and how his siblings look to the truth behind resurrection- that the only way possible to complete a perfect, working, resurrection, was if the deceased had a perfectly weightless, perfectly pure heart, so that the scale would not require a heart for a trade, but something else of equal weight- a feather

She remembered everything that he remembered and felt everything that he felt with her own heart

Ever since this revelation her powers had matured and grown in amazing strength, her eyes had started to glow more and more often, and she could almost, just faintly, see the outline of someone else in the mirror when she stared at the reflection

Sometimes it was a Jackal, and sometimes it was Asim

Sometimes still, it was both

"What will you do now? Now that you know the truth?" Bahiti asked once Akila explained all of this to her

"Isn't it obvious?" she replied, lacing up her boots and glancing in the mirror, her eyes glowing yellow

"We're going to find the Immortal Stones,"

Alexa Asagi Andres

The Invention Of Ancient Clay

Once upon a time

When our universe was young

There was a very special formula to creating souls

It was a very specific formula and even one single misstep could destroy the entire batch

This formula was used to create clay

And this clay was used to create souls

And a very long time ago, someone changed this formula

This clay consisted of stardust and magic

Of light and dark

Of sunlight and moonlight

Of iron and water

And of so many other things that no one ever really wrote down

And that was finalized by a Spark

A Spark of the celestial

Of Heaven

A Spark that brought these clay souls to life and created something so much... more...

Created something that existed under its own merit

It was called the Soul Spark

And all living things had it

Things became very monotonous in Heaven when it came to creating souls, for no one ever deviated from the process

Gather the ingredients

Mix them together

Create the clay

Add the spark

And a new soul- every bit as unique and different as each other soul- was born

But one day something happened

Something different

The angels were mixing together a new batch of clay, just as they did every day, when suddenly someone came bursting into the mixing room and distracted them

It was so long ago that no one can really remember what the poor soul wanted when they interrupted the angels

But they do remember what happened next

In the angels' haste to help the new arrival there was quite a commotion

And in the commotion one angel tripped out of step and fell against the giant pot of clay mix, unknowingly knocking in an extra dose of Stardust

No one realized the mistake right away and so the mix was sent to the next set of angels in line to bake into a clay

In fact, it was only after the Goddess added her spark of life to the two clay souls that the angels realized a mistake had been made

You see, each batch of clay is just enough to create exactly two souls

These souls are often called "soul mates" in human terms, for they came from the same batch

However, that is all they have in common

They are still individual souls, completely unique to themselves and connected only by being born together

They are not, as some people believe, two halves of the same soul

And they do not possess parts of each other in their own souls

But when the Soul Spark was added, the angels realized that that very basic fact, was not true of these two souls

The extra Stardust that had been knocked into the boiling pot caused just a little more clay to form than it usually would

And that extra clay formed a link between the two souls

Invisible and ever stretching, but a link none the less

The first soul had a little bit of the second in their very core

And the second soul had a little bit of the first in their very core

The angels feared what would happen to these two souls if they were sent to Earth

Feared that this link- once severed- would destroy them both

But before they could stop them, the two souls jumped down from Heaven's clouds and into Earth's atmosphere

And the angels could do nothing more

Although on the surface it appeared that the only change the extra Stardust made was a link between the souls, it was eventually discovered that the changes went far deeper than that

The very material it's self

The very clay that constructed the souls, had changed

It was hard to pinpoint the details in words

But undoubtedly, it changed

All of the other souls were made of the same material except for these two

And so as consequence, they would never find themselves capable of feeling truly at home with any soul but the other

For they were the only two souls in existence to be made of something different

They didn't know this at first though, obviously

For when souls come to Earth they're incapable of retaining any memory of their time in Heaven

All these two knew was that something was missing

There was a piece of them missing

And they couldn't seem to find it

No matter what they tried, nothing ever seemed to fill this gap

Five years passed

Then ten

Fifteen

And finally, after twenty years passed, they found what they had been missing

Neither knew it at first

Most people never know for sure who their soulmate is

But when they met again, they could feel something DIFFERENT there

Something that finally felt COMPLETE

Even if they didn't know it was

"What's your name anyway?"

"Hale, yours?"

"Robin, nice to meet you,"

They were only Earthly names

But as they were their first, those in Heaven recognized these as the names they would keep in their spirits

And they recognized Robin and Hale as the souls who had been born of extra Stardust twenty years ago

Everyone in Heaven watched them, for they were morbidly curious to see how the story of these two defective souls would live on now that they had found each other

And many angels had many theories

But no one quite expected what actually happened

Robin and Hale were the original love story

They were consumed with a love for each other that only exists in legends according to most normal people

To this day, there never has been and never will be two souls who love each other more than this pair

No matter how much it hurt

Or how little they seemed to be able to connect with other souls, they loved each other so much, that they could only ever find themselves smiling

It was a kind of love that was powerful

A kind of love that caused people to stare in amazement at them

For it was a love that it was wholly and entirely pure

And wholly and entirely meant to be

Some may have argued that it was only because of the link created between them

But when they returned to Heaven and were asked, they merely shook their heads

"We're made differently, but we're made of the same, we were meant for each other," Hale would say

And the angels would argue

Argue that the creation of such closeness was a mistake

And Robin would laugh at their beliefs

"All things in the universe- no matter Heaven sent or not- are meant to be, whatever caused that accident was meant to happen, because something stronger than even Heaven itself planned this, and wanted us to find each other,"

And the angels were confused, but they didn't know how to argue

Robin was right

Nothing was ever an accident, especially not in Heaven

"We're made of love for each other, and how could that be a mistake?" Hale would ask upon seeing their confusion

"It doesn't matter, love is love, and clay and clay, what's wrong with just letting us have this?" Robin would return

And the angels never knew how to respond

So one day, many centuries after Hale and Robin were created and now living just another of their many lives together, one of the angels went to the Goddess and asked her

"How did this happen?"

The Goddess smiled and watched from the clouds as Hale and Robin- now with different names and different faces and different lives- found each other again and embraced as if they remembered each other upon sight

As if they were merely two lovers separated by a few days and not entire lives

"Why are you asking me?" the Goddess asked as she watched the souls circle each other

Watched the link that had formed from their Sparks as it glowed with celestial light

Watched as the Stardust that had created them so very differently from all other souls drifted off of them as if it were traces of glitter, wanting to reconnect to the rest of its own

"I have a feeling this was intentional," the angel said

The Goddess only continued to smile as the souls experienced falling in love at first sight with each other for the seventh time all over again

Watched as their hearts bloomed with happiness and their spirits connected and their hands touched for the first time

"What would give you that idea?" the Goddess asked

The angel was silent and couldn't deny that even she felt her soul light up in happiness at watching such a Heaven blessed thing as soulmates- who were made for each other, of each other, and with each other- meet again for the first time and fall in love all over again

The angel considered this and thought that perhaps there was a reason for such souls to exist after all

That perhaps the Goddess wished to see two souls resemble herself and her own soulmate in smaller fashion

That perhaps these two souls, created of something entirely unique to only them, had been born of the love that the God and Goddess had for each other, and not just from clay and sparks

The angel considered this as she watched the two dance for the first time and laugh for the first time and fall into each other's arms for the first time in this life

And she decided not to tell the others, or to question things any further herself

For as new as they had been at the time, these souls had been right

What was the point in trying to dissect such a beautiful thing and turn it into something clinical and defined?

Sometimes even Heaven needed to witness something purely magical

Sometimes something needed to exist that even Gods and Goddesses could be in awe of

And to this day, all souls are still made with the same formula

Made from the same clay and blessed with the same Spark

But there are two souls who are different

And no one is entirely sure what they're made of

Only that whatever it is, for these two, it's the same

No one is sure exactly why they came to be how they are

But no one wants to ask either

The Jaguar And The Lady

Once upon a time

In a land of dazzling beauty

There lived a young lady who traveled by the river every night

Until one evening, that is, when she came to the river and found that it was blocked off

There had been some sort of accident and now the pathways were covered by fallen trees, meaning her only way of getting back home was through the jungle by the riverside

The jungle on its own was not usually a

frightening place

But with the darkness of night and many

nocturnal predators out and about, the

young woman felt a twinge

of fear at the thought of traveling through there to get back home

The very first night she began this expedition was a cloudy one no less, and the moon- her only source of light- was quickly being swallowed up by the clouds

And no matter how hard she tried, she couldn't manage to get the panic to go away

So, with no other option left, she prayed to the higher spirits that somehow, something would come along to help her find her way home

The higher spirits must have answered her prayers, because not even a moment later, a beautiful black jaguar stalked out of the greenery around him and towards the young woman

At first, she was understandably afraid, not sure at all what to actually think of the large beautiful cat skulking her way

But after finding that there was really nowhere to run in this place, she gave up and waited for her fate

She never expected her fate to come in the form of kitty cat kisses, but she certainly wasn't complaining

Using some sort of telepathic language that she still didn't exactly understand, she was able to communicate with the jaguar, and in no time at all she was home

In fact, she got there faster tonight than she did most of the time

And when it came time for the jaguar to leave, she almost didn't want him to

"I have to repay you for your kindness- please don't say I don't, I really do, and I WANT to," she insisted

The jaguar stared at her, a little surprised but mostly gracious and humble

"I want to.... please Mr. Jaguar, I don't have much but... take this single silver coin and know that when all else fails, you'll have a part of me there to help you too,"

The jaguar took the coin in his mouth, bowed politely, and ran back into the jungle before the sun could rise

And that afternoon the woman hoped that the river pathway would be free

Sadly, it was not

And once again she had to travel through the jungle to get home

So once again she was helped by the beautiful black jaguar volunteer

And, once again, she paid him for his services when she arrived home

"It isn't much, but I hope that it'll help remind you, if you ever get lonely, that someone is here to support you," she said, handing him her handkerchief

The jaguar took it in his mouth, bowed politely, and ran back into the jungle before the sun could rise

And that afternoon the woman was indifferent to whether or not the river pathway would be free

Yet again, it was not

And so she fell into the quickly-becoming-familiar pattern of going into the jungle and meeting up with the jaguar

This time when she waved him goodbye, she took the tie from her hair to give to him

"I would like to give you this as a token of our friendship, so you can always remember that I am a friend of yours if you need me,"

The jaguar took it in his mouth, bowed politely, and ran back into the jungle before the sun could rise

And that afternoon, the woman looked forward to her evening walk and discussion with the jaguar, and didn't once think about the river

It was with irony and heavy frustration, of course, that she found the river pathway clear that night

But, not wanting to intrude on the jaguar who had been so kind to her, she took the river pathway and didn't go into the jungle

Although she soon realized how much she missed the talks they had, even if they had only had the arrangement for three days, it always felt as if she were walking with an old, trusted friend rather than a jungle cat

A mere halfway down towards her house the woman paused, struck in curiosity at the beautiful man in front of her, currently exiting the forest

But although the man was stunning in his appearance, this wasn't what held the woman's interest for so long

What pulled at her curiosity, was the fact that he was holding the same silver coin that she had given to the jaguar

Alright, she supposed, maybe on its own that coin wasn't so rare...

But he also sported the handkerchief in his pocket that she had given to the jaguar

And to top it all off, the string tying his hair back was none other than the hair-tie that she had given to the jaguar

"Where did you get those things!?" she shouted as she ran towards him

"You gave them to me..." the man replied in confusion

"I did no such thing! When would I have done that?!" she huffed, glancing up and seeing that his eyes were the same shade of gold that the jaguar sported

"Are.... are you the jaguar?" she asked suddenly, beginning to feel self-conscious

"You didn't know I was a shape-shifter.... I'm so sorry, I thought you knew," the man- or werejaguar as it were- said sincerely

"How would I have known!?"

"The way you spoke to me... it was as if you were speaking to another human so... I thought you knew, I apologize deeply for the inconveniences and if you'd like your belong-"

"Oh no, keep them, they were gifts," she said with a soft smile

"I don't understand though, why not just shift into your human form before?"

"I thought you may prefer the company of a jaguar after the first time when I didn't have time to shapeshift to begin with," he admitted with a soft smile

The woman smiled back at him, extending her hand

"Come then, the river path is clear, let's enjoy our walk back to the village," she said with a hum

The jaguar-man smiled genuinely, squeezing her hand tightly as they walked

"No gifts this time," she added as an after thought

"Madam, your company is more than gift enough,"

The King Of Crocodiles

Once upon a time

In a land hot and dry

There lived a man by the name of Adom

Adom was a very ordinary man, he lived far off from the cities as a farmer and had a small family; a wife and a daughter

Overall, his life was very normal and mundane... until one day, when he went to the river to fetch some water

Upon walking towards the river, Adom stopped short at the sight of a large crocodile caught in a net

Being a very kind, brave person, and knowing that the crocodile must be caught in the net by some mistake, he approached slowly and carefully unwound the rope from the crocodile's leg

"Go, you're free now," Adom said softly, rising to his feet and watching the crocodile hurry back into the water

Wordlessly, as if it hadn't even happened, Adom took the buckets of water he had brought with him and began to fill them

Things were calm after that, until he prepared to leave

For then, he looked out into the river and saw the bright eyes of a crocodile- bigger than the one before- staring at him

The reptile swam closer and Adom took several steps back, not wanting to make any quick motions

"I am the King of this River," the crocodile announced as he walked onto the land, stopping a few feet away from Adom

Adom paused, kneeling and bowing respectfully

"Rise, Human, I am the one who should be bowing to you," he announced

Adom looked up in surprise, but didn't argue and rose to his feet

"Me? Why would you bow to me?" he asked in confusion

"You have saved my son from a terrible fate, if the humans had caught him, it would not have ended well, I wish to give you a gift as a symbol of my deep gratitude,"

"You don't have to, it was just the right thing to do," Adom replied softly

"I insist, I will grant you whatever you seek, when you need help, simply call out my name- Shakir, and I will appear before you and lend you all of the power a crocodile can lend, you may call on me however many times you wish,"

Although Adom truly felt that the gift was unwarranted, he knew it was disrespectful to refuse the offer and so accepted with great gratitude

And although he was hesitant to use it, after several weeks, Adom called on Shakir for the first time

"Shakir, please help me, there's a terrible drought and our crops are dying, my family is very hungry but the closest area that's heavy in rain is too far for us to move, it would take too long for us to get there," Adom said sadly as he stared at his wilted crops

Shakir ambled slowly from around the corner, gesturing for Adom to sit on the ground

"Tell me, if you could move to this place quickly, would your problem be solved?"

"Yes," Adom said instantly

Shakir nodded and placed his front paw on top of Adom's hand

"I grant you the speed of the crocodile, may you move quickly to your next home,"

And to Adom's surprise, when he and his family left, they somehow cut a week's journey into a single day, and were now in a place closer to the city that rained often

The next time Adom called on Shakir it was only a few weeks later

"Shakir, please help me, it's my first time selling produce at the market and I'm afraid I'll be taken advantage of due to my inexperience, please help me find a way to be sure that I'm getting the money I'm owed," Adom said worriedly as he stared at the stand and baskets of vegetables in front of him with deep anxiety

Shakir appeared in front of him, staring at the food with a glint of curiosity, as if wondering if that greenery was really what humans ate...

"Tell me, if you could tell when an offer is too high or too low, would your problem be solved?"

"Yes," Adom said quickly

Shakir nodded and placed his front paw on top of Adom's hand

"I grant you the intuition of the crocodile, may you always know a person's intentions, as well as their sincerity,"

And to Adom's surprise, when his first customer offered him three coins for a bundle of carrots, he immediately replied with "Four," despite not quite knowing why

And yet, the customer gave him four coins without hesitation and walked away with the carrots, things like this continued for the rest of the day, until Adom began understanding his unusual power and allowed it to work its magic

Adom didn't call for Shakir again for two months

"Shakir! Please help me! My daughter is being carried down the river and I have no way of helping her!" Adom shouted anxiously

Shakir rose suddenly from the river and approached Adom with urgency

"Tell me, if you could swim to your daughter and pull her ashore, would your problem be solved?"

"YES!" Adom said immediately

Shakir nodded and placed his front paw on top of Adom's hand

"I grant you the strength of the crocodile, may you be able to fight the harshest currents and hold the heaviest weights,"

And to Adom's surprise, when he jumped into the river, he swam to his daughter with ease and then swam back upstream just as easily before pulling them both to the shore

Adom was surprised by the sudden power, but he was more glad for it than he had been for any of Shakir's other gifts

Adom didn't call on Shakir again for nearly half a year, but when he finally did, it was urgent

"Shakir, please help me! A thief has come to my home and is threatening my family, I'm afraid to leave my room and fight him off, it may lead him to my wife and daughter if he knows we're home," Adom said anxiously

Shakir slipped through the window and climbed onto the foot of the bed before Adom and his wife

"Tell me, if you could confront the thief without fear and protect your family, would your problem be solved?"

"Yes," Adom said urgently

Shakir nodded and placed his front paw on top of Adom's hand

"I grant you the bravery of the crocodile, may you always have more courage than fear and with it, the ability to act on that courage,"

And to Adom's surprise, he found himself leaping up and racing downstairs

As soon as he saw the burglar he grabbed a pan from the stove that had been used to cook dinner earlier and smacked the thief on the back of the head with it

And to Adom's surprise, he didn't panic

He tied the thief to a chair and called the police without a shred of fear in his body, and he was extremely relieved by this

Adom called Shakir forth just two nights later

"Shakir, please help me.. the thief had friends, there are too many of them for me to take alone, no matter how strong I am or how brave I am, no matter how intuitive or fast, I need to protect my family, please help me,"

Shakir slid out from under the bed, approaching Adom as he struggled to hold the door shut

"Tell me, if you could fight off these men and protect your family, would your problem be solved?"

"Yes," Adom said at once

"You must understand that this is the last gift I will give you,"

Adom felt his heart sink, staring at him worriedly

"But... why?"

"Because it is the last gift I CAN give you," Shakir explained

Adom fell silent and offered his hand

Shakir nodded and placed his front paw on Adom's hand

"I grant you the teeth of the crocodile, may you possess all of the powers that we have and more,"

And to Adom's surprise, he felt a strange tingling in his mouth

The thieves broke the door down a moment later and when Adom turned and growled at them, the men paused in shock and fear at seeing Adom's mouth filled with the razor sharp teeth of a crocodile

Having now had a moment to adjust, rage filled Adom's heart, furious that these men dared to hurt his family, and in that rage, he felt his very bones begin to shapeshift

A moment later he was staring up at the men, hissing as his long tale swept across the floor, for Adom now possessed the body of a crocodile, and easily scared the thieves away

It took time- a lot of time- for Adom to master his new powers of shapeshifting, and because his mouth was always full of crocodile teeth to keep away dangerous people, he became known around the land as The Crocodile

However, it was not just the humans who had respect and fear for Adom, it was also the crocodiles themselves

They had heard many tales of Shakir offering his gratitude to a human, only for it to be wasted on something such as silk or gold

But by Adom's heart being pure and simple, he was able to get the true gift Shakir had been wanting to give for so long

And because he had gained the respect and trust of the crocodiles, he became known by them as The King Of Crocodiles, for the crocodiles felt that he was one of their own, and the only one of them who had the power to shapeshift into a human

For all of his new found fame and glory, Adom did not change

He remained a simple father who only wished for the happiness and health of his wife and daughter

However, there was ONE thing that had changed

When a young woman rescued one of Adom's sheep from a being caught in a mess of vines and thorns down the way, Adom appeared to thank her in person

And just like Shakir had made to him, Adom made the girl an offer

"I will grant you whatever you seek, when you need help, simply call out my name- Adom, and I will appear before you and lend you all of the power a crocodile can lend, you may call on me however many times you wish,"

The Laughing Faery

Once upon a time

In a land that was here long before our own..

There lived a faery, named Ellie, who they all called The Laughing Faery

They called her this, because her laughter was as bright and boisterous as Christmas bells and wind chimes

Because she found amusement and happiness in every single thing, no matter how dark it may seem at first

And because, most of all, her laughter was contagious

Everywhere she went, and to everyone she met, her laughter spread and spread like a case of the sniffles, although, of course, far more enjoyable

Faery Tales, Mermaid Myths, And Other Fantastical Legends

At first, Ellie never took mind of the strange fact, it all seemed somewhat normal to her, being that, that was the way it had always been

She didn't notice it, in fact, until someone from another village asked her about it

"Why do you do that?" asked the Nixie in the lake in front of her

"Why do I do what?" Ellie asked in confusion

"Laugh so much, in all of my life, I have never heard someone laugh as much as you do, and you've only been here for less than a day,"

Ellie sat back and thought that over, combing her fingers through her long red hair

The Nixie was right, and the more and more Ellie thought about it, the more she started to realize that she DID laugh quite a bit more than anyone else she could think of

The more she thought about it, she started to realize that when she laughed, other people laughed with her

Even people who had been sad or angry or just having a bad day, they laughed along with her

She had always thought this to be a good quality to have, to be able to laugh so much and to make others laugh along with her

But when the Nixie asked about it, it sounded as if it were a bad quality to have

Now feeling self-conscious about herself and about her laughter in general, she flew to the woods in the hopes of staying alone so that she would never "bother" anyone with her laughter again

Ellie, who had once been known as The Laughing Faery, laughed no more

She spent a few days in the forest, hidden away from others, and trying to find a place for herself

It was after these few days that she was found by a fox, who had followed the tracks of the unusual faery

"Why are you out here all alone Little Faery?" the fox asked as he walked towards her and sat down

Ellie glanced up at the fox and heaved a deep breath

"I can't be around other people," she said simply

"Why not?" the fox countered

"Because... I have a problem," she said vaguely

"What kind of problem could that be?" The fox asked, his ears twitching

Ellie wanted to answer- she really did- but the fox's twitching ears were too distracting and she found herself giggling

It was a soft, low laugh, but one full of cheer and happiness

And within only a few seconds the fox had started laughing as well

"See? This always happens, out of the blue I begin to laugh and then the people around me begin to laugh as well," she explained

"Ah I see, you have The Contagious," said the fox

"The Contagious? What is that?" the faery asked rather worriedly

"The Contagious is a very rare and special gift, anyone who has it possesses the ability to find happiness in everything and to spread that happiness to anyone near through laughter, it's truly an outstanding gift,"

Interestingly, this is how the word "contagious" came to wrongly represent anything that was spread from person to person

Humans always do butcher the languages of other cultures....

"It doesn't feel very outstanding," Ellie admitted softly

"I'm sorry to hear that, but do not let one rain cloud push away a sunny day," the fox said gently

"But what if people get tired of my laughter? Or don't feel like laughing themselves?" she asked

The fox thought for a moment before looking back up at her

"Then you go where you are wanted, do not let negative people ruin your happiness, my dear faery, because those are the kinds of people who can never truly be happy themselves,"

Ellie nodded thoughtfully and leaned over, giving her new friend a hug and giggling softly at how soft his fur was

"Alright, thank you," she said with a bright smile, flying away, out of the forest, back towards the villages

Now, many, many centuries after her conversation with the fox, The Laughing Faery came to find her place in the world

And her place... is in fact, not one place at all

Her place is many places

Her place is all places

Her place is wherever sad or sick children are

Her place is wherever unhappy people are

Her place is wherever stress and gloom and melancholy ran rampant

And in those places she thrived, for she was able to spread her gift of laughter to people who really, truly needed it

Who really, truly, WANTED it

The Laughing Faery found her place where she was considered a gift to all who met her

She sang and danced for the children

She told stories and made wishes with adults

She imparted her wisdom, her joy onto anyone who wished to have it

Faeries, mermaids, dragons... it didn't seem to matter

Even humans were extremely appreciative of The Laughing Faery's abilities

Especially new mothers

For babies were The Laughing Faery's biggest audience

When a baby cries and cries and then suddenly stops in contentment or to laugh, you can be sure that The Laughing Faery is there

Making funny faces in the dark or singing songs of happiness and joy

Dancing around in the room and laughing until she herself was smiling so much that the baby couldn't help but smile as well

Babies, for all their innocence and in-born happiness, do not question moments of laughter

They appreciate them for what they are

And although it makes The Laughing Faery sad to watch people get older and lose that sense of happiness and joy that she had once given to them

It's never long before she's called into action again as another baby begins to cry

Somewhere, in some land, at some place

The Laughing Faery is there, spreading joy and laughter to whoever is willing to listen, and especially to those who are willing to laugh along with her

Faery Tales, Mermaid Myths, And Other Fantastical Legends

The Love Of The Moon

Once upon a time

In a land filled with night skies

There lived a werewolf

He wasn't really a special werewolf

Sort of a plain little thing in fact

But he was happy with himself and with what he was

That is, until one day when he decided to leave the comfort and safety of his own land to depart for another

"Are you SURE you want to do this and mingle among the humans?" his mother asked worriedly

"I'll be fine Mom, I'm 19, I want to experience the human lifestyle," he insisted

"And you know I support that, it's just.... the humans can be cruel and I don't want you to get hurt Noah..."

"I won't Mom, I promise," he smiled brightly

If only it had been a promise he was able to keep

For not long after entering the human world he met a girl

She was a fine girl, beautiful, smart, and talented, and with a smart mouth to boot

And Noah found himself absolutely in love with her

So it was no surprise that when the first full moon came around, he pulled her out to the forest to show her his shift

What WAS surprising however, was the reaction he received in return

After elegantly turning from his human form to his wolf form, he expected the impressed smile and endless joy that most creatures from his realm expressed when seeing a werewolf shift for the first time

What he received instead was a look of horror and disgust

"What are you!?" she shouted

Noah blinked, a little confused, did she not see that he was a wolf?

Or maybe ... she didn't know about werewolves?

Ah that was probably it, he knew the humans were dense about these things...

So he shifted back, taking a step forward

"Lisa, I-"

"Stay away from me!!" she shouted, picking up a rock and throwing it at him

Noah flinched and took a step back, staring at her as his he felt his heart break in two

"Lisa please, I'm no-"

"Monster!! You're a monster is what you are!! Don't ever come near me again!" she screamed, picking up another rock and throwing it at him as well

This time Noah didn't wait to be hit by it and shifted back into his wolf form, fleeing as fast as he could as he felt the sensation of other stones and rocks fly past him

Only after reaching the river, on the other side of the forest, did his adrenaline give out and force him to stop

He shivered slightly, tears welling up in his eyes as he licked the scrape on his leg from where one of the rocks had nicked him

He didn't understand

He thought she really liked him

He thought they were friends- well more than that even

He thought she cared about him...

Noah hung his head, shivering in the cold weather and staring up at the moon as he howled

From there, things only got worse

Every time he tried to make a friend they seemed to brush him off or not talk to him at all, which had been the experience he had before but... at least back then he had Lisa to help cushion the blow....

He couldn't find another werewolf in the dreaded human metropolis no matter how hard he searched and he became increasingly lonely every night, missing the warmth of his fellow packmates and friends back home

Within days after the first full moon he had been out in his wolf form running through the forest in the hopes of meeting another shapeshifter only to find that hunters were following him and he very barely missed getting shot in the leg with Wolfsbane

His mother had been right when she said the human world was cruel, but Noah still wished she hadn't been

He wanted so badly to stick it out

To be the first in his pack- or his family- to survive a full year of human life

But after only the second month the loneliness was digging at him so badly that he slowly began to hate himself, and what he was

He wondered day after day as he watched friends and couples and families walk past him why he was outcaste

He knew that not everyone he met knew he was a werewolf, so why?

What was so inherently wrong with him that people didn't want him near?

He thought back again and again to how things were before he showed Lisa the truth, and wondered how long they could have stayed that way if he hadn't told her at all

He imagined that things would have stayed that way forever if he wasn't a werewolf

He imagined a lot of things, because without anyone to keep him company, there wasn't much else to do

And so, by the time the third full moon of his time in the human world came around, Noah was completely and absolutely sick of himself

He had grown so bitter towards his wolf side that he kept it bottled up all month

And what happens when a werewolf keeps themselves bottled up for a month?

They shift on the full moon, of course, without being able to stop it or shift back until morning like they normally would be able to

And so he writhed on the ground in pain, shivering and shuddering as he tried to stop the shift from over taking him, and when he realized he couldn't, he became furious with himself

He howled and screamed, staring- glaring- up at the moon

"Why are you doing this to me!?" he shouted to the moon

"What have I ever done to deserve such a curse!?"

The moon, who was just as alive as any other being, stared at Noah in sadness

"Do you really think I've cursed you Noah? My dear child... what happened? You were so happy once, so in love with me and my power and YOUR power once, where has that love gone?"

Noah laid on the forest floor, beginning to sob

"I'm just so lonely.... I'm so lonely that it hurts, I don't understand, why does no one want me? It must be this curse... it must be my second skin... my power... how else am I different?"

"You are so lonely that you would forsake your very soul out of anger and bitterness?" the moon asked

"Yes...." Noah confessed, sitting up and trying to stop the tears

The moon had been watching Noah- as she had watched all Night Creatures- for many years, and to see him hurting so badly hurt her just as much

"If I were to make sure that you were never lonely again, would you promise me to love yourself again? To love your power again? To love ME again?" the moon asked

"Yes... yes..... just please, please make it stop hurting," Noah choked

And so, the moon did something that would change the world forever

For she loved him so much, that she split herself in two

One half to stay in the sky where she belonged, the other to be with Noah, to heal his aching heart

At first, Noah wasn't sure what to do with this half of the moon, who before his very eyes, turned into a beautiful woman with sweeping silver hair and bright silver eyes

"I swear to you Noah, I will never let you be lonely again,"

It was a promise she kept

And this is why the moon is as she is today

This is why the moon is full only once a month- and nearly completely gone once a month

For one day a month, is the day when all werewolves worship the moon, and their ancestor Noah, and in turn, worship themselves as the beautiful beings that they are

As ALL creatures should worship themselves for the beautiful beings that they are

And on this night, the two halves of the moon become one again, and the great, wise spirit of Noah, travels across the world to aid any other lonely wolves

On the night of the New Moon, however, when there is nothing but a sliver of moon in the sky, the moon takes nearly her entire self to spend in Heaven with Noah, where he spends the entire night as a wolf, so that they can be their full, true selves for one night

Every other night of the month, only half of the moon is in the sky, because the other half is with Noah, sometimes they stay on Earth, sometimes they go back to the Heavens, and sometimes they romp through the skies and visit other spirits like the sun and the many many stars

It never matters where they go, or what they do

Because with each other, both Noah, and the moon, are together forever, and most importantly of all, are never- not for a single night of all eternity- lonely

The Mechanical Heart

Once upon a time

In a land that existed many times ago

There lived a woman

The woman had always wanted only one thing out of life: A child

Yet it seemed that this was the only thing she could not have, for the woman was barren and theirs seemed to be the only town without an orphanage in need

So one day, not knowing what else to do, but craving the light and joy that a child would bring

The woman got to work on creating a child, even if the doctors told her that she couldn't have one of her own

She began by taking pen to parchment and making the designs

Then buying the parts

And finally cleaning out the lab in her cellar before construction could begin

It took many years to figure out how to design a living thing

But in the end, the two most important things about the design were also the two most important parts of a human:

The heart, and the brain

The heart was easy enough to construct with the right parts, all she really needed after all was a pumping device to keep fuel flowing

It was the brain that became the difficult matter

No matter what she did or how hard she tried, she could never construct anything close to the human brain, despite the fact that the mechanical heart she had crafted strongly resembled that of an organic one

And so, left without much choice, the woman decided that perhaps a FULLY hand-crafted child was not possible...

But PARTLY crafted.... now this could work....

And so she waited, she waited for the perfect opportunity and found herself a job at an elderly garden community

And, as she had hoped, when one of the residents fell ill she promised to donate her body to science

And creating an artificial lifeform.... that was science wasn't it?

So the woman took the dying brain with the last beats of life in it and installed it in the head of her mechanical daughter, applied the right amount of electricity to get her kicking, and waited

And with a shocked breath, the heap of metal and oil that had been constructed into the shape of a girl rose and blinked slowly, turning her head in the woman's direction

"Can you hear me?" she asked hopefully

And the results were even better than she had hoped for

For the mechanical girl began to smile

"I shall name you Mary Beth, after my late mother... for she would have loved you so... just as I will always love you, my dearest Mary Beth," the woman breathed, wiping a tear from her eye

Mary Beth tilted her head to the side, a small squeak occurring at the metal getting newly adjusted, but maintained her smile

No matter what, Mary Beth always seemed to be smiling

A full year passed and as it did the woman taught Mary Beth the basics of life

It was a long, often tedious process, but Mary Beth was a fast learner and always eager to know more, which made the process much more enjoyable

And at this point, Mary Beth had come to be quite accustomed to the simplest things in life, like running errands for her mother, why just that gave her so much joy it always looked like she was about to pop a screw out of her head from smiling so much

"Good morning Mrs. Higgins! Good morning Mr. Stewart!" she said happily as she twirled her burgundy parasol in her fingers and skipped across the dirt pathway to the bakery

Mrs. Higgins gave her a polite, if not somewhat curt nod, and Mr. Stewart just grunted as if bothered by her very existence

People had a hard time getting used to Mary Beth, as they claimed she wasn't really alive at all

Or worse, that by her being alive, some sort of grave sin had been performed, and she was a work of evil

But Mary Beth never noticed the criticism or judgement, for Mary Beth- for all of her human ways- was born without something that all humans possessed

She was born without hatred

And it was something that her mother refused to teach her

And so she skipped along, humming a childlike tune as she swung into the bakery doors and smiled at the woman working there

"Good morning Miss Matilda!" she said brightly as she sprinted to the counter and set her parasol on the floor

"Good morning Mary Beth, what can I get for you today?" Matilda asked with an equally happy smile

"A bag of sugar please! Mama is making pie today!"

"Oh really? I'm sure they're very good," Matilda mused as she walked to get the sugar

"Mama's pies are the BEST! Not that yours aren't good Miss Matilda- they are! I just mea-"

"It's ok Mary Beth, I think MY mother's pies are the best too," Matilda laughed, bringing the bag of sugar out from behind the counter and handing it to the bronze metal girl

"I'll tell you what, that sugar is on the house if you promise to bring me a piece of your mother's pie in the morning," she smiled

Mary Beth's eyes lit up- quite literally- and she nodded excitedly

"Oh I will Miss Matilda! I'll see you in the morning!" she said excitedly, grabbing her parasol and carrying it carefully in one hand as the other held the sugar close to her chest

Matilda smiled, waving and leaning down to tighten one of the bolts in her leg

For Matilda was much like Mary Beth

She too had metal were flesh could be

And because she knew firsthand how cruel people could be, just to someone with a mechanical leg, she made it her mission to insure that Mary Beth never felt the despair that people had made her feel

But of course, Matilda only had a mechanical leg

She feared for the cruelty people could possess against someone with a mechanical heart

"Skip, skip, skip to my Lou, skip, skip, skip to my Lou, skip, skip, skip to my Lou, skip to my Lo my darlin'," Mary Beth sang to herself as she skipped back towards the way of her house

She was so distracted in her fit of happiness however, that she barely noticed the boy in front of her and ran right into him

"Oh!! I'm sorry!" Mary Beth cried, blinking and rubbing her sore bottom as she looked up and saw, once the cloud of dust dissipated, the son of the local doctor

"Patrick!" she chirped happily

Patrick looked up, coughing slightly and smiling

"Hello Mary Beth, where are you off to today?" he smiled just as brightly, standing and brushing his pants off before offering her his hand to help her up

She took it gratefully and grabbed her bag of sugar as she did, smoothing her soft red and black dress as she looked up at him

"I was just picking up sugar, we're having pie tonight! Cherry I think," she mused

"Cherry? I love cherry! It's my favorite!" he said excitedly

"Really? Well would you like to come over and share it? I'm sure Mother won't mind!" she said happily

Patrick grinned excitedly and nodded as well

"I'd love to! What time should I be there?" he asked

"Well.... how about six?" she offered

Patrick nodded and took his pocket watch from his pocket, flipping it open to check the time

"Six- in four hours then," he concluded

Mary Beth nodded excitedly and bit her lip, both of them swaying a bit awkwardly and shyly before Mary Beth snapped her fingers

"S-Sugar! I have to get the sugar home! I'll see you later tonight Patrick!" she promised

"I'll see you then Mary Beth!" he laughed, waving as she hummed her song and went back to skipping her way home

Patrick took a breath, looking down in surprise when he saw Mary

Beth's parasol still in the dirt

"Mary Beth!! Mary Beth you left your parasol!!" he shouted after her

But she was too far away to hear him, so, thinking nothing of it, he took the parasol and resolved to simply give it to her later when he saw her again

"I'll get her flowers too... roses like her dress," he muttered to himself as he started off to the florist, and even he couldn't resist singing in joyfulness as he walked

"Skip skip skip to my Lou, skip to my Lou my darlin'..."

Mary Beth was so excited when she got home that she couldn't even stay still

She was constantly zooming and humming and buzzing as if her wiring had gone wrong

(Her mother had checked of course and no such thing had happened)

And when six o'clock came Mary Beth waited by the door

When seven o'clock came, Mary Beth still waited by the door

When ten o'clock came, Mary Beth was still waiting by the door

It wasn't until the clock struck twelve that Mary Beth gave up and went upstairs

She cried for hours, no matter how much her mother tried to comfort her, for it was the first heartbreak she had ever known, and it hurt worse than anything she had ever felt

The next morning when she went back to the bakery to deliver the pie to Matilda the other woman immediately noticed something was wrong

Gone from her face was any trace of joy or light, and it was all replaced by agony and misery and gloom

Matilda, fearing the worst, immediately dropped the pan of cupcakes she was baking and rushed to Mary Beth's side

"Mary Beth!? Mary Beth what's wrong? What happened!?" she cried worriedly

"I... Patrick was supposed to come over last night... he never came...." she said softly, holding the slice of pie out for her friend

"Oh Mary Beth..." Matilda breathed, hugging the younger girl tightly and setting the pie on the counter

Matilda knew firsthand what it was like to be stood up and the fact that this beautiful, innocent girl had just suffered the same... it broke her heart

"Come with me my darling," she said immediately, grabbing a pair of goggles and her net gun from the back of the store

"Where are we going?" Mary Beth asked innocently as Matilda slipped the bronze and green-lensed goggles on

"We're going to find that boy and he's going to apologize to you! Whatever excuse he has isn't good enough for hurting you that way!" she said, taking Mary Beth's hand and dragging her away towards the small doctor's office, just past the blacksmith's and a little south of the seamstress

Once there, however, the girls were shocked to find the office closed

"Afternoon Miss Matilda, Miss Mary Beth," grunted an older man as he walked towards the two of them

"What's that gun ya' got there for?" he asked

"Catching vermin.... where's the good doctor and his son?" Matilda asked in confusion

"I see ya' haven't heard the news.... they left town last night, just b'fore six they did, don't know as where they were goin' but it seemed rather rushed and unplanned... ah that reminds me! Mary Beth! The young lad had asked me to give ya' somethin'!" he said, snapping his fingers and opening the office door with one of the many keys on his key ring

"I know it's around here some- ah! Here we go!" he hummed, handing Mary Beth her parasol back, as well as a bouquet of red roses

"I think that boy is feelin' somethin' mighty special for ya' Mary Beth," he chuckled

Mary Beth felt even more crushed than before but gave the man a broken smile

"Thank you Mr. Gus, I appreciate it, I best be going now before Mother starts to worry," she said softly, sprinting away as fast as she could

"Now what could be the matter with her I wonder?" Gus muttered as he straightened his jacket

Matilda just rolled her eyes and trudged back to the bakery, disappointed in equal parts that she couldn't help Mary Beth... and that she couldn't use her net gun.... it had just been far too long and she was worried it was going to rust....

"Mary Beth!? What's wrong!?" the girl's mother called as she sprinted into the house and up the stairs, not even bothering to close the door

Her mother sighed, shutting the door and racing after her

"Mary Beth what happened?"

The mechanical girl looked up, sniffling and wiping away the oil tears that were pouring out of her eyes

"Patrick didn't stand me up... he's gone," she breathed, clutching the flowers close

"What do you mean he's gone?" her mother asked in confusion

"His dad made him leave, it's all my fault... isn't it Mama? I made him leave didn't I?" she cried

"Mary Beth..... don't ever, ever think such a terrible thing, you did nothing wrong and NEVER believe differently," her mother said sternly

She knew why the girl would feel that way though

The so-called "good" doctor had been against Mary Beth since the moment she had been even a thought

To him she was "an abomination", something that went against medicine, against humanity itself, against the spirit

And he was sure to express it at every given opportunity

There was no doubt in her mind that he found out his son had plans to court Mary Beth and had spirited him away out of town just to keep from that happening

But she couldn't let her daughter know that, or she would never forgive herself

"Then why?" Mary Beth asked between sniffles

"Because .... some people ... some people can't understand new things... or new people, or anything or anyone different from themselves.... and this town is very different, he probably was just fed up with 'different' and wanted to go somewhere else with his same pig-hea-. .. er... very wrong views," she explained

"It really isn't my fault Mama?" she asked meekly

"No my dear girl, it isn't your fault at all,"

She nodded, leaning forward and wrapping her arms tightly around her mother

"Do you think Patrick will ever come back?" she asked softly

Her mother smiled gently, hugging her back just as tightly

"I don't know my sweet child.... I just don't know...."

And so, no matter how much it hurt, Mary Beth willed her pain to fade

She willed herself not to listen to Mr. Stewart's grumbles or pay attention to the way Mrs. Higgins looked at her when she was wearing a new dress

She forced herself not to get upset every time she heard bad things said about her and pretended not to notice every time someone moved a rock in front of her feet to trip her or "accidentally" got her hair caught around one of their belongings

She pretended to stay joyfully oblivious to all of these things

For she knew not hatred, and had no will to wish them ill in return for the cruelty they showed to her

Another full year passed and although there was now a crack in her mechanical heart, one that ached as if gears were scraping it whenever someone did something unkind or she remembered Patrick, she always smiled her way through it

And so on a day much like the day before, she found herself skipping towards Matilda's bakery with a fresh basket of apples

"Hello Mrs. Jenkins! Hello Mr. Barnes!" she said happily as she waved to the other customers

"Hello Mary Beth, how are you today?" Mrs. Jenkins said gently

"I'm doing well," she smiled

Mr. Barnes leaned over, tapping her on the shoulder and making her look up

"Is there somethin' in your ear there Mary Beth?" he asked

She tilted her head innocently and giggled happily when he reached over and pulled a simple copper coin out from behind her ear

"I believe this is yours," he winked, setting it in her palm

Mr. Barnes was quite literally willing to pay anyone who would indulge him in letting him perform his sleight of hand illusions

And Mary Beth, who found the tricks sincerely enjoyable, was by far his favorite customer

"Mama picked some fresh apples from the orchard outside of town today Miss Matilda! She wanted to give you a basket!" she said cheerfully, setting the basket on the counter

Only to be surprised when the person who turned around wasn't Matilda at all

It was Patrick

"Patrick?" she breathed

"Mary Beth!" he shouted happily

"I.. I don't understand... when did you get here? Where's Miss Matilda?" she asked happily

"Miss Matilda had to run to the post to have a letter delivered before it was sent out today, I'm her apprentice so I'm watching the store,"

"When did this happen?" she breathed

"Just recently in fact... I've only been in town for a day, I wanted to come and see you later,"

"Oh Patrick I've missed you so!" she cried

"And I've missed you, I had to work as my father's apprentice all this time and save every coin I got to afford the travel fair to come back here... but I did, and I'm staying," he smiled brightly

"You're staying!?"

"I'm staying," he laughed

"I actually... would like to try having pie with you again, if you wouldn't mind it much," he said softly

"I... I would love to, I'll bake it tonight, Mama has been teaching me," she offered

"It's a date then!" he smiled

Mary Beth smiled brightly and looked down

"O-Oh um.. just... give the apples-"

"Right right..."

"So... I'll see you at six?"

"Six it is,"

And so once again, Mary Beth skipped away- remembering her lavender parasol this time- and began to sing

"Skip to my Lou my darlin'~" she hummed as she skipped

And so, by Patrick's return, Mary Beth's mechanical heart had one less scratch in it

Faery Tales, Mermaid Myths, And Other Fantastical Legends

The Night Children

Once upon a time

In a land in this general vicinity

There lived a family

They were quite the odd family, that was for certain

But mainly, the neighbors saw the children

And more importantly, they saw the children at NIGHT

There was seemingly no explanation but the only time anyone from the family appeared to be awake was night

It started in the evenings and just got later from there

Everything about these children was strange though, not just their penchant for being nocturnal

They acted strangely, they spoke strangely, they even seemed to breathe strangely

Or at least, that was the general opinion of the neighborhood

The children seemed like they had jumped right off the set of a horror movie

And the parents?

The parents were no better for sure!

Except that they were hardly seen

They didn't really leave the house.... or at least not during waking hours....

And normally this was fine

Everyone kept to their own business (Specifically keeping OUT of the business of the weird family at 825)

Except that now the very strange family at house 825 had been in the neighborhood for a full year, meaning one thing...

Someone would have to collect their neighborhood association fee

"President are you really sure this is the best way to decide who performs..... The Task?" one member of the Neighborhood Board asked

"Do you have a better suggestion?" she asked sharply

The other shook his head, looking down miserably as the president began the sacred ritual that would decide who had to collect the fee from the weird people at house 825

"Eenie meanie minie moe, catch a tiger by his toe, if he hollers let him go, eenie meanie minie moe," she chanted, her finger landing on a boy in the dead center of the line

He turned, quickly pointing to the person next to him and then the person next to her

"Larry, Curly," he said, grinning hopefully that the stunt had worked

It hadn't

"James, you know the rules, you're the moe, you have to go," the president recited

James sank lowly into his chair, sighing loudly

"Just... tell my family I love them and give my dog to my sister..."

Despite having been given three days to prepare before going to meet with the odd family in 825 James was still exceedingly nervous when he left the house that evening

"Come on James you can do this, your mom didn't name you after a space explorer for nothing," he muttered to himself as he walked across the street

"Lizzie Borden took an axe~" he heard being chanted from the yard

Well that couldn't be good

Clearing his throat, he slowly glanced over at the yard were two little girls were jumping rope

Both in lacey, almost Victorian style-ish black dresses with long black braids

And they were twins

Because obviously the only thing creepier than creepy little children singing about murder was TWIN creepy little children singing about murder

Of course

He swallowed, turning and ringing the doorbell at the house

"Who are you?" he heard, turning and screaming when the aforementioned children appeared right in front of him

"Do you want to go in our house?" one of the twins asked

"Um-"

"Are you the demon that's come to kill us?" the other asked

"Um...."

The door opened and James had never been so thankful in his life

"Mommy Mommy he's the demon that's come to kill us! Hide us!" the girls screamed as they ran into the house

"Oh girls you know there's no such thing as demons," the woman chastised

James sighed, finally someone with some sens-

"AND if he were a malevolent spirit or poltergeist would you be able to see him?"

Never mind, no sense it was then

"That's true..." one of the twins relented

"But he could be an Unseelie Faery! You can SEE Unseelie Faeries!" protested the other

"Yeah he's the Unseelie Faery come to kill us!" the first almost giggled

"Oh now come on, Unseelie Faeries can't come into this realm, what do you think the faeries at the Seelie Courts are doing? Lazing about eating cake all day? The Seelie Faeries have JOBS you know," the woman said

"That's true..." one twin mused

"Well, he must be something, he looks so unpleasantly weird," the other said

"Lucinda! That was very rude! He looks very PLEASENTLY weird!" huffed their mother

James honestly couldn't decide which was more insulting

"Really?" the girl- Lucinda- asked with a slight frown

"Ugh, just go find your father," the woman said with a tired sigh as the twins skipped away

"Sorry about Lucinda and Luna, they're just both so-"

"Imaginative?"

"-Perceptive for their age, I have to try harder to instill manners in them," she mused

James swallowed nervously, taking in the woman's appearance

She looked like she had just stepped out of a Victorian Gothic club or something with her dark jewelry, eccentric black dress, and long red hair

"I'm Annabelle, pleased to meet you," she smiled

"James, pleased to meet you as well," he managed to choke out

"Ah James... would you like to come in? I'm just finishing breakfast,"

He tried so hard not to dwell on that sentence...

"Um, no thank you, I just wanted to remind you that the association fee is due," he said awkwardly

Annabelle blinked, a little surprised and smiled

"Of course, just come in and I'll write the check for you," she offered

Every fiber of his being was screaming "ABORT MISSION! ABORT MISSION!" but what choice did he have?

So, saying goodbye to the outside world, he entered the house

And to his surprise, it wasn't the dungeon he expected it to be

It was just a normal house

Children's paintings hung on the wall

A dog barked and skated around the corner to greet him

The kitchen tiles were a soft rose pink and cream color and there was a little fountain by the window that had a calm, soothing effect

Either these people were the best at disguising their cannibalistic ways..... or they really weren't evil at all....

So far he didn't know which

"Now let's see... where did I put my check book?" she muttered, looking around the kitchen

"I left it in my purse I think... let me run upstairs, feel free to help yourself to anything in the kitchen," Annabelle said politely as she scampered off to the stairs

James waited before making a b-line to the refrigerator, jerking the door open and feeling shocked when most of what he found consisted of salad goods, condiments, and various drinks like juices, sodas, and milk, there was even little snack yogurts and cheese stars with a cartoon cow on the bag

Shutting the door, he went for the freezer (which he noted had a penguin magnet on it from the local aquarium, he'd have to explore the other magnets later) and was even more surprised when the only meat he found was ground beef and baked chicken patties- and a small supply of chicken nuggets but lately he had started seriously questioning the legitimacy of calling that a meat product

Or a food product

Most of it was pizza, french toast sticks, popsicles, more ice cream than he felt was healthy for any family, Italian Ice, and even frozen cheesesticks and macaroni dinners shaped like ponies

He was at a total and complete loss for words

"Is there something you require?" he heard, turning around and nearly having a heart attack at the man in front of him

The man with blue hair and piercings in his lip, eyebrows, and ears and staring at him quite judgingly

Maybe he was wrong, maybe this wasn't normal

Maybe this was all the clever ploy these people used to lull visitors into a false sense of security before taking them to the dungeon-basement and pulling a Hannibal on them down there

Maybe the upstairs was nothing but a gigantic belfry where the bats lived

"Frozen macaroni," was all James managed to say

The blue-haired guy heaved a loud say as if he was the one somehow put out by all this

"Rae!!! There's a person in our kitchen!!" he hollered, glancing at the doorway expectantly

Sure enough a beautiful young woman with long black hair and in similar style to Annabelle crossed the corner, stalking into the kitchen like a cat stalking into a den of mice

James was more than a little scared at this point

But also a little intrigued

"Please take care of this, all I wanted was some string cheese and a grape soda," the blue-haired guy said with a sigh

The girl rolled her eyes, reaching past James into the refrigerator and handing him what he asked for

"Alright now go back to catching up on the vampires in love, if you aren't caught up by the new episode tonight we're NOT waiting for you," she threatened

"You are the darkness in my heart little sister," he said melodramatically as he rushed to the stairs

"And you are gum in my hair now get out of here," she hollered back, turning back to James with a grin

"Mom is having a fit looking for her checkbook, I have a feeling Dad took it with him to the bank," she mused

James didn't speak, just stared with mild concern

"I'm Raven, what's your name?"

"J-James,"

"Ohh like the space cadet, very cute, very socially acceptable," she chuckled

He wasn't sure if that was a joke or a legitimate critique on society but either way he just laughed nervously and hoped he wasn't going to meet a swift death

..... Or a long, drawn out death....

"Relax, I'm not going to hurt you," she snorted, taking a few steps back and pausing

"I mean, not without your consent," she teased

James wasn't sure when he stopped breathing but he managed to choke on nothing anyway

"I.. um... I wasn't snooping," he said awkwardly

"You mean in the fridge? Don't worry about it, Mom has an open door policy on the food, except for Tiberius, he went on ONE candied apple binge last Halloween and he's had to have permission to feed ever since," she mused

"Your brother's name is Tiberius?" he asked

He thought that was a name that only fictional characters and Rottweilers had....

"My oldest brother- the one you just met, yeah, and my younger brothers are Casper and Bram, Mom keeps saying she's going to name the next one Draco but that wizard movie sort of ripped the uniqueness out of that one I think, now EVERYBODY thinks Draco is a cool name," she said with an eye roll

"How many siblings do you HAVE?" James asked suspiciously

"Seven, you've already met the twins and then my other younger sisters are Harlow and Tabitha, Mom's expecting in the fall though,"

The more information he had, the less James was scared and the more he was... mildly overwhelmed....

"Big family," he said lamely

"You could say that's a family tradition, my mom has twelve brothers and sisters, she was lucky number thirteen," she mused

....

LUCKY number thirteen?

Faery Tales, Mermaid Myths, And Other Fantastical Legends

Just then the door opened and a man with jet black hair and a simple, somewhat well-groomed looking mustache walked in, setting an umbrella in the umbrella stand

"I didn't know it was raining," James mused

"It wasn't, Daddy had to leave early to catch the bank," Raven corrected

....

And then there was that

"Dad do you have Mom's check book? She needs to pay the neighborhood people," she called

"It's right here! I'll go tell your mother!" he shouted back, hopping up the stairs

"Speaking of that.... you look awfully young to be on the neighborhood board," Raven mused as she hopped onto the counter and stared at him curiously

"Y-Yeah.... I'm only twenty-one... I uh.. studied some financial stuff in college last semester so... my mom got me to fill in the temp position that's open.... I-I'm not going into finances though, I'm going into pediatrics, hopefully," he said with a small smile

"Really? Huh, twenty-three, got you beat," she mused

"Oh? What field are you studying?" he asked

That's it James

Just keep it normal

So far the only thing to suggest that these people were two birds shy of a nest was the nocturnal thing...and their appearances... and it wasn't right to judge on appearances....

Or on being creatures of the night apparently....

"I'm not in college, I write graphic novels, Tiberius illustrates them, we have the first three books in the first series out already- Children Of The Night, have you heard of it?"

"No I haven't, but that's quite an accomplishment for being twenty-three," he mused

"I started young," she shrugged back

"I hope to have a massive library's worth by the time I'm my mom's age... I just want to tell stories," she mused as she stared up at the ceiling

James smiled softly, leaning against the counter

"That's a really cool dream to have,"

"Yep, and I'm lucky enough that my parents support it, they always say 'you're spending the same amount of time and much much less money doing this than going to college, these are your college years so just build your brand like you would at any other job'," she mused

"That's really neat," James smiled

Before Raven could answer further a distressed looking Annabelle flew around the corner and promptly delivered a check to James

"Sorry about all the wait!" she said with an embarrassed grin

"Oh no, trust me, it's fine," James smiled back, rubbing the back of his neck nervously

"I really should get going though, I... my .. cat needs dinner," he said, starting for the door

"Hey Space Cadet?" Raven called, catching James' attention

"If you like horror movies, we could watch one sometime,"

"I love horror movies," James smiled

Ok, love was a little bit of an overstatement

He tolerated horror movies

That was good enough right?

"Cool, eleven tomorrow?"

"Eleven is good,"

Eleven wasn't good

He was usually asleep by midnight at the latest...

"Good, I'll see you then," Raven said with a smile, hopping down from the counter and walking over to him

"James?" she added

"Huh?" he asked innocently

She smirked slightly, placing a hand on his shoulder

"I hope you don't think of me as some twisted, dark video game fantasy girl like the over-stereotyped ones in bad movies," she said seriously

"I don't, I would never think of anyone like that," he said honestly

"Good, because if you ever treat me that way, you'll wish I was Hannibal Lecter," she said with a small grin, patting his shoulder and walking away

"I'll see you tomorrow,"

James wasn't sure what unnerved him more

The fact that he had just agreed to what he considered a date with a girl that honestly scared him to the point of heart palpitations

Or the fact that she apparently had read his mind earlier

Oh well, at least he could report back to the neighborhood that these were relatively nice people (except for the twins who still scared him more than any horror movie ever) and that they shouldn't keep judging them solely based on appearance and what time their internal clocks were set to

With that thought in mind he headed back to his house, determined to call a meeting for the rest of the association

"Ugh, finally, breakfast," Raven said with a happy grin as she reached into the refrigerator and pulled a strange looking fruit out from the back of the fruit drawer

"I can't believe you've finally got your first date Raven!" Annabelle said with a delighted smile

She shrugged, taking a bite of the weird looking fruit

"I think he's terrified of me, and not in the good 'you better respect me or you'll get what's coming to you' way, just the 'I'm somewhat sure you have organs in your freezer' sort of way," she sighed

"Don't worry, the boy seems pliable, I'm sure he'll become more accepting and less frightened once you spend a little time with him, now I need to call your grandmother and tell her about this, she'll be so excited for you!" Annabelle said happily as she grabbed a few orange slices out of the refrigerator

Raven just shrugged, sitting on the counter again as she watched her mother take a bottle of fizzing liquid, drop the orange slices in, and drop it on the ground

Wouldn't you know, a swirly mystical portal opened up in the middle of the kitchen floor

"Are you coming dear?"

"Sure, haven't seen Granny in almost a week," she shrugged, stretching and getting down from the counter

"Exactly! And since you'll be home you won't have to keep up those pesky human appearances anymore, you can stretch your wings and everything!" Annabelle smiled, jumping into the portal

"Oh.... thank goodness," Raven grinned as her eyes turned red and she jumped in after her mother

Faery Tales, Mermaid Myths, And Other Fantastical Legends

The Owl And The Snowy Forest

Once upon a time

In a land that was usually quite warm

There lived an owl named Tiki

Tiki was a relatively normal little owl

A Barn Owl in fact

And she lived in a fairly warm forest far from human attention

At least, it was usually fairly warm...

Until one day, late into the colder months, when Tiki awoke to find that the mildly cold weather had turned into FREEZING cold weather

And when she stretched her feathers, she found an odd substance hit her wing

It was white and fluffy and most of all absolutely FREEZING

As she looked around and shivered, she realized that this was the substance she had heard many call "snow"

And it was a DELIGHT!

Tiki had the time of her life bouncing and playing and rolling around in the snow

It was so much fun that at first she didn't even realize how cold it was....

That was, she didn't realize it, AT FIRST...

But after only a very short time she bobbed her head up and started to feel just how cold the snow was and she suddenly yearned for the warm weather to come back

Just as she was flying up to her favorite tree, intent to look for a shelter of some sort in the hopes of more warmth, Tiki heard an odd noise

It was a voice alright, but not one like Tiki had ever heard

Curiously, the bird flew over towards the voice, ignoring how cold she was against the open air, and hoped to find the source of the noise

There, sitting in the forest, was a human in what Tiki had heard referred to as a "car"

The human was speaking to some sort of device that talked back to her and she seemed pretty displeased with the conversation given that she took the device away and tossed it aside in frustration

The human shivered, appearing to be as cold as Tiki felt, and rubbed her arms

Tilting her head curiously to the side, the owl fluttered down and landed on the top of that "Car" thing, letting out a squeak and tapping her feet on it

Luckily the human seemed to understand her and exited the "car" with little hesitation

"What is that noise?" the human muttered, looking around here and there until she finally met eyes with the owl on top of her car

Tiki let out a chirp, fluttering down to the car mirror and tilting her head again

"O-Oh um... nice.... nice owl.... I'm not... meaning to intrude on your land or anything... I just want to get home... well... I WOULD get home... but my car is ruined, I had a wreck in the snow and... and so I just need to stay here for now,"

Tiki didn't quite understand what the human was saying but the tone of her voice sounded distressed, so she resolved that perhaps the human was also looking for shelter and warmth and that they should seek it out together

So Tiki chirped again and began to fly away, getting only a few feet from the "car" before realizing that the human wasn't following her

Perhaps the human was injured and couldn't follow, Tiki considered, and so she turned around and went back, landing on the human's featherless wing appendage (arm) and looking her over- which would have been a MUCH easier task if she had stopped squirming and talking mind you

But to Tiki's surprise, there didn't seem to be anything wrong with her

So she flew about a foot away, chirping again, and waited on the human to follow

But yet again, she just kept standing there like a deer in the headlights of life

And now Tiki was becoming a bit frustrated

She chirped louder, flying back and grabbing some of the human's hair, giving it a gentle tug before letting go and flying away

The human seemed to say something in human language and FINALLY took a few steps forward to follow the owl

And so Tiki flew a little further, and the human followed a little closer

This cycle continued on for longer than Tiki would have liked- why the human insisted on wasting time by moving so slowly and refusing to fly were BEYOND her- but they did eventually find shelter

It was nothing exquisite or even all that normal

It was a very, almost overly simple log cabin

But that wasn't important at all

What was important, the only thing that was important really, was that the place looked warm

"Wow... this must be one of those cabins that was foreclosed on recently..." the human mused as she stared at the building

Tiki chirped, happy that she had found what they were looking for, and easily flew in through one of the broken windows

"Ah... little owl wait!" the human shouted, looking pensive as she carefully opened the door, feeling relieved that it wasn't locked

Of course given the multiple broken windows she could see why....

"I don't think we should be in here," the human mused, blinking in surprise when she realized the place was fully furnished... and exceptionally warm....

Especially if she started a fire in that fireplace just ahead....

"Well, the tow truck DID say two hours.... surely I could stay here for just a little while without getting caught..." she mused

The human walked over to the fireplace and grabbed the lighter on top of the mantel, lighting a fire quickly and heading back towards the old couch in the corner where Tiki was currently perched

"Thank you Owl, I never would have found this place without you," she smiled, wrapping a blanket around herself and placing a pillow on the arm of the couch for Tiki to sit on

The little owl moved down, settling peacefully on the pillow and waited with the human

Snow, Tiki decided, could be fun for a little while, but what was best without a doubt was being able to find somewhere warm to relax after playing in it, especially if you had a friend there with you

✤ Faery Tales, Mermaid Myths, And Other Fantastical Legends ✤

The Pig's Restaurant

Once upon a time

In a land very different from our own

There lived a pig, and this pig had a big dream

The pig dreamed of opening a restaurant of his very own

And so for many, many years he saved his money

He pinched and frugled and stashed away every stray coin he could find

And finally, after many, many years, he had enough to open his restaurant

And so he did

He called it Milo's, after himself

Milo spent many months preparing his restaurant to make it as perfect as could be

He worked and worked and worked

He painted the restaurant and prepared his menu and ordered his cookware

Even though the stoves and sinks and other such cookware was much, much taller than he was

Milo managed

It was a fine restaurant indeed, and the grand opening was even finer

People had heard of the wonderful food and gathered around the corner just for a taste!

It was Milo's dream, and it was happening

But his dream didn't last for long

For once the restaurant was open, Milo went out to greet his guests

"Welcome to Milo's! I am Milo, and I would be honored to cook for you today," Milo announced with a smile, standing on the bar so as to be tall enough to draw attention

The restaurant, once filled with an excited buzz of commotion, went dead silent

"But.... you're a pig," piped up one person from the back

"Yes, I am a pig, but I promise you, my food is good, and I would love to serve you," he said brightly

It started slowly, but then picked up into a hurried, rushed pace as everyone began to leave

The guests, as well as the staff, all left upon finding out that Milo was a pig

And Milo was heart broken

However, there was ONE soul who stayed, a beautiful faery, and her name was Danika

Her skin was midnight dark and her smile was as bright as the moon

And she, unlike everyone else, did not care that Milo was a pig

And so Milo served his only customer with the biggest smile his aching heart could muster

And Danika lamented the same thing that Milo's friends and family had told him for a very long time

"This food is delicious! I've never tasted anything so good in my life!" she proclaimed

"Thank you, I really appreciate it, if only others shared your opinion," he said solemnly

Danika stood, bending down and putting her hand on Milo's shoulder

"You'll get there, and I'll help you, I can't do much cooking but I'm not a bad waitress,"

"You really wouldn't mind?" he asked quietly

"Certainly not, I was about to quit my office job anyway, I would love to help you here Milo, if you'll have me,"

Milo smiled sincerely and nodded his confirmation

"I would love to,"

For many months Milo and Danika worked as hard as they could to make the restaurant a success

But even after all that time and work hardly anyone ever stopped in, even the other animals often cringed at the thought of eating what a pig would make

They had a few steady customers who visited frequently, but even on its best day the restaurant wasn't even half full

And Milo remained heart broken

One day, after a new customer arrived, Milo cooked the food as requested and took it out to her himself, being that Danika was occupied with a phone order at the time

"Please enjoy," Milo smiled brightly as he presented the food

The woman stared at Milo and stood wordlessly, racing to the door and never turning back

Milo fell back on his rump, staring up at the table where he had placed the food and beginning to weep

He cried and cried, for it seemed that nothing he did ever mattered

No one would ever make his restaurant a success, because no one was willing to even try his food

And the thought of this, of his dreams failing because people refused to open their minds a little, made him sob harder

"Darling Milo, what's wrong?" Danika asked as she rushed over to him

Milo cried and cried, snorting and honking and wiping at his teary eyes and runny nose with the back of his little front foot

"I'll never succeed Danika, never," he wept

"I could work for years and years and no one will ever try my food, because when they look at me, they only see a pig, that's all I am to them, nothing but a pig,"

"Dear Milo, don't despair, why, pigs are one of the loveliest animals in the world," Danika said gently

"No one else seems to think so, they think terribly of us, and even the other animals are wary of my food, I can't take it anymore Danika, the hatred and the loneliness.... I try so hard and no one seems to care, I work night and day, I'm tired, and my feet hurt from constantly straining to reach the stove and counter, I can't take it anymore, I just.... I just give up," he cried

Danika sat down next to him on the floor, one of her giant, feathery wings wrapping around him as she brought him closer

"Precious Milo, would you believe that I've been through the same thing you have?"

This stopped the crying for a moment, as Milo stared up at her in shock

"You... you have...?"

"Yes, like you, people judged me because of my appearance, and never thought of me as a person, or as the potential of what I could do, and just like you, I wept for not being the ideal that they wanted,"

"But... but you're beautiful!" Milo insisted

He was absolutely shocked to think that anyone, ANYONE, could see Danika as any less than the most beautiful creature in the world

She may have been just a faery to most, but to Milo, she was the very sun and moon and stars

"And you are too, you, Milo, are beautiful," she insisted, reaching down and clearing his tears away with her thumbs

"No... I'm not, I'm just a pig..."

"And why do you believe that?" She frowned

"Because no one else believes what you believe Danika, no one else thinks I'm beautiful, or special, or worth anything at all,"

"And who are these people to be listened to?" she frowned deeper, moving Milo closer to look into his eyes

"I am telling you the truth Milo, you are beautiful, I find you beautiful, and who are these people- who say less and refuse to spare you even a glance from their eyes- that you would listen to them and not listen to me? Are my words somehow less?"

"Never," he said immediately

"Then Milo, believe in your beauty, your talent, and your worth, because I am telling you- I, who loves you as much as a brother- that it is true,"

Milo nodded, wiping his eyes again and leaning in as Danika gave him a tight hug

"I'm sorry Danika, I just feel so awful all the time,"

"I know, which is why I'm going to make you a promise," she offered, pulling back and smiling at him

"Milo, if you promise me- SWEAR to me- that you will never give up, then I will grant you what you need to reach the heights you wish to reach, ok?"

He nodded slowly, taking a breath of confidence and nodding a little harder

"I promise,"

And so it was done

A small pair of wings, as white and feathery as Danika's own, sprouted from Milo's back

"Now, dear Milo, you can fly, and you can reach the stove and the counter and anything at all that you wish to reach with ease, now, Milo, you can reach the very stars if you try,"

And Milo, elated with his new gift, believed her

Weeks passed with no change, but Milo was no longer as unhappy as he once was

Things had fallen into normalcy and Milo didn't suspect that he would ever see a new customer, which he was fine with, as there were a few who were very loyal to him

Why, he suspected that every person in the kingdom had heard of the pig who owned the restaurant.....

.... Except, incidentally, for one

And that one person, was the queen

One day in the summer the queen and her young son arrived at the restaurant, completely unaware of who owned it

"It's my son's birthday and he was just dying to come here, he's such a picky eater you see," explained the tired queen as her son looked around and kicked his feet and hummed to himself

"Well I promise, if he tries it, he'll like it," Danika said as she took their order to be placed with Milo

"Milo come out here, you have to meet the queen!" Danika insisted excitedly

"I.. I can't.... I can't handle being rejected again," Milo said as he prepared the food

"Nonsense, if she rejects you, why.. I'll... I'll tell her what's for," Danika said with determination

"But Danika she's the QUEEN,"

"Queen she may be, but that does not make her more right than me," she argued

Milo, trusting Danika's words more than his own instinct, reluctantly agreed, and walked out with Danika towards the table

"And who is this?" asked the queen as the food was placed down

"Your highness, my name is Milo, I own this restaurant and I am the chef," he said softly

The queen stared at him in shock, unaware that her son- who was but a child, and far too young to understand why pigs cooking was uncommon- took the sandwich off of the plate and took a great big bite of it

For a long, tense moment, everything was completely silent

"Mommy," said the prince

"I LOVE IT!! This is the bestest food I've ever had!!"

The queen sighed with relief as he dug into the food, watching silently

"Try some Mommy! Try some try some!"

Ever eager to please, the queen put aside her own prejudice and reached for the other sandwich, pausing a moment, before taking a small bite

Her eyes lit up and her expression loosened

"Why.... this is the best food I've ever had," she observed

"Thank you your highness," Milo said with a bow

"Tell me little pig- Milo wasn't it?- Milo... tell me, what would it take to get you to become a chef at the palace? My son has such picky tastes... to have someone cook for him who's food he actually enjoys would be a dream,"

"I'm sorry your highness, but there is nothing you could do, for you see, my dream has always been to own a restaurant, nothing more and nothing less, this is what I want to do," he explained

"I understand," the queen said with a gentle smile

"I must at least tell the land- nay... the WORLD- of your brilliant food though, is that alright?" Milo smiled brightly, nodding excitedly

"Yes your highness, I would be honored!"

And so the queen told the entire land- and later the world- of Milo, the pig with wings who made the most delicious food

And although many were hesitant to believe her, soon others started to overcome their prejudices and try Milo's food as well

He was successful, so much so in fact, that he opened an entire CHAIN of restaurants

He of course shared his success with Danika, and finally, after a very long time of misery and heartache, Milo's dream of owning a restaurant, of making people happy with his food... had finally come true

Alexa Asagi Andres

The Prince Of Mordackee

Once upon a time

In a land called Mordackee

There lived a prince named Nicoli

Nicoli had just turned twenty-two, a rather old age for a prince to be unmarried in lands such as Mordackee

But that was not something Nicoli was worried about

He was more than content to focus on the political affairs of his country and to be single when doing so

His father, however, was not in agreement with this, and only three weeks after Nicoli's twenty-second birthday, he informed his son that he had arranged a marriage for him in another country, claiming that it would strengthen the weak alliance of the two lands

Nicoli was a flexible, peaceful type of person who cared about his country above all else, even above his own happiness, and so the prospect of an arranged marriage didn't bother him

As the prince was soon to learn, however, it was not as easy to submit to the marriage as he thought it would

Because on the way to meet the queen, who Nicoli only knew by the name of Suzume, something happened...

Half-way there, the prince found his carriage pulled off of the road with no apparent reasoning behind it

"Guards? Why have we stopped?" he asked, looking around anxiously

Upon receiving no answer, Nicoli became quite worried and got out of the carriage, feeling himself begin to sweat when he saw the coachmen and guards were gone

"Hello?" he shouted

No answer

"Hello!?" he called out again

This time instead of receiving dead silence, he turned around and found himself face to face with the lord of Akanti, a land at war with Mordackee

"Well well well... what's this we have? The young prince is traveling so far from home... I wonder why that would be..." the lord hummed, pointing his sword at the prince's throat

Nicoli swallowed, but when he attempted to discreetly remove his sword from its sheath on his hip he found the tip of the blade touching his skin

"Don't make another move Prince, or it will be the last move you ever make," the lord threatened

"That's funny, I was about to mention similar sentiments to you," came a voice from behind the lord

And when the older man turned his head, he found a blade pointed against his throat as well

"Unhand the prince," the stranger demanded

Cursing, the lord stepped aside, sheathing his blade

"You haven't heard the last of this Prince Nicoli, I will return for you!" he threatened, mounting his horse and riding away quickly

"Are you alright your Highness?" the stranger asked

"I am... but I'm afraid I haven't the foggiest idea of who you are,"

"My name is not important, Queen Suzume sent me to insure your safety, I see I'm well needed,"

Nicoli frowned at that, he was well versed in the sword and even in firearms, he just had been caught off guard...

"M'lady requests your presence immediately so please come along," the stranger- who was a little bit more than a stranger now- requested

And, having no objections, Prince Nicoli followed

The journey was shorter than he had realized and it didn't take long at all for them to arrive at the palace- and for that matter, the prince's new home

"It's beautiful..." Nicoli said breathlessly

The grounds were the greenest and purest of nature he had ever seen and they were layered with trees and flowers and other plants in bloom

Everything around him felt astoundingly natural and he didn't know how quite to adjust to that given he had been part of a fairly industrial kingdom with polluted air and mechanical skylines

He hadn't even been in this foreign country for a full minute yet but he already preferred it

"You must be the Prince of Mordackee, Nicoli wasn't it?" came a soft voice from in front of him

When Nicoli looked up, he saw a beautiful young woman standing before him with long, fine black hair and a sweet but wise expression on her face

"I am Suzume, ruling Queen of this land, I hear you're to be my bridegroom," she stated

"A-Ah.... yes Ma'am," Nicoli replied awkwardly

Suzume smiled brightly, barely able to stop herself from laughing

"You needn't call me 'Ma'am' Nicoli, you're going to be my husband soon, doesn't that make us equals?" she asked

"Well... yes... sorry... I'm just... not quite used to foreign royals," he admitted

Although Suzume suggested they were equals, there was something that made Nicoli feel like Suzume had a bit more of a powerhold than he did, perhaps it was because they were in Suzume's land now and he was surrounded by only her guards and servants and none of his own, but something felt almost... tipped... in Suzume's favor, and he wasn't sure why

"Don't worry about it, really, would you like to have some tea with me?" she proposed

Nicoli agreed and stepped forward, noticing the way Suzume helped him up the steps of her porch the way he usually helped ladies at home to climb steps

It was unnerving, and he had no idea why

The initial meeting aside, everything from there went off without a hitch

Nicoli found himself falling in love with Suzume easily and the concept of marrying her felt much more organic than the heaviness of an arranged marriage

Suzume, for her part, seemed to be falling for Nicoli too, and although they had to be sure their political views were kept at the forefront of their minds, it was nice to fall in love all the same

It may not be easy, but it would be better than a mere political contract, and Nicoli was more than willing to go the extra mile to insure their happiness

However, with all that being said, there still seemed to be a perpetual air of dominance that hung over Suzume that extended past that first day

For now, Nicoli had settled with the reasoning that they were in her homeland, and this was first and foremost her Royal Court, not his

At the end of the day, although he was addressed as a prince should be, the loyalties and respect of the people around him all lay first on Suzume, and only second on him

Not to mention the fact that Suzume was actually a queen, and Nicoli only a prince

That would change by technicality when they were wed but not in many other ways

Despite being roughly the same age it was clear that Suzume held more power and had more choices and responsibilities than Nicoli did

And even after becoming her king, Nicoli would only be a prince in his homeland of Mordackee

And even here in Suzume's home that wouldn't change

His mother had told him before departing that unlike Mordackee, Suzume's land- Aikahou- was a matriarchy, meaning that the queens held more power than the kings and although a queen could rule for any length of time without a king, the reverse was not true

If something were to happen to one of them Suzume would always be a queen, no questions asked

However, Nicoli's position was in constant peril, if anything were to happen to Suzume, his only claim to the throne of Aikahou would be if they had children, at which point he would only be an acting king, his child would be the true ruler of the land

And if they had no children, Nicoli would lose his position entirely and be sent straight back to Mordackee

It was a frustrating concept to understand when he had always lived knowing the opposite in his homeland, that a king's position would be secure no matter what happened to his queen

He decided that this must be the reasoning for the strange feeling he often had, and decided to ignore it and not think of it any further

That, he soon learned, would be a mistake

It was a mere three nights before the wedding that it happened

Things started well enough, of course

Nicoli found himself fast asleep that night, exhausted from meeting with some of the generals of Suzume's army and sparring with a few of her personal guards, all of who had been women, thus he not only felt exhausted from trying to keep up and from the physical strain, but also from trying to make sure he acted respectfully

He was sleeping well... until he heard an odd cracking sound at his door

After opening his eyes and lighting his lamp, Nicoli turned and screamed when he found the lord from a few weeks prior standing above him, the sword aimed once again at his head

"I've got you now Prince Nicoli," the lord chuckled lowly

Nicoli swallowed and stood up as soon as the lord gestured for him to do so

"You really don't want to do this," Nicoli said softly

"Oh I disagree, with you out of the picture I'll be next in line to rule over Mordackee, do try not to take it personally, its politics you see," he mused

Nicoli glanced at the entrance to the bedroom, heart skipping a beat when he saw Suzume slip inside without the lord even noticing her there

"Then I hope you don't take this personally," he replied

The lord stared at him in confusion, tilting his head

"Take what personally?"

Out of the corner of his eye, Nicoli watched in amazement as Suzume changed shapes, going from a young woman, to a fox

"This," he finally said, ducking at just the right time as Suzume- now in fox form- lunged at the lord

And within seconds the danger was gone

"I'm sorry that you had to find out this way," Suzume said once she was human again

"It's alright.. what exactly ARE you though?" Nicoli asked curiously

"I'm a Kitsune, and I promise, you haven't seen so much as a quarter of what I can do yet," Suzume promised with a small smirk

"Really?" he asked in shock

"Really.. I wanted to show you right away but.... I never found the right time," she sighed

Nicoli smiled, reaching his hands out and taking her hands in his

"It's alright, really... I.. I love you for WHO you are, not WHAT you are, even if you're a fox or if you were a wolf or a raven... it doesn't matter to me," he promised

"You promise?" Suzume asked with a smile as she turned towards him

It was then that Nicoli began to understand why he felt such an unusual air around Suzume

Yes, it was in part due to how much power she had versus him in this kingdom

But it was also due to the fact that she really- literally- had more power than he did, a very striking, otherworldly power

And a power that Nicoli was more than ok with

He squeezed her hand, leaning closer

"I promise," he smiled, sealing it with a kiss

The Princess Dresses

Once upon a time

In a land a little east of our own

There lived five princesses

These five princesses were sisters, you see, and were very, very close

So it was no surprise that when a grand ball came, they all wanted to wear matching dresses

When the tailor came to ask for what the princesses wanted, they described five dresses in the same style but each in a different color

The oldest princess wanted her dress to be a light, spring blue

The second oldest princess asked that her dress be a soft tangerine orange

The middle princess described her dress as being a gentle wisteria purple

The fourth princess imagined a dress that was a prim baby pink

And the youngest princess dreamed of a fresh, seafoam green

The princesses were all very excited to see their dresses next to each other, especially when matched with their mother's dark cranberry red dress and their aunt's vibrant sunshine yellow

The princesses spent over a week dreaming of, thinking of, wishing for their dresses

But when the day finally came, the princesses were... disappointed...

The dresses all looked so ... different... even though they had asked for them to be the same

The blue dress was exceedingly long and thin and didn't have nearly as big of a skirt as the others

The orange dress was shaped oddly with a wide bodice that shrunk and narrowed out around the hips before poofing out into the skirt

The purple dress was just right and looked like nearly all of the dresses that one would see this time of year in the ballroom, but it looked so... so plain...

The pink dress was tiny, barely a slip of a thing, short and thin with a wide skirt at the bottom

And the green dress was different still, a little longer than the pink one but not by much, however, much, much wider, and not just in the skirt either...

The princesses stared at the dresses in despair and then all turned to the tailor in charge

"These are not what we asked for," the oldest princess said with a deep-set frown

"We asked for all of the dresses to be identical," the second princess added

"These look nothing alike," the middle princess protested

"We'd like them to be changed," the fourth princess put in

The fifth princess stayed quiet

"You'd like me to change them so that they're all identical?" the tailor asked

"Yes," the four oldest princesses replied

"Very well, I'll return tomorrow," the tailor replied with an affirmative nod as he walked out

No one noticed the youngest princess gathering all of the dresses and taking them away

The next evening arrived, the night of the ball, and the princesses were all excited to see that their dresses, as requested, were now all identical in everything except for color

But when the princesses went to try on the dresses, they found that none of them fit

The oldest princess found that her dress was much too short and too wide in the bodice and kept falling down

The second princess found that her dress was too narrow and couldn't lace up the back

The middle princess found that although the proportions looked right, the dress was too long and too tight in the middle

The fourth princess found that the dress was far too big and swallowed her no matter how tight she tried to make it

And the fifth princess, who knew right away that the dress was too long and too tight, didn't bother to try on her's at all

"NOW what are we going to do?" the oldest princess sighed heavily

"The first dresses may have not been identical but they probably would have fit," the second princess added

"And yet we passed them up," the middle princess complained

"Now we have nothing," the fourth princess expressed

"Actually that isn't true at all," the youngest princess replied, smiling as she revealed the dresses that she had saved from the day before

"Our dresses! Why did you save them?" the oldest princess asked in shock as she rushed to her gown

"I had a feeling this would happen," she confessed

"But how could you have known?" the second princess asked in confusion

"We're all different, we may be sisters and we may be similar but each one of us is different, tall, short, thin, wide, something in between, that's just how nature is, everyone- every single person- is shaped differently, and adjustments have to be made for that, you can't expect to all fit in the exact same clothes, it just isn't how nature works," she explained

"Then... do we need to change so we CAN fit?" the middle princess asked quietly

"No, it isn't US who need to change, it's the CLOTHES, we're shaped the way we are for a reason, why change it just so we can fit in to someone else's standards?" the youngest princess said with a smile

"Even though we're all so different?" The fourth princess asked in amazement

"Yes, in fact, it's our differences that make us who we are, I think we should look just like this, and wear our different dresses," the youngest princess added

And so they did

And when they went to the ball they found that being different was actually a rather good thing

So many other princesses had tried too hard to fit into clothes that they were simply not meant to fit into and were now miserable because of it

By daring to be different and embrace that, the princesses not only stood out, but they were comfortable too, not just in the clothes, but in their own skins as well

Faery Tales, Mermaid Myths, And Other Fantastical Legends

The Queen Of Beasts

Once upon a time

In a land that was in a far off corner from our's There lived a faery named Anatalia

Anatalia was a beautiful woman, with long, fine black hair, soft golden eyes, and soft full lips

She was stunning on her own, but perhaps what drew most people in were her beautiful tattoos, she had several of them, a couple on her arms, a few on her legs, a smattering across her back, her front, her shoulders, they were spread out like little groups of freckles in designs of flowers or patterns or symbols, whatever meant something to her

But this story is not about her tattoos, or about her beauty, this story is about her life

A very specific, important part of her life

Specifically, those who live in her life...

Anatalia lived underground, not in a tunnel or a cave or a hole as most people assumed underground to be like

But in a type of palace, as expansive and vast as the ones above the surface

There was a long, crystalline stream from the lake above that ran through the underground and carried clean drinking water as well as the occasional fish their way

"They"... because Anatalia didn't live alone

She lived with many, many different souls

She lived with the outcasts of society, the "odd" ones, the "ugly" ones, the "bad" ones, the "rejects", the "monsters", the "beasts"

And the only time she left her palace beneath the ground was when she needed to bring in another "Beast" from the surface world

For that, however, she relied on her imp companion

The imp was rather small and a bit stubby with gigantic ears and paste-white skin and big eyes who often went on missions above the surface world for Anatalia

This was a bit difficult for the imp at times, for you see, the imp was blind

But he asked Anatalia not to dwell on the fact- as he did not- and she agreed

For being blind did not make him any less capable than any of the other many lives in Anatalia's palace

Some of them stayed for only a short time, needing to rest or recover from something traumatic or simply needing to find a better place to stay than where they currently were

Others stayed for longer, until some outside force like falling in love or finding a magnificent career or traveling came to them

And then there were those who never left at all

Anatalia loved them all equally

Today she was brought out of the palace by Thyme, her imp, to retrieve an injured werewolf

Anatalia had a questionable relationship in general with those such as werewolves and vampires, although often considered as monstrous as goblins or yetis, they were also almost always born beautiful, and were appreciated for their surface beauty even if people treated them like a plague

Well actually, these days they were more often treated like a taboo

Fallen for due to their beauty but shunned for what they were

There were many who felt that the beauty of these creatures didn't belong underground with Anatalia, even if they were treated nearly as badly as the others

But she disagreed, when someone was suffering- outcaste- no matter if they were beautiful like vampires or privileged like faeries, she wanted them

Because she wanted to heal them

Today was a bit of a different matter, she would soon learn, as the werewolf did not possess the same beauty that most people would think he did

Anatalia braced herself, taking several deep breaths and leaning against her closest dragon friend, Clove, and fluttered towards the entrance to her little underground world, removing the covering and wincing at the harshness of the sunlight

But she persevered and flew upwards anyway, even if it pained her

There was a reason that Anatalia lived underground, and surprisingly, it wasn't because of her "beasts"

They came later

Anatalia lived underground because she had severe anxiety about being in open spaces

Or cramped, small spaces too, actually

The brightness of day and the crowdedness of the surface world as well as all of the sights and sounds and overloaded senses that they brought easily forced her into a corner of panic, and so she decided, one day, to live underground, where she could be at peace with the darkness, the loneliness, the lack of cramped spaces and yet the lack of open spaces as well

It was like a giant closet really

That was until she met Thyme, who already lived there

The two became friends and when he went on one of his many food gathering missions he brought Clove back with him

That was the start of it, how their little family grew into something else

Into... whatever this was....

Anatalia had slowly been forced out of her comfort zone, as many were more willing to listen to her than anyone else- Thyme called it a gift- and she blended into the outside world with her beauty and grace

Beauty and grace on the outside, at least, because on the inside, stepping out of her safe haven created chaos and panic on the inside...

She could make these trips now, but it took a long time for it to happen, and she never said she liked them....

"Who are you?"

It was usually the first question she got when she approached someone and today was no different

"My name is Anatalia, I just wanted to meet you," she replied simply, sitting down on the porch steps of the apartment building

The werewolf tensed, staring at her for a long moment before he relaxed slightly

"You wanted to meet me?" he echoed in disbelief

"My friend told me you were in pain, I just wanted to help," she replied simply

The werewolf looked down, his hand instinctively going to touch the vicious burn on the side of his face

"Is that the only reason then?" he asked with a long sigh

"Well... yes and no, I'm not here because of your BURN, I'm here because of YOU, I want to help, I think I CAN help," she explained

"I'm not a broken object to be fixed Miss," he replied softly

"People can need fixing too, that isn't a bad thing, and no one said I had to FIX you, I said I wanted to HELP you, there's a difference,"

The werewolf stared at her for a moment before taking a breath

"And ... how exactly do you plan to 'help' me?"

Anatalia smiled softly, standing and offering him her hand

And with great hesitance, the werewolf took it

Many called her the Queen Of Beasts

And at first she wasn't fond of that title

At first she hated it

But now, years into doing what she was doing

She was coming to a realization

People would never end hatred

It was the way of the world

All she did was spare those who were suffering it from suffering it any longer

She was not a queen

And those around her were not beasts

But, as she sat back in her chair and Clove curled up next to her beneath the stream, and she waited for Thyme to come to her with news of how the new werewolf was adjusting, she started to consider that maybe the title was rather fitting after all

She was not queen of the people here

And they were not beasts

The REAL beasts were the ones on the surface who drove her people to her

Who burned the werewolf, who taunted the goblins and bullied the trolls, who feared the dragons and then mocked them behind their backs

Those were the REAL monsters, the real beasts

And so Anatalia considered, smiling as the werewolf came around the corner with a nervous smile on his face and talking to small griffin, that maybe she WAS deserving of that title

Maybe she WAS The Queen Of Beasts

The queen of taking innocent people AWAY from beasts, that is

The Quiet Banshee

Once upon a time

In a land you may yet know

There lived a banshee

She was a kind and beautiful banshee who, despite constantly calling out death, was relatively cheerful

When not signaling that death was abound for a member of her clan, she tried to stay away from the negativity and misfortune that many banshees sought after

However, there was a problem with this banshee

The problem was that she could not scream

She could not scream, and she was far too shy to sing

This was a problem because of all the banshees in the land, she was by far the most quiet

And banshees are notorious for being loud

She may not have been able to scream or sing, but she did wail

This banshee wailed the longest and mourned the hardest, for her soul was so sensitive, that according to legend, merely sweeping a lock of her hair would cause her heart such a shock that she would poof away in shock and fright

But it did not matter how long the banshee wailed

Or how hard she mourned

Because the other banshees only cared for how loud she could scream or how beautifully she could sing

No one seemed to care that the banshee was a sensitive and peace-filled being who prayed for the well-being of her guarded human family

Nor that she wandered the grounds of their homes day and night picking flowers and leaving small gifts of coins and candies for the children

All they cared about was her screaming and her songs

And so, as she so often did, the banshee sat by the lake off the hill of her guarded family's home and began to weep

But she didn't hear the sound of tiny footsteps crossing towards her

"Excuse me? Miss Ghost?" she heard, jumping suddenly and trying to wipe away her tears as the voice startled her

When she turned around, standing there, was a little girl, no more than the age of six, with long wavy red hair and a face full of freckles

Children were not nearly as frightening as adults, and so she paused, not fleeing just yet

"Oh, you're our banshee aren't you? Why are you crying? Is someone I know about to die?" she asked worriedly as she walked closer to the spirit

"Oh.. no, no dear child nothing like that I'm crying for myself this time, not for your family," she smiled gently as she slowly sat back down

The child neared, sitting on the rock next to her

"Oh... is someone YOU know about to die?"

"Well... no..."

"Then why are you crying?"

There was a generous pause as the banshee took some time to consider that

"Because ... I'm different from other banshees, I cannot scream, I do not sing... there's something wrong with me you see, I'm not normal," she explained softly

"Oh... well I know how that feels then," she mused with a small shrug

"You do?" the banshee asked in surprise

"Uh-huh, there's something wrong with me too," she explained, pointing at her eyes

And it was only then that the banshee saw it, the girl had one green eye.... and one blue

"Why my sweet child, there's not a thing wrong with you! Look at you, you're beautiful,"

"I'm not, my eyes are different colors, it's not normal... I'M not normal,"

"And what's so good about being normal?" the banshee scoffed

"Well you seem to value it,"

There was a pause before she spoke again

"That's different, your eyes are beautiful my dear, you see eyes are the windows to the very soul, and your soul must be so big and vibrant and beautiful, that it couldn't decide between green or blue, so it decided that it must have both, no other way could it be contained in such a tiny little thing as yourself," she explained

"But why are my eyes a good different thing, when your different thing is bad?" she asked in confusion

The banshee thought on that for a long moment, biting her lip

"Because... because I'm not what a banshee should be,"

"And I'm not what a person should be either, I like having you as a banshee Miss, you're not so loud and boisterous like the others, and you aren't so depressing and sad all the time... and you visit a lot more too,"

The banshee gave the girl a small smile, thanking her for her understanding

"Of course! I'm Alannah, what's your name?" she smiled happily

"Ashling," the banshee replied softly

"What a pretty name!" Alannah smiled more

"Thank you, it's been a long time since anyone has asked for it," Ashling smiled gently as she twirled a few strands of her long, pale blonde hair

"That's too bad... would you like to play a game with me Ashling? We could be friends," she offered brightly

And so Ashling did something again that banshees frowned upon, she made friends with a living, human girl

Ashling and Alannah ended up becoming very good friends

They spoke often and spent an increasing amount of time together

For a few weeks, things seemed to be improving in Ashling's life

Until one night she woke, gasping as the sense of death loomed over her

One of Alannah's distant relatives in a far off land was dying, and as a banshee, it was Ashling's job to alert the family

Rising from her bed, she spirited herself away to the home of the relative, tears already pouring from her face as she crumpled down on the hill outside of the cottage and began to weep

She took the bloody clothes from the clothing line and summoned a bucket and washboard, sobbing harder as she began to wash the blood stains from the clothes

It wasn't something that all banshees did these days, washing the bloody clothes of the dying that is, but it was something that Ashling still enjoyed, it gave her something to do as she grieved

And she grieved a lot

Her tears fell down her face and into the wash bucket, keeping an endless supply of clean water coming in as she scrubbed the red stains out of the clothes

And when she felt the man take his last breath, she dropped the clothes and cried harder, cupping her hands over her eyes and wailing terribly

But her distress was paused, for a moment later a sharp, terrible scream interrupted her mourning and she looked up as an older- though you could hardly tell it-banshee flew in above

"What are you doing here?" Ashling asked softly as she wiped her eyes

"I am the banshee of the McNeal family, and who are you?"

"I am the banshee of the O'Donnovan family," she said softly

"I see, one of mine married one of yours and now we're joined," she mused

"Yes it appears so," Ashling replied quietly, sniffling and picking up the clothes again

"Tell me, why weren't you screaming?" the older banshee asked curiously

"I cannot scream, I'm not sure why, I just... can't.... I wail though, I sob and grieve and mourn as deeply as my spirit can withhold,"

"You cannot scream, and yet you call yourself a banshee, how is the family supposed to hear of this death? Your sobbing does nothing," the older banshee huffed

"I... I know.... but I just... I just can't..." she said quietly

"Well singing then, can't you at least sing a lament for him?"

"I cannot sing," she said quietly, curling into herself defensively as the older banshee circled around her

"You cannot scream, you cannot sing, I doubt you even wail properly... what good are you as a banshee if you can't even use your lungs the way they were meant to be used? You are neither alive nor dead, neither a body nor a ghost, you're a spirit of the in between, the only place you belong- and ever can or will belong- is with the other banshees, yet you can't even act like a REAL banshee in the first place, so what are good you at all?"

Ashling looked down, a single tear slipping down her cheek as she tried to muffle her sobs once more, though this time, they were not sobs of mourning

"I suppose I am no good at all," she submitted, hanging her head and slumping her shoulders

And for the first time since meeting Alannah, she was reminded of her worthlessness

Ashling did not visit Alannah for several days

And she didn't plan to visit her again, for she did not wish to continue to inflict her worthlessness on the girl any more than she already had

But a few days after the funeral was held, Ashling felt herself pulled to another side of the land

The side, as it were, that Alannah was in...

And when she arrived there she felt the overwhelming urge to wail... yet she did not

She refused to wail for the only one who had ever shown her kindness, because it meant that she would soon be dead, and Ashling couldn't accept that

She spent two days on the grounds, forcing herself not to cry

Over the two days she heard Alannah's mother mention that it had been a horseback riding accident that caused the bright girl such pain

Lightening had scared the horse she was riding and the horse reared back, knocking Alannah off of her and kicking her in the head on accident

It was tragic, but Ashling still refused to weep

Ashling refused to weep, because she refused to lose the only friend she had ever had

And much to the surprise of Ashling- as well as many others in the surrounding area- the banshee was invited upstairs to Alannah's bedside, something that never happened to banshees

For banshees were guardians

Heralds

Workers

They weren't friends of the family

Yet... Ashling seemed to be...

She sat by Alannah's bedside and took her hand

And though she tried and tried, she couldn't stop herself from mourning

She stayed as silent as possible, but the tears were beginning to fall from her eyes and there was nothing she could do to stop them

As she bit her lip, trying her very hardest not to begin her wailing, something absolutely magical happened

Just as her first tear hit Alannah's hand, the little girl fluttered her eyes open, first the green one, then the blue, and stared up at Ashling's face

Immediately a smile overtook her as if she had been holding it in for days

"Ashling! Ashling you're back! Oh I was so worried I'd lost you forever!" she smiled, wrapping her arms tightly around her shoulders and squeezing gently

"You were afraid you'd lost me? My dear you almost made me weep for you!"

"I know... but it was that ... your tear on my skin that brought me back! I could feel myself slipping away, but feeling that... it reminded me where I belong and so I came back," she smiled

Ashling stared at her, completely and utterly stunned by this

"I'm sure it would have worked just as well if not better if I had screamed, surely you could hear me," she reasoned

"I could hear vaguely yes, but no matter what I heard, none was good enough to wake me from my stupor, when I felt your tear on my hand.. it reminded me that you were crying, and I never wanted to see you cry again," she explained simply

"Ashling please... please promise me that you'll always be my friend?"

Ashling smiled gently and willed herself not to cry again

"Of course my dear child, of course," she promised

Banshees were known for detecting death, for mourning it, but not for preventing it

The concept was new to them all

It was different, it was strange, just as so many things were for Ashling

And though she was still criticized by some for not being a "proper banshee", she came to realize over spending more and more time with Alannah that none of that mattered

SHE mattered

Different or not

"Broken" or not

Ashling mattered

She mattered to someone else, but over time, Alannah taught her how to matter to herself

And that was more than good enough for her

Faery Tales, Mermaid Myths, And Other Fantastical Legends

The Ram And The Crab

Once upon a time

In a land worlds away from our own

Before our own was even created in fact

There lived the twelve signs of the Zodiac

Aries, Cancer, Capricorn, Sagittarius, Leo, Virgo, Pisces, Aquarius, Gemini, Scorpio, Taurus, and Libra

These twelve signs held very large and heavy spirits and decided that, before they departed a blessing of their souls unto the newly forming creatures of earth, they should make sure that they were all relatively compatible first

So, all of the twelve signs of the zodiac split off into twenty-four different souls, twelve male and twelve female, this, however, is another story for another time

The focus here is on two of those souls in particular

A soul of Aries, and a soul of Cancer

Though the other signs had all predicted with as much certainty as possible that the relationship was toxic, that it would fail before it began, that Aries and Cancer were just TOO different, these two souls decided to try anyway

After all, if not to try and get along, then what was the experiment for in the first place?

And so the soul of Aries- Arabella- and the soul of Cancer- Carista- decided to embark on this journey together

And to their surprise, it was not nearly so trying as the others tried to say it was

Alexa Asagi Andres

Arabella and Carista were soulmates

It wasn't specifically romantic, for one's soulmate can be truly anyone, their true love yes, but also their friend, their sister, their partner, their mother, whoever it is that they feel has a twin soul to match their own

And for Arabella, Carista was her's

And for Carista, Arabella was her's

Even the deepest of loves the rest of the Signs' souls had for each other could not rival the purity and the depth of Arabella and Carista's

And some even looked onto them with jealousy

But they cared not

Their souls were so deeply and evenly matched that there was talk around the circles that they were not twin souls at all- but the same soul, somehow split into two halves and forced apart only to join together again

Again, it mattered not

Arabella and Carista were part of each other in a way that defied words

They were inseparable in a way that made them physically ache to be apart

They were truly soulmates

But even soulmates do not always get along

Even soulmates fight

And Arabella and Carista were no exception

True, they got along exceptionally well

But when they did fight, it shattered the very ground they stood on

It destroyed the skies and concaved the walls

It was heard throughout all the land and the other signs fearfully ran for shelter from the fall out

Because when two souls who are so very much alike and so deeply connected to each other fight, there is truly nothing left to hold them back

When two souls who so deeply orbit each other are at odds, there is absolutely nothing left to anchor them from their negative emotions

And so, although they were usually more in love than love could explain

When a quarral arrived, it created thunder and lightening

It lit the skies and broke the earth

It was the heaviest of burdens and it left the lands in ruins

For a love that loved too much to feel a fracture was the greatest of injustices, and the very ground they stood on knew that

And to make matters worse, their fighting began to escalate as time went on

Arabella, first and foremost, was born as a part of Aries

Aries, who channels war and violence and anger

Aries, who has the sharpest tongue and the hardest punches thrown

Aries, who savors the blood of a battle just long enough before picking up her blade and starting another one

Aries, who to some, is the God of War

Carista, first and foremost, was born as a part of Cancer

Cancer, who happily makes the home and hearth and nurtures every single soul like a mother

Cancer, who channels love and adoration and kindness

Cancer, who loves with every ounce, every cell of their being, until they can love no more

Cancer, who when hurt too deeply too much, will hold the worst grudge that any world has seen and will never, ever let it go

It was predicted long before Arabella and Carista found each other that any Aries and Cancer pairs would fall into a tragic hatred for each other

For, as one can see, it simply is not in their nature to get along

Where Aries wishes to move on to the battlefield and fight day in and out, Cancer begs to pull them in, nurture them and keep them safe, and who can no longer find it in their heart to love Aries anymore after one too many indiscretions

Arabella and Carista were doomed from the start

From the moment they met, they were destined to fall apart

But Arabella inherited a part of Aries that stayed strong to all of Aries' souls, but that stayed the strongest in her's

Arabella inherited stubbornness and passion

Arabella inherited the gnawing need to keep going until she got what she wanted and never give up a moment sooner

Arabella inherited the desire to win her wars

And for Arabella, Carista was the breath of fresh air at the end of each one

For Arabella, Carista was the princess she was privileged to rescue after defeating each and every dragon

For Arabella, Carista made it worth it to fight through the wars

But this was where the fighting came in

Carista, who inherited a part of Cancer that stayed strong to all of Cancer's souls, but that stayed strongest in her's

Carista inherited nurturing and caring

Carista inherited the bleeding and gasping need to mother and nurture, to keep safe and protect

Carista inherited the desire to stop any and all wars that threatened to step over her threshold before they even began

And for Carista, Arabella was the softness of sheets after a long and hard day

For Carista, Arabella was the knight in shining armor who always needed more tending to than they were willing to admit

For Carista, Arabella made it worth it to continue nurturing and caring for souls who didn't always even want to be cared for

And this is where the fighting came in

For Carista held her tongue too long

Carista, who wanted Arabella's happiness more than her own, bit her lip shut every time she wanted to ask Arabella to stay

Every time a war began and she saw Arabella reach for her sword

Every time a fight broke out and Arabella was through the door before she could even say goodbye

Carista held her breath every time

And she waited by the door

But the anger and resentment of keeping her wishes to herself began to build

The frustration she felt over every waking moment that Arabella was away, not sure if she was alive or dead, began to claw at her very flesh

The deep, earth shattering fear and loneliness that she may never see Arabella again threatened to tear her very mind apart

But Carista was too kind for her own good and stayed quiet, for she could not bear the thought of ever seeing Arabella unhappy

The anger, however, the deep and painful anxiety, all began to grow and grow and blacken out the sweet, darling pink of Carista's love for Arabella

And one morning

Any morning

Just like all the other mornings that came before it

Arabella reached for her armor

And Carista snapped

Carista did what she had been trying so hard for so long not to do

She asked Arabella to stay

And Arabella, in not knowing the pain Carista felt, and not being capable of holding back her own thoughtlessness

Told her no

And Arabella gave her a goodbye and left

Carista's heart, which was such a very big, very vulnerable heart, shattered into pieces

Carista crumpled to the ground and sobbed for three days and three nights in grief

For the love that she had believed Arabella to hold for her was not as strong as her own

The love that she had valued and treasured and nurtured for so long was not returned as strongly as she always believed it to be

Arabella had refused to stay with her- just one morning, just ONE morning out of all of the mornings she had asked, and Arabella refused her

Carista misunderstood Arabella

She believed that her refusal was due to a lack of love

She believed that her refusal was due to a selfish desire

She believed that her refusal was due to Arabella understanding why she asked

Because she believed that Arabella had understood her pain every time she left for war and left Carista alone

Arabella did not

Because Arabella felt her own pain

Arabella's pain was being away from the battle

Her pain was the searing in her veins to pick up her blade

The rush of adrenaline that stayed caught under her skin because she was unable to get it out

The way her fingers curled at night and her breath released in ragged, frustrated huffs

The always coming, never going away for long, anger that was fueled by her very nature

She needed to release it all

War was her opportunity, her ONLY opportunity, to undo the nerves that tied themselves into her muscles

It was her release, much like a breath of air or a note on a song

It was to allow the building adrenaline and twitching muscles an escape

And although being away from Carista hurt, she knew she would return

Arabella was the Goddess of war, surpassing all of her brothers and sisters by far

Arabella would always return to Carista

What frightened her enough to bare the pain of being away from her soulmate

Was the fear that the building aggression in her bones may one day break and harm Carista

Her flesh was made of fire and her bones burned with anger

It was her natural way, it was how she was born

Her head was a vengeful spirit that shouted terrible things to her

And when she needed it most it ghosted away completely and left her to her body's ache for battle

Arabella hated her body, for it was sin itself, anger, violence, resentment, and constantly attacking her

Her soul could find peace at home with Carista, her soul was content with being in a world of peace and love

It was her mind and body that were not

Her body ached for fighting and her mind screamed for chaos

And she had no way to shut them out

She had nothing she could drown her thoughts in or cool her skin with

And so she, who was the most stubborn of all, gave up trying to fight her own personal war

She would gladly fight a thousand wars and face death a thousand times than to ever harm Carista or make her unhappy

Arabella had thought her love knew that

But Carista did not

It was miscommunication, as so many fights begin, that caused things to turn out so terribly

When Arabella arrived home that evening, after a relatively short battle, she found that Carista was not waiting for her as she usually was

She searched the house and looked through the woods

She went everywhere she thought she could go

And when she found that Carista was nowhere near

Arabella assumed the worst

Arabella assumed that for Carista to disappear so suddenly there must be foul play afoot

And never had she felt rage burn through her body the way she felt it when that realization hit her

And that rage, that burned her bones and boiled her blood and ignited her flesh, it made the voices in her head stronger

It powered her to follow through on the chaos and destruction that her mind always drifted to

It shut down the love and gentleness that Carista had always caused her to maintain as the forefront

And now she was nothing but a spirit of violence

She searched for Carista for three days and found nothing

She searched every part of the surrounding kingdoms for three days and found nothing

It was on the morning of the fourth day that Carista was finally found

And when she was, Arabella changed again

When Carista was found it was as if she was able to breathe again

The anger and violence that had coated her body for three days fell apart

The voices that had driven her forward were quieted

The very ground she stood on shook due to the weight that Arabella dropped in that moment

And the only thing that she could feel was gratitude

Was relief

Was love

But when she approached Carista, and saw the angry look in her eyes, all she could feel was pain

Pain more immense and immeasurable than any buildup of war tensions had ever felt before

The anger built behind Carista's eyes- anger that she had never once seen there before- was like a bullet to the heart

And when Arabella reached for her, and Carista shied away instead of reaching back

Arabella could swear that that, that very sensation, was exactly what death felt like

It was all the absence of pain replaced with the worst, most darkening numbing to consume every single inch and cell of her

"Carista... why?" she asked

Carista turned to her, angry, but behind that also hurt

"Because you did not love me enough to stay,"

This, in this moment, was when the first battle began between the two of them

Arabella insisted that she didn't know how Carista felt

Arabella persisted that the ache in her bones when she became restless was enough to drive anyone mad

Arabella shouted that the screaming in her head for horrible things that she fought to ignore time and time again sometimes escaped past her control

And Carista, for all of her quiet joy and comfort, actually shouted back

Carista shouted that Arabella must have known how she felt for she couldn't have made it more obvious every time Arabella left and returned

Carista persisted that the crushing pain in her heart when Arabella left was enough to choke the life out of anyone

Carista insisted that the nagging anxiety and grief in her head was too much for anyone to have to bare regardless of the circumstances

Each blamed each other for their own pain

And each had fault in this

Arabella should have tried harder to understand Carista and to resist a little harder

And Carista should never have assumed anything about Arabella and been as blatant as possible before she ever asked her to stay

Neither of them, however, should have fought about it

By nightfall they had both nearly lost their voices and their hands still twitched and shook from the emotion flooding through them both

Carista stayed inside the palace that she had been staying at, belonging to a Taurus friend of her's

And Arabella stayed on the steps

Before Carista went to bed that evening, she heard something odd coming from the steps of the palace

Reluctant to show any care for Arabella at the moment, but worried none the less, she stepped just an inch outside to see what had made the sound

And without a doubt, she found that it was Arabella

The Aries sister who was the most stubborn, hard-headed, and anger-driven of all of the Aries brothers and sisters

Sat crumpled on the ground with her long, brilliant red hair covering her face

But the sound was unmistakable

Alexa Asagi Andres

This sister of Aries was crying

She was sobbing

In the first time in her life

Arabella was in so much pain that she was sobbing

The thought hurt Carista even more than anything else she had ever hurt over

And with more caution than reluctance, she approached Arabella and set a hand on her shoulder

The sister of Aries turned with tear-soaked brown eyes and reached out her hand again

And Carista, for all the many times she had cried, could suddenly muster only a single tear, that slipped from her blue-green eyes down her cheek and onto Arabella's hand

But before she could withdraw it

The sister of Cancer took her hand in her own and held onto it

The wind blew through her short blonde hair and gave her skin a chill

But just like always, Arabella was there wrapping her shawl around Carista's shoulders before the goosebumps had a chance to rise on her skin

For of all the violence and anger that Arabella held against the world

Of all the tension in her fingers and voice in her head pulling her down the path of war

There was a force stronger than all of those things

And that force was five feet tall and softer than a newborn rabbit

That force was Carista

Carista, who always brought out the best in Arabella, who always made

Arabella strive to be better, who always pushed Arabella's violent nature away and brought her kindness to the surface

Carista, who Arabella would gladly lay her life down for over and over again

It was at this moment that the sister of Aries and the sister of Cancer made a pact

Never again would Carista disappear from Arabella without a word

And never again would Arabella depart from Carista when Carista truly asked her to stay

It wasn't easy

And sometimes the pact was almost broken, from one side or both

Sometimes the tension built up too much in Arabella's bones and sometimes the anxiety screamed too much in Carista's head

Sometimes they had to compromise

And sometimes those compromises shook the earth with thunder and tossed down barbs of lightening

Sometimes it wasn't even the mornings that caused the fighting, but the aftermath

Sometimes Carista waited too long or Arabella waited too late

Sometimes Arabella's cuts and bruises were closer to scars and shattered bones

Sometimes Arabella was too tired to fight her urges any longer and lashed out without meaning too

Sometimes Carista's patience melted away after too long of staying quiet and she picked up an instrument of war herself

Sometimes things just happened

Like any relationship it was not problem free

And although their fights shook the very earth

Although everyone in every other sign ran for hiding when the sister of Aries and the sister of Cancer were at odds

This senselessness was only temporary

It was a passing cloud on the beautiful sunshine that was the love that Arabella and Carista had for each other

And like all clouds it passed soon enough

Like all short things it dissolved soon enough

And Arabella and Carista, though always remembering and wearing the verbal scars that the other had given them, come back to each other

Just as in love and adoring as before

For one cannot simply stop loving their soulmate, no matter what their nature tells them

Faery Tales, Mermaid Myths, And Other Fantastical Legends

The Shark Spirit

Once upon a time

Deep under the sea

There lived a shark named Mano

Mano was nothing special, just an average fish

Until one day, something terrible happened

The day began normally, the fish and water all seemed at peace, until late in the afternoon when the sun was highest in the sky reflecting in the water

And the water became red

Mano was used to blood in the water, he was a shark after all

Many times the red water was even due to his own hunting

But something about this time seemed vastly different

Something seemed.... wrong....

The red color wasn't fading or drifting as it usually was

In fact it only seemed to be getting worse

And for the first time since becoming an adult, Mano started to feel afraid

He swam closer to the source of the red and paused in shock upon the sight he was confronted with

Nets

Nets from the surface world

And although Mano was used to seeing the nets- collecting fish and the like- he wasn't used to seeing his own brethren being the ones to suffer the fate of being hauled away from the water and onto the human ships

He couldn't bear to stay and watch and so, with fear increasing in his veins, he hurried and swam away, too afraid to try to help them

As the day went on Mano found his mind haunted by the sight

And worse, he found himself growing increasingly angry

Angry at the nets

Angry at the fishermen who were abducting his own from their homes

And angry.... at himself, for not trying to help them, even though he felt certain that he could have done nothing, he always could have tried

As the anger filled his cartilage he found himself swimming towards a certain place, instead of just aimlessly around the sea like he usually did

Where he was swimming to was the home of the local Mer-Queen

The waters of the planet Earth were expansive and every region had their own hierarchy of merfolk, for Mano's area, they were led by a queen named Kanani

Kanani was beautiful with thick black hair, dark brown skin, and a midnight blue tail

Pearls and jewels decorated her body and a spear rested faithfully at her side, for Kanani was somewhat of a legend even among non-native merfolk

Kanani had once saved twelve pods of dolphins in a single day by bringing stormy weather down upon the humans who tried to poach them in her sea

And Mano was desperate now for her help

He swam closer and closer to the palace and was stopped by Kanani's husband and personal guard just outside of her throne "room"

"Please let me through, I need to speak with the queen! I need help, please!" Mano shouted desperately

"Let him in Kai, let me hear what he has to say," Kanani said

Kai, a massive creature with hair as long and dark as Kanani's own, tattoos of magic rippling across his dark skin, and more strength in the tip of his dark green tail than Mano had in his entire body, was a force to be reckoned with, but moved passively like a wave upon Kanani's orders

Mano wasn't sure which force was stronger, Kanani's power, or Kai's devotion to her, but merely being in their space made him feel like his nerves were being torn apart

"Your Highness.... today I witnessed the worst thing I've ever seen, sharks being slaughtered, and for no reason except for the hatred humans have for us, we're not safe in our own home anymore because the humans have decided they have a right to be here, and whenever they see us- no matter how at peace we are- they see us as a threat, they swim further and further into our territory, take more and more of our food each year, chatter about us as if we ascended from the Netherworld itself, they fish us, poach us, massacre us, and for what? Trophies on a wall? Ingredients in a soup? A photograph to show around pridefully as some sort of ... some symbol of dominance over the sea? We have hurt less humans than the electric lights in the sky, but they never run at the sky with the spears and nets, they take our home and blame us for swimming too close, they take our food and blame us for being hungry, they pollute our waters and blame us for breathing, please, Queen Kanani, grant me the power to protect my own," Mano begged

Kanani rose from her throne, stabbing her spear in the sand and swimming closer to him, cupping her hands beneath his jaw

"My dear shark, your people have suffered more than any other in the ocean, the most powerful and awe-inspiring creature in the sea and you've been reduced to begging for your life because of human ignorance and selfishness, my heart weeps for you, the ocean weeps for you, even the sky weeps for you,"

Mano glanced up and could faintly tell that the sky water was beating down on the surface of the sea, no doubt mourning for Kanani's breaking heart

"I will grant you the power you need to protect your own from the humans, but I warn you, always act with kindness, though these creatures have done you nothing but wrong, it will cause only war and further destruction for us all if you lash out with your teeth, move your cause with strength and kindness, dear Mano, and you will protect all you wish to protect,"

And with that, Mano felt himself fill with a strange type of warmth

A bright glow enveloped around him, and when he swam to look at the mirror in Kanani's room, he found that he was no longer a Reef Shark

He had transformed into a Great White Shark, and a truly massive one at that, now dwarfing Kanani and even making Kai seem small

"You will have three forms that you can become Mano, this form, a mershark, and a human, when you wish to change shape, merely think of what you'd like to become, and so it shall be," Kanani added

"Thank you," Mano said sincerely

And with that he left from the kingdom of the merfolk and swam back into the open waters

He was surprised to find that maintaining his massive form didn't require any more food than he had needed in his smaller form, but wasn't surprised that whenever he neared, every other creature swam away

He didn't blame them

If he had seen a shark of this size when he was a mere Reef Shark, he would have fled too

But he didn't mind the loneliness, it kept him focused

For weeks Mano patrolled the seas and easily snapped any nets that he found to be disturbing his fellow sharks or thought were taking too many fish

He occasionally swam close enough to the surface to allow his large grey fin to breach the waters in order to send a message to the humans

A message that told them of his presence

And for a long time, the small acts of defense seemed to work

He didn't see anyone try to take away his people or destroy his home for a very long time indeed

But as all things did, the peace eventually ended

And on a chilly autumn day, the humans invaded his home again

Once more Mano found himself swimming upon the scene of his brethren being hauled away in nets and once more he swam quickly and snapped the nets in his jaws to release them

But that wasn't all

Why it seemed that for every net he broke, another one came down right after it!

Nets weren't even the biggest worry, the humans were using spears and hooks and other weapons to take his people from him

And Mano had finally had enough

He envisioned himself as a mershark and swam to the surface, anger seething in his newly formed bones as he stared at the boat ahead and gripped onto one of the nets, pulling himself up and envisioning himself as a human as he climbed aboard

As expected the humans screamed and shouted and caused a ruckus but Mano didn't care, he walked straight towards them as the sky darkened above him

"You are destroying the sea," he bellowed, his voice shaking the boat as his feet took each and every step with deliberation

"You are destroying MY HOME, you take our home, you take our food, you take our people, and still you DARE to call sharks the monsters, still you shout and scream whenever one of us is near despite being in OUR waters, still you believe yourselves to be righteous in slaying us and wearing us like trophies, and still you delight in spreading the lies and the fear of us with your stories and robotic creations, you think you have some sort of RIGHT? You think that you newly formed creatures can take away what has belonged to my kind for MILLIONS of years? What arrogance! What ignorance! What selfishness!" Mano shouted

With every word the sea became angrier, with every breath the sky turned darker, and with every step the boat shook harder

The humans found themselves huddled in the corner as thunder boomed and lightening flashed around them and the sky and the sea both sloshed water at them

Mano stopped before them, snarling with his still pointed teeth bared and ready to tear through the monsters that had destroyed his home

"You humans will destroy the waters until there is no water left for you to destroy, and knowing you, you will find a way to blame us for it, my ancestors were a great and mighty people, we have evolved over millions and millions of years yet barely changed at all, the form you use to frighten each other in your movies and scary tales is the very form I take, and it is the form that was taken by my grand ancestor the Megalodon in his hay day, I have inherited his strength and power, and what have you inherited from your people besides a sense of ownership to this planet, violence, and greed? You think we are a simple folk, so easy to figure out just by splashing us with labels, 'man-eaters', 'monsters', pressing names to our shapes as if that's really going to help you understand anything, there are more of us in all shapes and sizes out there than your human minds can even fathom, brethren who have survived things that would make you humans disappear in the blink of an eye, how many lives of my people have you taken in comparison to your own? For every one human my kind kills, one MILLION of our own is taken by you in revenge, tell me, how is that number equal!?

How is that number even!? We are not a sport, we are not a fashion, we are not a trophy, a food, or a scary story, we are living, breathing, descendants of the great divine, just like you are, you want revenge? You want equal? I should kill each and every one of you, invade your land and kill each and every person on it, then, maybe, we'll be equal," he said, snapping his teeth at them as the humans screamed and cowered in fear

Mano took a breath, and then a step back

"But I won't, for it is not in my nature, and it would not be right, although YOU have hurt us, your children have not, I will not take away their futures, or the guardians who protect those futures, because if I did, I would become the monster you say I am, I would become like you, and I do not wish that, I wish for your children to grow up to be smarter, and kinder, and gentler than you did, I wish for them to see us and our home as living creatures, not as monsters or whatever it is you'd like to call us, I wish that they will protect us, and we will protect them as well, and that is why I am letting you live, NEVER forget how easily I could take your life away, as you have taken the lives of so many of my own people, and always remember that the reason I left in peace, is so that you can tell THIS story to your children, not one of terror, not one of predators, not one of fear, but one of kindness, one of mercy, one of sadness, for you have done nothing but cause me sadness, YOU are responsible for the blood in the water, not us, tell these stories to your children, so that they can end the mistakes that began with the first of your kind,"

And with that, Mano left

He freed the sharks that had been in the last net and watched with held breath until the ship moved away and not another thing was heard from the humans

And for many years, Mano repeated this process

He roamed every ocean and sea and even some rivers and lakes, and whenever he saw humans hunt his kind, he told the story of the fishermen from that day and repeated what he had said to them

It took a very long time for Mano's message to spread through every part of every land

But eventually it did

Time changed as it moved, and with it, so too did the opinions of the humans and what they thought of sharks

And though Mano often grew tired of his quest and wished to rest, he continued to trek on until the days of violence against sharks were a thing of the past

Until the days when humans swam in the waters and did so with respect for the ones who already lived there

Until the days when the sharks inhabiting human aquariums were not viewed with fear or as some sort of challenge, but with respect and honor and who were healed from their wounds instead and rested from their hard journeys

Until the days when Mano could shift into his human form and wander the human lands but find no trace of the death of his people

Mano continued his mission until those days came

And when they finally did, something very surprising happened, something that even Mano did not expect

When the days came of respect and kindness from the humans, so too did the days that Mano's story spread even further and to even more ears than the horror stories told by old fishermen and Hollywood screenwriters

Mano became a legend in his own right, and the people spoke- not with fear, but with admiration and gratitude- of the massive shark who could become a human

The enormous shark who swam through the seas

The shark named Mano

Faery Tales, Mermaid Myths, And Other Fantastical Legends

The Skeptical Vampire

Once upon a time

In our very own land

There lived a vampire who didn't believe he really existed

Or, perhaps better put, he didn't believe in vampires

For this vampire you see, first and foremost, was a scientist

And science does not support the idea of vampires

It didn't seem to matter to him that he burned when he walked in the sun or that he had fangs and could only survive by drinking blood

He would still dispute- for the entire ten years that he had gone without aging so much as a hair- that he was not a vampire

Because vampires, according to science, did not exist

"How can you say that vampires don't exist?" asked the faery that sat next to him one day at the park

"Because scientifically they're IMPOSSIBLE, one cannot simply die and come back to life, there is no such thing as immortality, and drinking blood is every kind of bad idea, not to mention insufficient nourishment," he replied as he adjusted his glasses

The faery stared at him, clearly in disbelief, and pointed to the cup he was drinking out of

"You're drinking blood RIGHT NOW,"

"That proves nothing,"

She shook her head slowly and frowned

"Science also claims that faeries can't exist, yet here I am," she pointed out

"You aren't a faery, for whatever reason you BELIEVE you are a faery, but you really aren't,"

"I have WINGS," she shouted, placing his hand on her wings as proof

"That is some very clever makeup but they aren't real,"

The faery was quite honestly enraged by the bull-headedness of the vampire- who claimed he wasn't a vampire- and flew away in frustration

"I am not a vampire, vampires are not real," the vampire said stiffly

"But you just got burned by walking in the sun..." pointed out the mermaid who swam near the docks

"No no, you see I've always tanned so easily that even the smallest exposure can burn me," he explained

"Well why can't there be vampires? There are mermaids, after all, I'm a mermaid," the mermaid pointed out

"You aren't a REAL mermaid though, you're wearing a very nice costume, but it isn't real,"

The mermaid frowned, her tail flicking across the water

"I AM a real mermaid, I can breathe under water," she insisted

"Nonsense, you just can hold your breath for much longer than most people, I'm sure you practiced for many years to develop that talent,"

The mermaid huffed in anger and swam away, too infuriated to stay any longer

"I am not a vampire, vampires are not real," said the vampire as he slid a toothpick between his fangs

"But you have fangs," protested the ghost that haunted the bar the vampire was currently at

"Not at all, my teeth just happen to be longer than average and can retract at will, that doesn't make them FANGS," he argued

"But.. you can see me, and I'm a ghost- that means you must be more than just a normal human," she explained

"Not at all, you aren't actually a ghost,"

The ghost frowned, narrowing her eyes and putting her hands on her hips

"I am a ghost! I died twenty years ago and remember it well!"

"It was all a dream I'm sure, next you'll be telling me you believe in reincarnation," the vampire scoffed

"You can put your hand right through me!" the ghost shouted, swarming around him as proof when his hand went straight through her with no resistance

"This is a very clever camera trick but you can buy the software at any office supply store,"

The ghost was so stunned by his display that she vanished in rage

"I am not a vampire, vampires are not real," said the vampire as he watched his paper cut heal right in front of him

"And I am not a werewolf, werewolves don't exist," said the talking wolf next to him

"I'm glad we can agree on something," the vampire said with a bright smile

"Well of course we agree, who would ACTUALLY believe in something as evil as vampires and werewolves existing? It's very wrong,"

"I don't think its evil, I just think it's ridiculous," the vampire clarified

"Hm, seems we disagree on something after all, I believe that creatures like vampires and faeries and the like- and werewolves of course- must be evil, they aren't ... natural, they aren't part of what we were always taught growing up, they're too different, and I know for a fact that all different things are evil, that's what I was always taught as a child," the talking wolf said as she lapped at the bowl of water on the counter

"I don't believe there's any such thing as evil, or good or bad or anything in between, there is only logic and ignorance, of course humans have an emotional system that drives their actions and beliefs, but who's to say if one is good and one is bad?" the vampire pointed out as he took a drink of his blood

"The natural order for one thing," argued the werewolf

"There IS no natural order, there is scientific order," argued the vampire

"Here's an idea," the bartender said suddenly, drawing the attention of both the vampire and the werewolf

"How about you two believe whatever you want to believe, and stop trying to push those beliefs down other people's throats?" he suggested

The concept seemed absolutely foreign to them both

"But.... other people are wrong, we have to correct them," the vampire said in surprise

"Why? Why do you HAVE to correct them?" the bartender asked sorely

"... Because otherwise they're all stupid and we don't need any of that in the world," compromised the werewolf

The bartender took a deep, deep, DEEP breath, letting smoke flow out of his nostrils

"Just because someone's opinion is DIFFERENT from yours, doesn't mean you're right and they're wrong, and it doesn't mean they're right and you're wrong either, an opinion is an opinion, let people have theirs," he explained

"Science is NOT an opinion, it's a FACT," argued the vampire

"And so is good and evil! It can't be argued, bad things will happen if it is," the werewolf agreed

"Why do you CARE? It isn't hurting anyone to let a mermaid swim or let a faery fly, why does it MATTER if you agree or disagree about someone being a ghost? You're entitled to your opinion- that means that if you don't want people to call you a vampire, they should respect that and not call you a vampire... even if you are one, but that ALSO means that if someone says they're a ghost- you need to respect them and not argue with them about it, they know what and who they are better than you do, stop trying to control other people's thoughts and beliefs just because they're different from yours,"

"But-!" the vampire and werewolf said at once

"No buts, if you two want to be miserable and refuse to believe what's right in front of you then go ahead, you have every right to, but you DON'T have the right to take that away from someone else, or make them feel stupid for their own personal beliefs and opinions, if you want to be a skeptic, go ahead, have fun, but don't pee on the parade of someone else just because they believe in something you don't, it's not a nice thing to do, and it isn't constructive either, what? You think that because you argue with someone and make them feel bad for what they believe that means they'll suddenly change their mind and agree with you? Even if they did, you'd know that you changed their mind in an unspeakable way, let people have their difference of opinions and beliefs, it's not gonna kill you,"

There was silence between the vampire and the werewolf for once, each thinking over these words

"Now I don't suppose either of you believe in dragons do you?" the bartender asked

"Of course not!" the vampire and werewolf protested in unison

The bartender nodded thoughtfully, grabbing a kabob of raw meat and holding it in front of them before inhaling deeply and breathing out a massive breath of fire, effectively cooking (well.. charring..) the meat on the stick

"How about now?" the bartender challenged

There was silence for a moment before the vampire cleared his throat

"........ Maybe......."

Alexa Asagi Andres

The Story Weaver

Once upon a time

In a land quite a ways from our own

There lived an elf, who was appreciated as one of the wisest of elves

The elf was not only considered to be very wise

But creative as well

And soon, she no longer became known as an elf at all

But as the Storyweaver

Now, how this change came about is almost as interesting as what happened after it began

It started with a child

A very young child, who asked the wise elf, her grandmother for that matter, to tell her a story

At first the wise elf was uncertain, not knowing if she should try to come up with a story or just repeat one of the ones she had heard her children tell over the years

But as none were coming to mind, she decided eventually that she must simply make one up on her own

And so the wise elf, who was called Marie, began to weave a story

No one quite knows what the story was that started it all- except Marie's granddaughter, who refuses to tell, for she wishes to keep that one story her own-

But the beauty behind it was stunning

For when Marie wove the story she didn't just speak it

Nor did she write it down

When Marie wove a story, it played out in Pixie Dust in front of her

All it took was speaking the words and careful crafting of the Pixie Dust for it to work

She would tell a story of a princess and a dragon, and beautiful multi-colored dust would rise from the many Pixie Dust pouches around and form a princess and a dragon

The princess and the dragon would become friends, and so the dust would depict the princess and the dragon giving each other a hug

The princess and the dragon would witness fireworks and so the dust would form small fireworks lighting and going off above the child's head

It was all very dramatic and really quite spectacular

It was all so beautiful that Marie's granddaughter simply had to tell everyone about it

She told her parents

She told her friends

She told anyone who would listen about her grandmother's powers to create stories

And not just TELL them, but SPIN them

And before long other children started to come to her to request stories of their very own

And the wise elf, would of course comply

And not long after that more and more children came

Until eventually she became known for them

And all the children, in lands both near and far, had heard of the mysterious Story Weaver

And all children- and even some adults- wished to have a story told to them with such spectacular magic

And so began the great journey for many folks, be they small or large

Be they human or Fae

May they be light or dark, young or old, of any belief and any class

All wanted to come to the Story Weaver to experience her magic

And no matter how much time has passed between the very first stories she wove being told and the present

The results are the same

All still wish to take part in the magical experience of the Story Weaver spinning them a story

But of course, there is one person who has the privilege of being woven a story at will

The very first person to ever experience the magic of the Story Weaver

Marie's granddaughter

For no matter how many stories she tells, spins, or weaves in a day

No matter how tired she is or how much creativity has been drained for her

At the end of every day, she still sits with her granddaughter and weaves a story

A very special one

Just for her

The Sun King And The Moon Queen

Once upon a time

In a realm that existed long before our own

There lived two spirits who ruled over the stars

One was the Sun King, Tristan

The other, the Moon Queen, Tsuki

For a very long time, the Sun King and the Moon Queen never met but on one very fateful night, that changed

One very fateful night, in which the sun and the moon were directly aligned in an eclipse

The Sun King, deciding to finally meet the queen of the other world, created a bridge of sunlight and crossed it towards her

When his feet landed on the moon, he was immediately surprised

The moon was frigidly cold and dark and he came from a place of heat and light

He looked around and found nothing in his line of sight

Everything about this new land was foreign and he wasn't sure where to even start

"Who are you?" came a smooth voice from across the moon

"My name is Tristan, I am the Sun King, and you are?"

Emerging from the shadows across from him was a beautiful woman with long black hair as dark as the night around them

She was as pale as the very moon itself and she was draped in gorgeous white fabrics and jewels

She was so beautiful in fact, that the Sun King forgot how to breathe

"I am Tsuki, the Moon Queen,"

Tristan smiled gently, bowing deeply to her

"It... feels a bit silly to just call each other 'Your Highness'... would it be alright if I call you Tsuki?"

"Only if I may call you Tristan," she replied softly

"Of course," he agreed

Tsuki moved closer, bowing to him in return and holding her hand out to him

Tristan smiled slightly, shaking her hand gently

"It's a pleasure to meet you my Queen,"

"And you my King,"

This was the beginning

The first- but far from the last- meeting of the Sun King and the Moon Queen

No one is quite sure why they seemed to take on life- only one on each of their respective domains

But legend has it, that it's because the sun and the moon themselves had fallen deeply in love with each other and personified the King and Queen as a way of finally being able to meet

Ever since that day Tristan and Tsuki began to meet

And over the course of time, they fell in love

People these days often ask what happens to the sun and moon when they set

When the moon rises in the night, it's so that the Sun King and the Moon Queen can rule over the moon

And when it sets in the morning, it's so the Sun King and Moon Queen can rule over the sun

During the meantime, it's left up to their children to rule over the abandonded domains

Over the centuries and millennia's that passed, the Sun King and Moon Queen had many children and every eclipse they met on the same bridge that the Sun King had created all that time ago and share a kiss as a way to remember their love for each other

However, legend has it that every now and then, when Tristan and Tsuki get bored, they decide to leave the care of their worlds in the hands of their children and decide to explore other worlds

Like this one, for example

So the next time you see a happy couple walking near you, and you feel the heat of the day or the cool of the night

It may be time to wonder if those you saw were not merely a happy couple, but in reality, the King of the Sun and the Queen of the Moon

Alexa Asagi Andres

The Troll Who Ate Dishes

Once upon a time

In a land a hop skip and a jump from our own

There lived a troll

He was a rather cute little troll with fluffy, springy, poodlish brown hair and gigantic round glasses

He was short and stubby and rounded and rather resembled a rollie polli

And more than anything- he was always hungry

The little troll was a fan of food, to put it mildly

Well, ALL trolls were, but this one especially enjoyed a good meal

And by "a good meal", of course, I mean everything he could find sloshed together

This troll, you see, was a Forest Troll/Stone Troll hybrid

That meant that he had two completely different diets

On the Forest Troll side he enjoyed food, ACTUAL food

Fruit, vegetables, bread, dairy, even some types of meat

Basically, Forest Trolls ate mostly the same things that humans would eat, besides the occasional grass or moss

Stone Trolls on the other hand... well now they were quite different

Stone Trolls had no desire for human food

What THEY craved was minerals

And lots of them!

Rocks, stones, sand, cement, even materials like clay and china that had only small traces of minerals

And the troll's FAVORITE mineral delicacy?

Dishes

He LOVED to eat dishes!

Plates, bowls, cups, glasses, even silverware!

He had to be wary of the knives though, if he ate from the wrong end he could get indigestion

But regardless, dishes were his FAVORITE

When people asked what kind of token he wanted as payment for crossing through his woods, he always asked for dishes

Some folks- usually the humans- found it off putting to watch him chomp away at a nice wine glass or nom on tea cup but the troll didn't care, he loved his dishes

And then the worst thing in the world happened

He found out he was being transferred

The forest he currently occupied was going to be taken over by the big Mountain Trolls from upstate due to the increasing rumors that humans were going to try to take over this part of the land, they needed the big, strong, brutal Mountain Trolls to detour them

And the hybrid troll, for all his delightfulness and charm, was far from giant

He was rather small, in fact, no bigger than a tree stump

And although he could certainly wrestle with the best of them and chomp through bone if he wanted to, he wasn't very intimidating

So the chances of him running off the humans was considerably slim

And thus, he was forced to relocate

The problem was that his new home by the river was... well... bad

It was VERY bad

It was a cardboard box in fact

No, that isn't an analogy, that's the truth

And the worst part was that no one ever seemed to need to cross the river so his food was severely limited

Or at least, his delicacy of dishes was...

The troll was becoming rather disgruntled....

And then something very strange and very spectacular happened

The troll met a dog

Or rather, the dog met him

It was in the early evening and he was just finishing up a handful of acorns when suddenly a dog came barking his way

To most people the dog was rather small, as most Yorkshire Terriers are, but to the troll, who was only a few inches bigger than the dog, she was rather large

Still though, determined to defend his home and more importantly his acorns, the troll stood his ground, putting the remaining acorns aside and puffing out his chest

The dog barked and so the troll growled

The dog seemed surprised and pawed at him

The troll reached over and petted the dog

The dog licked the troll on the cheek...

He adamantly refused to lick the dog back.....

"Izzy! There you are!" shouted a loud voice

Craning his neck to look up, the troll spied too beautiful faeries

One with sweeping long red hair and another far more beautiful one with short framing blonde hair

"Oh Darling look! It's a little troll!" shouted the red head with a smile

"And it seems to have made friends with Izzy," the blonde faery concluded

The troll was awestruck by the two faeries, having never encountered faeries before

He was mostly used to humans and ogres and other trolls- those who didn't live in the forest

He'd get the occasional elf from out of town but most of the Forest Folk- of which the faeries belonged to- didn't bother interacting with him for the forest was their home and a toll didn't need to be paid

However, he no longer worked in the forest, now he was working by the river, and it occurred to him that faeries didn't usually live around rivers, some did, but it wasn't common

So, puffing out his chest, he put his hand out and attempted to ask for payment

Only....

He found himself unable to...

He was so mesmerized by the light and happiness of the faeries that he seemingly lost his voice and all that came out was a scratchy, grunt of a noise

The faeries looked at each other, confusion written all over their faces as the blonde picked up the dog

"Aw you don't speak faery language do you little guy?" the red-head smiled

The troll frowned, yes, as a matter of fact, he DID speak faery language

But when he tried again, he only made the same stubborn sound

"I wonder if he understands us..." the red head mused, leaning down and poking the troll in the forehead

The troll squeaked and screeched and tried to fight her off- because seriously? Rude

"Oh leave that poor creature alone Alexandra, I'm sure he doesn't want you messing with him," the blonde sighed

"But Darling he's so round and cute! Don't you want to squish him?"

The troll began to turn pale

No, no thank you, he didn't want to be squished today

...

He didn't want to be squished ANY day but you know...

"Is he living in that box?" Darling asked with confusion as she peered over his shoulder

"Must be the economy," Alexandra nodded

The troll was starting to get annoyed with these two

And that dog kept staring at him and licking her lips like all she saw was a big chew toy

Really, the entire thing was unnerving, but he wanted payment for once!

The good stuff too, not the horrible little pennies and bags of trail mix he had been getting lately

He screeched again, holding his hand out and wiggling his fingers

"I think he wants a hug," Darling commented

The troll rolled his eyes and slapped himself in the head

For the love of crud these two really didn't get out much if they didn't understand the concept of paying him...

"I know! Let's take him home with us!" Alexandra said excitedly

What.

"I mean look at him! He lives in a box, he eats acorns, he obviously craves physical contact, and just look at that! He's got a stubbed toe and a bruised knee to boot!" she said

That happened to be from ONE accident down the hill and she really didn't need to point that out, thank you

"Well he clearly IS in distress about something," Darling agreed as she held the dog a bit more tightly

"Then let's take the little creature with us! We'll patch up the toe and knee- ... that's it... that's what we'll call him! Toe-nee! Tony! We'll name him Tony!"

It didn't seem to occur to either of these two butterheads that he might actually already HAVE a name

That was the thing about faeries, or so he had been told, they were kind to a fault

Every unhappy looking or down-and-out creature and the faeries had an insatiable urge to "fix" them or "adopt" them and it ended in more than a few trolls unwittingly becoming house pets more or less

Of course, those trolls never seemed to complain when they waddled out of their fine houses draped in nice clothes and eating elegant desserts....

But it was the principal of the matter!

It's why trolls didn't seem to care very much for faeries, they saw them coming and flashes of adoring kidnappers came through their heads

And sure enough, before the troll- Tony, as he had now been dubbed- knew what hit him, he was in a house far from the river and staring at the dog again

The dog, who barked excitedly and head-butted him, knocking him down

"Izzy! Leave Tony alone! You two have to be friends now," Darling chastised

Tony stared at the dog and wondered how he was supposed to be friends with.... that..... but he couldn't seem to voice his concerns even if he wanted to, and so he didn't

The biggest problem, among many, became that he was rather shy around the faeries

Even if he held a minimal grudge that they more or less abducted him from his job and was positive that they were both missing a couple of screws in their heads, the faeries were still beautiful and kind and soft-spoken in a way that he wasn't used to

And they were so close to each other that they seemed to be twins

Even the dog appeared to have an almost unnaturally close bond with them

And Tony

Well...

He just wasn't sure how to get involved without miscommunicating like he had earlier

For all he knew he'd ask them for a piece of toast and end up in a freezer

And so he waited and when the faeries or dog came around he ran and hid to keep from confronting them

They were all a little bit crazy and he didn't know what they were capable of yet...

"Tony! I don't know where you are little fella but I'm leaving your dinner by the fireplace!" Darling shouted, setting a huge bowl of spaghetti with a big piece of garlic toast on a saucer and a large glass of orange soda down by the fireplace

"If you spill it on the carpet I'll skin you and wear you as a hat!" she threatened as she went back upstairs

Tony barely even heard her, in his head all that could be heard was the word "Food" being sung by the voices of angels set to some tune he had heard in passing

And even better than the food- though surely it was delicious- was the fact that he had THREE dishes, a bowl, a saucer, and a glass, all waiting for him

There was even SILVERWARE!!!!

Tony ate well that night

And when the faeries came down the next morning they had assumed him to be kind enough that he had washed the dishes and put them in the dishwasher for them

Well, he HAD cleaned his plate....

....

He then ATE his plate but he did lick every bit of sauce off of it first

This happened again the next night when Darling made chicken and rice

A big plate full of chicken, rice, and vegetables, a glass of lemonade, and a big bowl of ice cream for dessert

Also, a plate, a bowl, a glass, a fork, two spoons, and a knife

He did get a bit of a stomachache from not chewing that knife all the way through but it was worth it

It kept happening too

Night after night

The more time passed, the more Tony became accustomed to the faeries- and their dog

It started with the dog ironically enough

He learned that she loved to wrestle as much as he did and before he knew it they were wrestling and playing fetch and he was riding her around the kitchen like a tiny horse

It was a pretty good thing they had going, especially since she only occasionally tried to bite off his fingers

And after getting used to the dog he became getting used to the faeries

He learned when was and wasn't the appropriate time to socialize with them- feel free to jump into a conversation unless it's on the phone, yes you can watch TV whenever you want, no you can't make rude noises or laugh at inappropriate moments

It was about two weeks into his unusual stay that the faeries really started getting concerned about their missing dishes

"I swear Darling, I am COMPLETELY out of forks!" Alexandra huffed

"And you're SURE you didn't break any of my glasses?" Darling frowned

"Would I lie to you?"

"Yes but I'm asking anyway,"

"How insulting! I wouldn't lie, besides if I had broken a glass you would have heard it!"

This went on for a while and Tony began to feel bad about the fact that the faeries were fighting because of him

But being that he couldn't properly speak to them, he didn't quite know what to do

The guilty look, however, didn't go unnoticed by the faeries

And that night when they set out his dinner- a big steak with mashed potatoes, a salad, cola, and a big slab of apple pie- they watched him secretly

And when they saw him take a bite out of the glass, it was all they could do not to start screaming in horror

The next morning was a somewhat long one as they waited for Tony to wake up

And when he finally did, walking downstairs with a yawn and rubbing his eyes beneath his glasses, well....

They ambushed him

The faeries asked why he ate the dishes, but more importantly, why he never tried to tell them that he was eating the dishes

And for the first time since meeting the peculiar faeries, Tony did something rather new

He spoke

In THEIR language

"I wasn't TRYING to lie to you," he explained

"I just.... couldn't talk to you, I don't know why, I just couldn't, I mean you did sort of kidnap me, so trust me, if I could have talked, I would have," he insisted

"So... you WANTED to live in that little box?" Alexandra asked in confusion

"Um...." he decided not answering was probably best

"We understand," Darling smiled

"AND if you want to go back to the river, we'll take you back,"

Tony made an indifferent face and shrugged

"No no, it's fine, I like living here, your untamed beast wouldn't know what to do without me anyway," he mused, sticking out his tongue childishly at the dog

Izzy stared at him and then jumped, making him scream as she started to lick him all over

"Oh sure, SHE'D be the one at a loss," Alexandra snorted

"Well I guess this just means one thing," Darling sighed

"What's that?" Alexandra asked

"The grocery bill is about to get a lot higher..."

 Faery Tales, Mermaid Myths, And Other Fantastical Legends

The Unicorn Queen

Once upon a time

In a land full of light

There lived a unicorn

She was beautiful, with a shimmering white coat, coal black eyes, and a flowing mane and tail

Not to mention her sparkling winding horn But unicorns are not known just for their beauty, but also for their freedom and peacefulness

Unicorns are revered for their beauty and non-confrontational attitudes

And because of that, are often hunted

One unicorn in particular, Adelaid, would know a lot about that

When she was merely a foal her mother did everything she could to keep Adelaid away from harm- away from potential hunters

But, despite her calm and content nature, Adelaid could not always be protected from harm, no creature could

And one day, not long after entering adulthood, that became a proven fact to unicorns everywhere

Adelaid had wandered off from her normal path to graze in some greener fields and hadn't noticed herself exiting the faery realm that she was from and entering the human realm, she was just too caught up in the delicious grass and flowers she was munching on

And it was only then that... it... happened...

Before she knew it an arrow whizzed by her and pierced the tree behind her

Adelaid jerked her head up, heart pounding, as she locked eyes with the human

And a moment later he was drawing another arrow

So she ran, back into the forest, desperate to get away

She didn't know what she had done to deserve this

She didn't know how anyone could be so cruel

As she ran, she nearly didn't see the elf that was just up ahead and had to skid to a sudden halt to avoid running into her

"Whoa.. easy now.... what's wrong little unicorn?" she asked gently

Adelaid shook slightly, nuzzling against the elf's hands

The elf smiled softly, stroking her muzzle gently

"The humans tried to hurt you didn't they?" she asked softly

The unicorn let out a soft whimper, nuzzling her again as confirmation as she was too tired to try to communicate telepathically

"Those humans... always thinking they can just do whatever they want.... would you like to be able to show the humans that they can't do that? That they can't get away with that?" the elf offered

Adelaid stared at her in surprise and slight confusion

She was a unicorn, by her nature she wasn't confrontational, and her nerves were so on end from that one encounter....

But at the same time, she couldn't help but feel intrigued by the idea of being able to help others like her

She WANTED to help others like her

To ensure that this would stop, even if it were only for a day or only one human who took the message back with them, she wanted to help....

And so, despite how shaken and twisted up her nerves were, she nodded her head in agreement

The elf smiled gently and placed her hands on Adelaid's chest, closing her eyes

A strange, warm sensation traveled throughout the unicorn's body and when she opened her eyes again she found herself staring at life through a new perspective

Quite literally at that

She looked around, moving on two feet, and peering into the beautiful crystalline lake before her

Adelaid gasped in surprise and stepped back, for what stared back at her was not a unicorn, but a woman

A human looking woman with long, stark white hair, beautiful brown eyes so dark they looked nearly black, and the palest skin

"You now have the voice to speak your peace, and I suggest that you do," the elf said as she gestured towards the forest where Adelaid knew would lead back to the human realm

No matter how nervous she felt or how loudly her heart was pounding, she knew that this was a job that had to be done

So she walked forward, stepping out of the trees and met eyes with the hunter again

"Fair maiden.... what beauty!" the man breathed, immediately replacing his arrow in his quiver and strapping his bow across his shoulder

"Beauty?" Adelaid scoffed

"You were hunting a unicorn- a creature who has done NOTHING to you, and yet you dare speak to me of beauty?"

"Ah, fair maiden," chuckled the hunter arrogantly

"You know nothing of hunting I'm afraid, why the unicorn may be PRETTY but it's just an animal, like a deer or a boar," he said with a cocky laugh

"And you would hunt them?" Adelaid huffed

"...Well.... yes... of course," the hunter replied, apparently confused by this

"Why?"

"Well for many reasons! You wouldn't fault a wolf for hunting a sheep now would you?"

"I wouldn't fault any creature for needing food or warmth or shelter, but tell me, what does a unicorn provide you with?"

"Pride!" laughed the hunter boastfully

"Pride and honor! Why if I sold a unicorn horn do you have ANY idea how much gold I could get? I could have myself- not to mention any wife I might take- set for life!" he insisted

Adelaid felt an unusual sensation bubbling up in her veins, something she had never felt before in her life

Adelaid felt anger

"So that's what it's for then? To show off as a prize? You'd take the life of another living, breathing, feeling creature for the sole purpose of stroking your ego and making coin?"

"Of course!" the hunter laughed

"See now my maiden? NOW you're getting it! But you still seem to be under the wrong impression, unicorns are ANIMALS, animals don't FEEL, they don't have emotion, that's a human quality!"

Adelaid felt her blood suddenly run cold

The warmth that usually soothed her body had vanished and now her fingertips were so chilled that they were nearly numb

The only warmth she felt now were the tears falling down her cheeks

"We don't feel? We don't have emotion? Just because we don't look like you? Talk like you? Walk like you? That makes us emotionless, painless, drifting beings? Is that what you're trying to tell me? That we haven't any souls? That we feel no pain? Can you really look into my eyes as they grieve tears that I feel nothing?" she breathed

"M'lady please, you're getting entirely too upset, it's merely a dumb animal!" he exclaimed

Adelaid began to shake, and without being able to stop herself, she felt the same warmth as before overtake her and when she opened her eyes she was on four legs again

A unicorn again

The hunter gasped in surprise and fell backwards, staring up at her in shock as Adelaid took a leap forward, landing over him and hovering her hoof above his throat

She shapeshifted back into the form of a woman again, gripping the sleeves of her pure white dress as she grabbed one of his arrows and hovered it over his throat

"A dumb animal? Tell me, who of us is the dumb one now? Who of us is on the ground? If I were really a 'dumb animal' who lacked emotion or reason or a SOUL would I have been able to knock you down? Would I have been able to hold this arrow above your throat? Would I hesitate to plunge it in? You wouldn't hesitate if our positions are reversed, why should I hesitate now?"

"P-Please! I beg of you! I-I... I didn't mean it!" shouted the hunter

"Oh yes you did," Adelaid said calmly, coldly

"I know that you did, it's how human men think, YOU are the emotionless ones who feel no pain, you feel your own- sure, but you feel no pain for ANOTHER, you have no empathy, if I were as cruel to you as you have been to me I would say you had no soul at all.... but I am not that cruel," she sat back, laying the arrow in her lap

"I am not that cruel, I am not that person, I have empathy for you, I have

MERCY for you, which is FAR more than anything you have ever harbored for me, I mourn the lives you have taken, my heart ACHES for the souls you have ripped from this world with the ignorance that anyone who does not look or sound like you must not possess emotion or a soul or the ability to feel pain... to feel joy... to feel love... what terrible ignorance you've been cursed with, I pity it, I pity YOU," Adelaid stood, wiping the tear from her eye and stepping back

"Go, tell everyone this tale, stop this disease of stupidity and hatred before it can spread any further,"

She stepped back further, clutching the arrow

"I will be keeping this, for the next emotionless fool who dares to lecture me on feelings,"

Without waiting or confronting her further the hunter ran as fast as his legs could carry him

Adelaid sat in the grass and sobbed over the arrow, her heart aching from the knowledge that such cruelty existed

And as she sobbed, the arrow began to glow with her tears, with her magic, with her POWER

And although she yearned to go back to the forest

Back to her contentment, her happiness, her peace

She knew now that she never could

Not for long at least

Her life was dedicated to protecting those beautiful souls from now on

To ensuring that no other unicorn would fear or suffer as she had

To teaching the truth about the unicorns- about all animals, all BEINGS- wherever this arrow would lead her

And it lead her

It lead her all over the world to anywhere that such horrible beliefs were held

It was hard work

It was draining work

But it was work that needed to be done

And during the many, many years of her travel, the word spread of her

Of a unicorn who could become a woman and who confronted evil face on

Word spread of her courage

And the unicorns revered her and called her their queen

And so, without ever even being present when the decision was made

Adelaid became the queen of the unicorns

For Adelaid possessed the bravery to keep them all safe by speaking up for the truth

Alexa Asagi Andres

The Vampire And The Faery

Once upon a time

In many, many lands as it were

There lived an elf

This elf was very wise and very kind but was also... very old, by elf standards

And so when the elf found a basket sitting on his doorstep one day with a baby inside it, he realized that he would be incapable of caring for the child

Especially upon finding out that the baby was a faery

Faeries are notoriously more energetic and harder to raise than elves...

And so the elf began his mission to find a home for the baby faery

There was just one problem...

The elf lived in the more... suburban area of the faery world

And by "suburban", he meant the very outskirts where there were maybe three houses and no young vibrant people looking for children

Faery Tales, Mermaid Myths, And Other Fantastical Legends

The central part of the faery world was quite a bit away and so the elf would have to make do if he wished to find this child a home before too much time had passed

So he decided the only thing he could do, really, would be to knock door to door until he found someone willing to take the baby

The faeries all told him "no"

... As did the other elves...

And the Pixies

And the Nymphs

He wasn't even sure why he bothered asking merfolk really, considering...

Basically all creatures that could be filed under the tab of "Fae Folk" turned him down

This, of course, was not for lack of compassion, but much like the elf they just weren't equipped to suddenly have a child thrust upon them at the time

And so it was time to start thinking out of the box

But sadly three werewolf packs, two witch covens, and a dragon nest later he was starting to get low on options

One of the werewolf couples had been THIS CLOSE to saying yes- being that all of their children were adopted and they already had three faeries, it looked like he had finally found her a place...

... And then a chain of events was set off inside the household that started with the sound of breaking glass and a loud "IT WASN'T ME" followed by screaming, a dog barking, a baby crying, and a ball hitting the slightly smaller werewolf in the back of the head

"Oops..." had come the reply

The slightly larger werewolf took a deep breath in that special way that only a fellow parent could understand as his pupils dilated for a moment and he gave a gentle "Maybe next year" before closing the door

The elf, being tired and already down to his last options, had been ready to bargain with the couple if they would just open the door again...

He gave it a good ten minutes before deciding that they had, in fact, reached their annual limit for children before insanity would start to seep in

And given that the only other person to consider it, a gentle dragon mother with six hatchlings of her own, had nearly agreed when one of her children sneezed and almost caught the elf (and thereby the faery baby) on fire...

Well....

That went downhill fast...

He was now at his last- and by last, he means VERY last resort

The vampire that lived on the top of the hill

The last house in the tiny suburban town and the one that bordered on the edge of the woods

The house that seemed to be cloaked in perpetual darkness and that housed a creature who didn't seem to ever leave

The vampire didn't even have a proper nest of fellow blood sucking creatures of the night

The elf was gaining certainty that he would, in fact, be stuck raising this child

Taking a deep breath, he knocked on the door and waited....

..And waited....

.....And waited....

.....And waited.....

Just as he was about to give up, the door creaked open and a dark haired, tired looking man approached

"What is it?" he asked in a low voice

"I ah... you see... well... there's this child-"

"Yes yes, the faery child that was left on your doorstep, so I've heard, you've come to ask me to take her?" he asked in a bored, if not slightly irritated voice

The elf had to think about that

Was it worth it to give the child to someone who probably had a stack of bodies in his basement?

".....Yes," he decided

Because you really never can be too sure and he didn't stare down the face of fear himself for nothing

The vampire stepped closer, peering down at the baby in the basket and reaching out

The elf swallowed tightly, watching as he picked up the baby with such gentleness that the elf forgot, for a moment, that the child was not the vampire's own

He held her the way one would hold a precious piece of glass, far too afraid to squeeze too tightly or yet lose support and risk dropping the small faery

And then the vampire did something that the elf never would have thought he'd see him do

He smiled

Not in a menacing, "I'd like to have you for... 'dinner'..." kind of smile

But a gentle, sweet smile that only a parent could give to their child

"Yes," he said in a soft voice

"I would like to have her,"

He turned, placing the faery baby back in the basket, and picking up the basket by its handles

"Please excuse my voice and my lateness to the door, I had been cleaning the basement and inhaled quite a bit of dust," he said with a slight cough, careful to cover his mouth

"It's.... no.... problem..... I understand?" the elf said quietly

"Thank you," he said, clearing his throat as he took the baby and stepped fully inside once more, a foot on the door to nudge it shut when he paused again and stared at the elf

"Thank you," he repeated, shutting the door

The elf stood for a long moment on the vampire's doorstep, really very uncertain about what to do now or what he just did

Finally, he moved, walking back down the hill and hoping that he hadn't just made a mistake that would cost the little faery her young life

Incidentally, he had become more invested in the baby faery than he realized and went to check on her the next day... mostly to make sure she was still alive

The vampire, whose throat was much clearer now and voice much kinder, invited him upstairs without hesitation

"Please excuse the state of the house, I've been trying to do some remodeling after a recent flood and it's ... not going as well as I'd hoped,"

"You could hire a professional," the elf suggested as they walked up the old, creaky stairs

"No no, they won't do it right, the last time a professional was in here they painted my walls YELLOW, not even a soft, muted yellow either, that bright sunshiny muck you'd see in a crayon box,"

The elf muffled a laugh, he was beginning to feel sorry for the vampire, given everyone's perception of him

When they arrived at the top of the stairs the vampire opened a door, that on the outside seemed as rotted and old as the rest of the house, and revealed something that made the elf nearly stop breathing

It was a nursery

Painted a soft lavender and carpeted and full of rugs and stuffed animals and pictures of ponies and teddy bears with a crib in the center of the room and a music box that projected little hologram stars in the ceiling playing in the corner

Upon inspection of the child, who was already wearing fresh clothes and wrapped tightly- but not suffocatingly- in a blanket, fast asleep, the elf determined that yes, this was surprisingly a good choice

The elf began visiting the vampire and the faery quite often

At first he tried to give them space, he didn't want to seem like an intruder, and wait months at a time, but as he talked to the vampire he began to develop a steady friendship with him

The reason, as it turned out, for his not leaving the house was his work, he was a writer and often became so engrossed in his work that he forgot the outside world even existed, and then when the flood happened he had to spend so much time on home repair that he never had time to leave anyway

His basement was full of blood bottles that he ordered through the mail- as many vampires in the modern age had started to do- and he found that most of his favorite shopping places and eateries were in or just past the woods anyway, thus, on the few occasions he did leave, he didn't go into town

He was also a quiet, sensitive, socially anxious soul who had trouble getting along with people- even other vampires- due to his nerves, thus his lack of a nest

His family still lived in the bigger city and thus, no family

The more the elf visited, the more these things started to make sense, and the more sorry he felt for the vampire, who more than likely had no idea what the rest of town thought of him

However, now that he had the faery child, he was forced out of many of his own home comforts in order to give her the best things in life like friends and the outside world

He still was a homebody and often preferred spending his time with just the faery and himself

But at least these days he made use of his car

By the time six years had passed things were very different, and it was almost hard to remember a time when the kind vampire was thought to be such a nasty thing

"Bella my darling! Come downstairs so your uncle can see your new dress!" he shouted

"I'm coming Daddy!" the faery shouted back

"And no flying! We're still practicing and where are we NOT going to practice?"

There was a pause

"..Over the stairs..."

"Because what happens when we fall over the stairs?"

"... Ouchies and booboos..."

"Ouchies and booboos, you bet," he replied back, looking back to the elf and smiling

"Would you like some tea before the birthday party begins? I'm sure once the other children and parents get here you'll be able to find nothing but soda and juices," he mused

"Tea would be lovely," the elf replied, following him into the nicely renovated kitchen

"I hear that the werewolves have adopted another one," the elf mused as he grabbed the kettle from the counter

"Last week, what is that now? Sixteen? And they've been married for twenty years," the vampire said with a shiver

"I can't even imagine..."

"And to think they almost had Bella," the elf chuckled

"No, you almost forced them to have Bella, we met them right after that little visit you know, one of their werewolf children was teething and if I were them I wouldn't have brought in another child at that point either,"

"Have you ever considered taking in another now though?" the elf asked curiously

The vampire shrugged, leaning against the counter and pouring the boiling water into two mugs

"I may, I may not, we are not like the humans, you and I, we're blessed with lives that have the potential for endless adventures, perhaps I will have another child, perhaps in a year, perhaps in a decade, perhaps in a hundred years... perhaps never, I don't like to plan ahead, the better things in life seem to be spontaneous," he explained

"I suppose that's true," the elf nodded, both turning around upon the sound of footsteps racing into the kitchen

The little faery twirled in a black and pink flower petal dress, showing off her pink and white striped socks and black Mary Janes

"What do you think!?" she asked with an excited smile, her little wings fluttering beneath her bright copper hair

"I think I have never seen a more beautiful creature in my entire life, my darling Bella," the vampire replied with a smile, reaching out to pick her up and give her a tight hug

Yes, the elf decided as he sipped his tea

This was a very good decision

Alexa Asagi Andres

The Vampire Who Loved The Sun

Once upon a time

Many, many, many years ago

There lived a vampire

He was a very unusual vampire

For he was a vampire who loved the sun

He was born a vampire, not turned, he had his entire life to get used to the fact that he couldn't enjoy the soft heat on his face or the bright light in his eyes or the smell of fresh morning dew

Yet he never did

Twenty years after his birth he stopped physically aging, a bit of a late bloomer for vampires but not unheard of

And when his aging stopped, so too, stopped his enjoyment of the sun

Vampire children mature like human children, for the first ten or so years of their lives they're like everyone else

Save, perhaps, for acute hearing and healing from scrapes and cuts a little more quickly than most

It isn't until puberty hits, like for all other children, that the change takes place

It's gradual, the first step is coming to crave blood, the last is that physical aging stops, and in between is the rest

Most vampire children develop their sensitivity to sunlight very early on, and for many it's one of the first signs of changing into their more permanent state

But this vampire especially resisted

The sun made his head ache and his eyes seer with a dull throbbing behind them

His skin itched and burned at the same time and he was out of breath in only a few steps by the time he was in his late teens

But yet he still loved the sun

Sunrise especially

He would stay up to all hours of the night and go outside just to watch the sunrise

Only when the burning was too much to take would he go back inside

"Vincent, what have I told you about going outside in the daytime? You know better... now come back inside and sleep like a normal vampire," would chastise his mother

He never blamed her, he wouldn't want his children exposed to a lethal substance every morning either

But what could he do?

He loved the sun, the light, the early morning dew, far too much to keep his health at the forefront of his mind

But now, twenty years after his birth, the sun had become unbearable

Standing for even a moment outside in the sunlight gave him severe migraines and his eyes burned in their sockets

His skin burned in minutes to an unhealthy red and if he stayed in the sun for more than a minute or two it would start to smoke, threatening to catch fire and burn him alive

He never hated being a vampire until the sun was taken away from him

But now he looks at his reflection with disdain and stares longingly at the mortal humans who walk beside him in the early evenings

It was once in a while, on very rare, special occasions, that the clouds of rain or snow hid the sun just so

Just enough to be able to see its beauty and not be harmed by the thing he found so breathtaking

On those days he always went out

He went to the busiest part of town to soak in everything he could about the sun, instead of staying on the edge below the hills where sunlight was harder to capture

It was during one of these such outings that he met a girl

A girl who would change everything forever

"What are you staring at? Have you never seen the sun?" came a soft laugh from behind him

Vincent turned on his heel, umbrella held tightly above him as he stared at her

She was.... beautiful

Beautiful was such an understatement but Vincent was never good with words

Her hair was soft blonde, like droplets of the sun's rays, dripping over her shoulders in big, loose curls

Her eyes were ocean blue with a bit of lightness to them that made them look like the sea in the middle of the day- with the sun shining directly on the water

Her skin was as pale as his was and her smile could put even the beauty of the sun to shame

She clutched her parasol tighter and lifted up her petticoat, stepping a step closer

"I... I don't get out much," he explained, suddenly remembering that he had been asked a question

"Don't get out much? What do you do then?" she chuckled

"I... am a poet," he concluded

It was the furthest thing from the truth but it was the best he had

"A poet? Like Sir Edgar Allan Poe?" she asked with surprise and a bit of excitement

"Yes," he nodded

He hoped she didn't ask him to recite something

"Well, it's an honor to meet a poet then," she smiled

"The honor, m'lady, is all mine," he promised, bowing at the waist and very gently capturing her white gloved hand, laying a kiss just above her knuckles

She smiled brighter, her eyes crinkling as she slowly withdrew her hand and he stood up

"My name is Angelique, and what is yours?"

"Vincent," he added

"Well Vincent, I hope we do meet again," Angelique said happily, nodding her head respectfully as she turned and walked away

Vincent watched her go until she blended in with the crowd and even the soft pinkness of her dress no longer stood out, and once she was gone, he stared up at the sky and searched for a ray of sunshine

He took his glove off slowly, reaching his bare hand into the ray and hissing a breath in as he began feeling the familiar burn

"I see I've met your daughter," he said, withdrawing his hand and slowly placing his glove on it again

"I see she takes after you, for all her beauty, I may never gaze upon her for longer than a moment, or our fates would kill us both,"

Vincent did not see Angelique for six days

The next time he did, it was night and he was searching with the rest of his family for a quick meal

Instead of sticking to the outskirts of town where he could catch easy prey, he did the unheard of and stepped into town for reasons that, to this day, he could not explain

And as soon as he did, he realized the reason for it

The smell of fresh blood hit him like a brick to the head and he felt his eyes turning red as his fangs began to grow out

He quickened his pace, hurrying towards the scent and rounding into a small ally behind a bakery

There, laying in the mud and dirt, her baby blue and white dress soaked and dirtied, was Angelique, blood spilling over the already wet dirt around her

"Angelique?" he breathed, unable to move for a moment

But he snapped himself out of it, as quickly as he could, and raced to her side

"Angelique!?" he shouted again, falling to his knees beside her and cradling her head in his hands

She opened her eyes weakly, staring up at him and smiling sickly

"Vincent.... won't you.... recite a poem to me...?" she asked breathlessly

He felt a pang of hurt in his chest that he had never felt before

Not even being away from the sun had caused so much pain to fill his body

He shook his head slowly, watching her eyes grow dimmer and dimmer

"One.... poem....?" she asked quietly

He gritted his teeth, hands clutching her body tighter as he leaned down

His family had a personal rule against turning humans into vampires like them

They were too uncontrollable, too unpredictable, they brought nothing but pain and strife, they often forced the existing vampires to pick up and leave because they couldn't control themselves

But Angelique had the sun in her

Drops in her hair, rays in her eyes, and the shine of it over her entire soul

And Vincent, for as much as his life was made to be against it, loved the sun

And so he bit into her soft flesh and felt her jerk in shock and pain against him

And that night, with rain falling down around them, Vincent turned Angelique into something he hated

Something that could never love the sun again

Something like himself

And as he waited for the bite to do its job

As he waited for Angelique to wake

He stared hopefully before him, hoping to see the sun rise

And although it certainly did rise, there was too much rain covering it for him to see it

For several days Angelique stayed with Vincent and his family and they taught her everything they could about being a vampire

They taught her control, they taught her to hunt, they taught her to conceal, they taught her everything in a few days that Vincent's mother had worked to teach he and his siblings in the course of years

And like anyone with the stamina of a newly turned vampire, Angelique absorbed it all with ease

Vincent had started to feel happy with Angelique in his life, even though he could see the sun less than ever now, with people searching for her

But that came to an abrupt end, as Vincent woke one morning and Angelique was gone

He did not see her again for twenty years

Well... even in twenty years, he didn't technically "see" her

He heard of her

It was one summer night that seemed at first like any other that he heard the name "Angelique" again and knew that it was in reference to the daughter of the sun

"These are brand new, guaranteed to protect against all ill effects of the sun,"

Vincent stared at the bottle of pills with skepticism and turned to frown at the vampire who had handed them to him

"And why did you seek me out to give these to me? I don't recall ever meeting you before," he noted

"I don't know, it was the request of Lady Angelique, she invented those tablets, she said they were for you, I'm not sure why," the man replied with a nod and a tip of his hat as he tried to walk away

"Angelique? Where is she?" Vincent asked urgently, taking the other vampire's shoulder

"I don't know, somewhere in France I think," the man replied, shaking Vincent's hand off of his shoulder and being on about his way

Vincent spent five years in France looking for Angelique, but did not find her

It was at the end of those five years that he had heard of several scientists going to America for some reason, and decided to go to America to find her there

He didn't hear a single breath of the name "Angelique" for fifty years

And at the corner of those fifty years, he saw her face again

Though it was not in person, it was a photograph on a poster

Advertising the beautiful Angelique Beauchamp, an expert violinist giving a concert in Philadelphia for one night only

Vincent hunted down a ticket and went to the concert with certainty that he would see her again

And he did

Performing on the stage, looking not a day older or a hair less beautiful than she did the day he met her seventy-five years ago

But tragedy always seems to come in threes

Before the concert was over and he could find her and reintroduce himself, the concert hall fell under the attack of vampire hunters and Angelique's manager (he assumed) rushed her away

The hunters kept Vincent from giving chase and he was so angry that he didn't even bother to feed on them before snapping their necks

It was another twenty-five years before he saw Angelique again, and this time, things were much different

Sitting on a park bench he felt the same twinge of pain that he felt whenever he saw the sun

The sun, that had once been an object of longing and desire, was now a bitter memory of pain and something that could have been

Something that may have never been meant to be

And then, as soft as fresh morning dew, came a voice

"Vincent?"

The black haired man turned around, stunned and frozen in silence as he stared at her

She carried a parasol similar to that day a hundred years ago, and though her dress and jacket were drastically different, they were still the same, fresh spring pink

"Angelique?" he breathed in shock

A bright smile spread over her face as she walked forward, eyes as bright as the sun it's self

"You cut your hair," he said dumbly as he stared sadly at where the locks ended at her chin

"Vincent Kellar, we've been apart for a hundred years and you want to speak with me about my hair?" she gasped

"I'm sorry... it's different," he concluded

It was the only thing different about her

"Well perhaps I should go away again until it grows out," "No please don't," he begged quietly, holding his hand out desperately for her

Angelique smiled adoringly and placed her hand in his

"You MUST work on your social skills, what would your mother say?"

"She would likely be very disheartened to hear of it if she were to ever to come to the states," he chuckled

"Is she still in England?" Angelique asked curiously as she walked to the side of the bench, never letting go of his hand, and sat next to him

"She, my father, and Elizabeth, yes," he nodded, wrapping his arm gingerly around her shoulders

"Well what about Sebastian and Kirsten then?" she hummed

"Mmmm... Kirsten has traveled to another continent and I haven't heard from her in a few years... Mother says she's doing fine though, Sebastian followed me to the states like the lost puppy he thinks he is and hasn't left my residence since," he grunted in frustration

"In seventy-five years your brother hasn't moved out of your house?" she laughed

"Oh you know Sebastian, he has the independence of a five-week-old kitten," Vincent snorted back

"Well as long as he's housebroken I would consider it a win," Angelique pointed out

"Oh, certainly a win, IF he were housebroken, I am STILL cleaning up blood from the carpet every now and then, just last month in fact he got into the raw steak and... I should have KNOWN an apartment with white carpeting would be a TERRIBLE idea," he sighed loudly

Angelique laughed loudly and happily, her voice ringing like bells, and they talked and talked until the sun began to threaten going down, it was as if they had never spent an hour apart, no less a hundred years

They began to calm once the sun had begun to go down and knew they would have to part soon so as not to raise suspicion

"I didn't wait for you," Vincent said suddenly as he walked Angelique home

"I searched for you," he concluded a moment later

Angelique paused, looking up and staring at him in amazement

He didn't look back, merely kept his eyes on the road

"And how did know that I waited for you? How did you know I hadn't gotten married and become wildly happy?" she asked curiously

"I didn't, but I hoped," he replied

"You hoped... for a hundred years? You hoped?" she asked, clearly in disbelief

"The first twenty was the hardest, when your pills were delivered to me I knew you were still thinking of me, when I saw you at the concert our eyes locked and you smiled at me, it meant that you remembered me, and so yes, with the reminder that you remembered me, I hoped,"

There was a long pause as they walked

"You are a VERY foolish man," she noted

"So would agree my mother, who had to reel me away from the sun every day of my youth,

"And I see that hasn't changed," Angelique teased

"No, but now that I have the sun in my grasp I hope to never let go of it again," he said softly

She nodded slowly, looking at the ground

"I'm sorry Vincent, I never intended to be gone for so long,"

"What's a hundred years between vampires?" he shrugged

She chuckled softly, leaning her head on his shoulder "Out of curiosity though.... why did you leave?" he asked softly

They stopped outside of a small house in a relatively suburban neighborhood, their hands taken in each other's as Angelique stared at the ground

"I ... didn't want to ruin your life, you had a life where you were and I knew if I stayed for too long... unable to control myself as I was... I would have ruined that for you, and so I left, I was on my own for those twenty years and occupied my time with finding a way to fix this... eternal war we have with the sun, and when I did... I had intended to go back to you I swear it but..."

"Life got in the way?"

She nodded slowly

"And you think I'm foolish, you left without saying anything, going off on your own barely adjusted to your new skin, you could have found yourself on the unfriendly end of a stake or a laced bullet so easily...." he said sadly

"At least I never stood out and burned myself in the sun," she replied softly

He shook his head slowly, squeezing her hands a bit tighter

"If I let go of my hands, will it be another hundred years before I hold them in my own again?" he asked softly

"I am not going anywhere Vincent, of that I solemnly swear,"

And to that, Angelique kept her promise

A hundred years later Angelique lived in that very house

Only by this point, she was not alone

"You haven't eaten today have you?" Angelique frowned as she stood over Vincent's shoulder

The vampire glanced up, tilting his head innocently at her

"It's such a warm spring day... I wanted to be under the sun,"

She rolled her eyes, slapping his head playfully

"Come inside and eat before you start getting cravings for the neighbor's sister again," she said with a huff

"Good smelling blood in that sister," he muttered to himself

Angelique raised her eyebrows, putting her hands on her hips

"Vincent Kellar, are you coming or not?"

He looked up at her upside down, taking her hands and cupping them in his own, he gave her a light tug and she walked forward with ease as he kissed her palms

"Is there something you want from me?" she teased

"Only everything," he hummed back

She rolled her eyes and sat down next to him, leaning her head on his shoulder as she stared at the flowers in the garden

"I like your hair longer like this," he hummed, playing with the ringlets of curls in her hair

"Oh trust me, I know that, the seven years of you begging me to grow it out again are proof," she snorted

He smirked teasingly, placing the curls against his lips and kissing through every strand he could capture

"Vincent don't start that!" she laughed as she shoved his shoulder playfully

"Mmm can't stop me," he hummed back

"Oh we'll see if I can stop you, I can roll you down that hill into Poison Ivy, will that stop you?" she teased

"Hrn.... I do not care for that...." he muttered with a cringe

Angelique just laughed harder and pushed him again, the force of the push barely budging him

"If you need me I'll be inside making food and making sure the baby is still asleep," she hummed

"Mm when are the other kids going to be here?" he asked, laying back with his head on her legs

"Margret, Stanley, and Grace will be here at five, their entire families included, grandkids and all... I'm not sure when the others are going to be here.. I'll have to call Emily and ask when she's planning to get here..." she muttered

Vincent nodded slowly

"And the little ones? Aren't they at a birthday party today?" he asked with a hum

"Yes, they're at... oh... I think it was Kathrine's..." she mused

"Is she the blonde at the end of the street or the red-head we have to drive thirty-five minutes to get to?"

"Red-head,"

"I've got to pick them up haven't I?" he groaned

"Oh hush, you can enjoy your beautiful sun anytime," she said playfully

"But that doesn't mean I shouldn't worship every moment with her," he said seriously

She looked down at him, cupping his face in her hands

"I thought you said you lied about being a poet,"

"I did,"

"I wonder," she snorted, pressing her forehead against his

"Everything has changed in a hundred years... hasn't it? Us, our lives, the people around us... the world, technology... everything has changed, everything keeps changing... it's like... a big tornado of constant change that never stops or even takes a break.... so why do I feel like nothing has changed at all?"

He took her hand, kissing it again

"Because nothing has, only the exterior to our world has changed my darling, those of us within the universe- our hearts, our souls- those will never change, much like my love for the sun, it will never change,"

"Oh is that so? Even with global warming?"

"Mm... it could burn me to ashes and I would still beg to bathe in the rays of it..." he said softly

"I can believe that," she agreed

He stared up at her, leaning up and pausing a breath from her lips

"As long as the sun is shining upon me," he said, lips touching against her's as he spoke

"I will never change, nor stop loving it, nor stop loving you,"

Angelique closed her eyes, leaning down so their lips were pressed lightly against each other

"Then by God, may the sun shine forever,"

Faery Tales, Mermaid Myths, And Other Fantastical Legends

The Wish Granter

Once upon a time

In a land not too far from our own

There lived a wizard, a faery, and two little pixies

But the wizard was not just any normal wizard

He was a Wish Granter named Jamie

Now one may be confused, can't all wizards technically grant wishes?

All wizards hold magic, after all, as do faeries, merpeople, and any other Fae Folk

So what is it about a Wish Granter that's so special?

Wish Granters are, unlike most wizards, specifically capable of using their magic to grant wishes

Each Wish Granter presides over a certain type of wishing so that no one wizard or witch is ever overwhelmed

The Wish Granter in question, who lived with the beautiful faery and the two adorable pixies, was a Story Granter

His specialty is granting wishes in concern to stories, legends, and all written word

This is a very special talent indeed, for not only is it one of the rarer Wish Granting talents, but it also is a bit more.. expansive than most other talents

For most Wish Granters, their powers are limited

Rain Granters for example can control rain, bringing it forth, sweeping it away, creating more or less in any given place, but their only control is over the rain

Cloth Granters can create anything out of any kind of cloth without so much as batting an eye, a simple idea is all it takes to summon the fabric and create stunning gowns or tailored suits or an entire nursery full of different fabricated necessities, but their only control is over the cloth it's self

Garden Granters can control any and every type of plant, flowers, fruits, weeds, and every single thing in between, they can grow anything at will or detour its path to grow elsewhere, but yet again, their only control is over the plants themselves

This is what makes Story Granters so very special

For Story Granters are one of the Creative Talents, meaning that their magic takes many more forms than simply bringing rain, sewing cloth, or growing plants

The talent of a Story Granter is the ability to not only summon any written word ever created at will, but also to create written word out of thin air

How, one may ask, is that possible?

Story Granters are able to see into the hearts and minds of whoever they grant wishes to and see what stories are swirling around in their heads, where their imaginations lie as well as their happiness and passions, and just by seeing those things, a Story Granter is capable of summoning a pen and page and with a snap of their fingers create whatever it is the wisher truly wants

This, of course, is a rare talent indeed

And due to its rarity, the Story Granter was often overcome with swarms of people all asking for any number of books, scrolls, or pages

He was in such demand that it was almost impossible to keep up with on his own

So it was lucky then, for the Story Granter, that he had a brilliant faery to help him

Before the faery, things seemed to be in such a constant disarray that one could easily lose their mind just walking into the Grantiary

But as soon as the faery Desiree found the Grantiary she decided that her talents would be best used there and decided to stay

It didn't take long before people traveled out of their way, past even other Story Granters, to request their written words from Jamie and Desiree

For their very presence was light it's self

The Grantiary was always filled with love and joy and it was more than enough reason for others to make the long journey

Before long Jamie and Desiree found themselves greeting travelers from lands so far away that they had never even heard of them

And as if they hadn't had enough visitors before then, the Grantiary was almost always packed once the Pixies arrived

It started with the bouncy and energetic pixie, Rebbecca, who arrived to fill the Grantiary with even more joy shortly after the faery Desiree decided to stay with the Story Granter Jamie

And a few years after that, arrived the younger and quieter Emma, who brightened the Grantiary even more

And all were devoted to the same thing: Stories

Stories are an expression of one's self, of every range of emotion from joy to sadness and everything in between

But often times, stories are rather difficult to track down, especially in a land so very full of them, and people are always so sad when they're unable to find the story that lights their life so

It is for this reason that Jamie, Desiree, and their pixie daughters, wished to devote their time to finding and weaving stories, so that others could be as happy as they were

It was certainly not an easy thing, even for the Story Granter himself it was sometimes hard to remember where books from lands and lands (and lands and lands) away had gone off to

But he always managed to find them before long, and with a snap of his fingers, the book appeared before him

Word continued to spread and spread across so many lands and seas of the beautiful family who brought stories to any who asked, that even our land, that is mostly disjointed from the magic lands, has heard of them

In fact, there is, in part, a legend to this tale...

According to this legend, the Grantiary just became too big and too overstuffed with people for even the happiest family to run alone and the beautiful and brilliant faery Desiree came up with a solution for their problem...

Her solution was to project Grantiaries in other lands, without, of course, telling anyone that they were merely projections and not the REAL Grantiary

With the help of the magic from her Pixie children, the lovely and excitable Rebbecca, and the wonderful and cheery Emma, the three were able to create a strong enough magic that they could project a Grantiary anywhere they wished

This made things exceedingly easier for the Story Granter and his family, now that he had room to move and could hear himself think

And thus they were able to grant even more story-wishes than before

According to legend, if one is to believe it, there is even a Grantiary in our world, located somewhere in the woods where things are more quiet, where one can go and see the four magical beings and have a story granted to them

But of course, this is just a legend, and usually, there is very little truth to legends, even in true stories such as these....

..... Unless you know where to look

 Faery Tales, Mermaid Myths, And Other Fantastical Legends

The Wizard's Garden

Once upon a time

In a land a good distance from our own

There lived a wizard

This wizard was unusual, for unlike most wizards who rode around on steeds shoving wands and staffs around like it was their job, this wizard preferred to stay quiet and keep to himself

His preferences were less the adventurous, hazardous, life-threatening type, and far more the low-laying, relaxed, gardening type

He didn't have a need for the grand city life and so lived in a cottage just outside of the woods that he frequented to get fresh herbs from

It was in this cottage that magic happened

With a wave of his wand or a snap of his fingers food seemed to come out of nowhere

Although, as all followers of magic know, nothing can simply appear out of nowhere

The gardens surrounding the cottage were full of all fruits and vegetables and the woods just outwards of there held many herbs and spices that thrived in such an environment

And so the wizard spent his days cooking anything and everything he could think of

He baked fresh bread and pastries and chopped fresh salads and conjured all kinds of soups and sauces and exotic flavors

He wasn't a famous wizard, as he preferred it that way (all of the famous wizards seemed to have a tendency to get themselves involved in trouble...)

But he was quite popular in the surrounding area and often brought the overabundance of food to the bakeries and markets nearby, or when the weather was less than ideal had an owl fly it out to them

All came to be excited when the Great Grey Owl graced the villages and towns with his presence, for it meant that the wizard had been cooking and conjuring in the kitchen once again

Yes it was a quiet life, but that was what the wizard preferred....

Until it stopped being quiet that is

One day, that wasn't any different at all from any usual day, a beautiful Blue Bird suddenly flew straight through the Wizard's window and landed in a pot of flour laying out on the table

Startled, the wizard dropped the grapes he had been washing and rushed to the table to check on the little bird

"Are you alright little bird? Why were you flying so hazardously?" he asked with concern

The bird stood up and shook the flour off, becoming a bird once again instead of the white puffball she had momentarily turned into

"I'm fine good wizard," the bird chirped

"I simply have encountered a bit of a ... problem,"

"A problem?" the wizard asked in concern

"Yes, you see the lords of the neighboring villages have torn down my home- the trees that were once part of the forest are gone and with them went the only home I've ever known, I was trying to escape from a much larger bird and didn't see your window here, why, I hadn't a clue that anyone even lived out here,"

"I have been here for many years little bird, but I don't make noise so I realize most people don't notice," he said with a small chuckle, frowning with sympathy when he realized that the little bird was now homeless

"I cannot go against someone else's wishes and grow trees that they've cut down, combat is not in my nature, but if you're looking for a place to stay you are more than welcome to stay here,"

The bird lit up, chirping excitedly and doing a little dance on the table

"Oh thank you! Do tell me kind wizard, what is your name?" she asked

"My name is Scott, and what is your name?"

"Ella," the bird replied

"Alright Ella, you are more than welcome to stay,"

And from that moment on, Ella never left

It soon became apparent to the little bird that she couldn't exactly help in the preparation of food that the wizard so loved

And with magic abundant there were very little things that Ella COULD do to help

Still, she felt she had to find a way to repay the wizard for his kindness

Thinking hard on it for a few days, Ella finally came to an idea

And the next day when the wizard began gardening, Ella began to sing

It was small at first, a few chirps, an average bird song

But when she noticed how much the kind wizard seemed to like her singing she began to sing more

Unknowingly, the sound of a bird singing with such joy began to attract other birds

And a few days after Ella's there came another bird, this one a robin, who had the same problem that Ella had- her home had been destroyed by the nearby humans

And so the wizard Scott, being the kind wizard that he is, invited the robin, Meryl, to stay

And when Meryl found out what Ella was doing, she decided to join in

And before long the wizard had two birds who delighted in singing along when he cooked

The songs of happy birds, however, continued to attract more birds

A cardinal was next, he had been Meryl's neighbor, and like the other birds, the wizard invited him to stay

After the cardinal came a finch

And then a dove

And a chickadee and a hummingbird

A sparrow and a woodpecker and mockingbird

And before very long at all the kind wizard, who had at first invited one bird to live in his shelter, had an entire chorus full of birds who sang every day in gratitude for his help and kindness

As wonderful as it was to have the company and as much as he delighted in the music he found that the birds were starting to take over the relatively small cottage

He noticed it shortly after the fifth robin came in but it wasn't until the arrival of the first raven that things really started getting out of hand

The birds, although singing together in harmony, were beginning to fight over the small space

And if there was one thing the wizard couldn't stand, it was fighting and discord

However, he couldn't just turn away or turn out any bird, he felt as an inhabitant of the forest it was in part his job to help look over the wildlife- such as the birds

So the wizard did the only thing that he could logically do:

He constructed a place just for the birds

He made a large row of trees, cutting off parts of his garden, to surround the cottage

And he even made a smaller cottage off near his so that if the birds preferred cottages to trees they could still be just as happy as the birds who preferred trees to cottages

"Scott," said Ella, as she noticed what he had done

"I don't see all of your garden... did you replace it with trees?" she asked with concern

The kind wizard nodded and smiled, humming to himself as he walked to the oven to check on the baking bread

"I did, the trees would better serve the birds than a third row of strawberries would serve me," he replied with a shrug

"But you love your garden," she insisted

"I do, but I love you and the other birds more, after all, you are the rightful owners of this forest, I am the guest, it's only fair anyway," he reasoned

Ella stared at him curiously before flying away, leaving Scott a bit confused but not very worried as he watched her go

And when he woke the next morning to begin his routine, he was surprised to find an entire gaggle of birds perched outside that weren't there before

"Ella, where did all of these birds come from?" he asked worriedly, fearing that the humans had destroyed yet another precious section of trees

"They're my friends from the forest, I asked them to come so that we could thank you properly for all that you've done," she explained

"There's no need to thank me," he insisted gently

"Of course there is, and there's only one way we birds can thank someone,"

At the realization, the kind wizard began to smile and all of the birds lined up outside of the window

And as if on cue, they began to sing

Faery Tales, Mermaid Myths, And Other Fantastical Legends

The Wonderful Magical Stevie

There are creatures who are not of this world

Creatures who possess nothing but kindness and joy and light in their very souls

Creatures who look at the humans from the highest of trees and beneath the smallest of stones

They fascinate themselves with human delights and find it curiouser and curiouser the more they observe us

They find themselves drawn to this world and all of the many strange things it holds

Their world is so vastly different and just as we would have an adventure exploring it, so they would have one exploring ours

These creatures vary from faeries to merfolk to trolls to witches to shapeshifters and everything else one can imagine

They find our world to be something of a mystery and enjoy watching the humans to try to unlock more and more clues

But, for the most part, that's all they do- they watch

They observe

They take their research down from a safe distance away not unlike how humans watch wild animals

And I suppose that all things considered we really must be like wild animals to creatures as light and lovely as the Fae Folk

But I digress

They watch

And sometimes they'll play a harmless prank to let us know they're here

Moving a necklace or dropping a penny

But most Fae Folk are far too afraid to integrate themselves fully into our society

And who can blame them?

Humans are very frightening, our society possibly even more so!

But there was one creature who was born in the land of the Fae who dared to do more than most

One who was brave enough and curious enough to take a chance

One who found herself so drawn to the curiosity that the human world had to offer that soon simply watching wasn't enough

She wanted to explore for herself, get to know things the others never would

This creature, a divine and darling Fae, possessed the name of Stevie

And although she left much of her faery self behind in order to blend in with the humans, such as her wings and her Pixie Dust, she did bring with her, her spirit- her very soul- and her appearance

Blonde curls and bright, otherworldly eyes brings with her the hint that she's not from the cruelty of this world

And her spirit is something else entirely

Even other Fae marveled at that

Soft spoken and energetic, sweet and gentle, the most peaceful soul to ever incarnate, no matter the land

She roams the world- our world- studying us silently and imparting her own wisdom on us whenever she can

She has encountered many problems along her journey and the Darkness has tried to claim her many times

But in the end no dark matter can touch such a purely light being

And so she continues on her journey

For Fae Folk, time moves so very differently

One day to them is probably a hundred years to us

So I wonder, having had the personal privilege to meet and befriend this brilliant soul, if she'll return to her own Realm when she's seen all she can see of this one, or if she'll choose to live out her life in the very human way that she has been for many years now

Although it doesn't much matter I suppose

Fae Folk have an uncanny knack to bond with people of all kinds and species

And Stevie is no exception

In only one meeting my life has been changed forever and no matter how many times she must flutter back to another realm or to further explore this one

No matter how many times I've waited for her return

The light she carries with her remains at the forefront of my mind until we meet again

Alexa Asagi Andres

The Yorkie Who Swallowed Pixie Dust

Once upon a time

In a land crossbred with our own

There lived two faeries-

But much, MUCH more importantly

There lived a Yorkie

Now for those who are unfamiliar, "Yorkie" is short for Yorkshire Terrier, which sounds like a very proper and distinguished name

And on any other dog it would be

Yorkies, however, are TERRIERS

And unbeknownst to most, "Terriers" are another word for "terrors"

Now obviously not all Terriers are this way

Not all YORKIES are this way

Just as not all flowers bloom in the spring

There are those few Yorkies out there who DON'T make their human companions question the meaning of life on an hourly basis

....

This Yorkie was not one of them

This Yorkie, in fact, was one of the spawns of Trouble Incarnate

In fact, this Yorkie, many have come to believe, was their LEADER

For this Yorkie was not just any plain ol' Yorkie

THIS Yorkie..... was the Yorkie that ate Pixie Dust....

Yes, the magical substance that allows for things like flying and baking cakes without so much as snapping your fingers...

This dog had EATEN it

Just swallowed several spoons of it like it was sugar

But let's start at the beginning

Because Once upon a time there were two faeries who were grieving

They were grieving the loss of a dearly beloved, and they sought comfort in bringing new life into the house

This new life, for reasons the universe is surely laughing at as we speak, came in the form of a long-tailed, long-legged, loud, destructive, taunting, toddler of a Yorkie

To be fair, the Yorkie looked like an angel in her pictures....

The faeries blamed that on camera quality

The faeries though, unknowing and a little desperate at the time, brought the Yorkie home with open arms and open wings

And for the first hour or so, the Yorkie, who they had named Isabo McKenzie, was the little angel they were expecting

And like Cinderella, once the hour was up, so was the glitz and glamour

Because this Yorkie, as cute as she was- and she was, mind you, EXTREMELY cute- had a penchant for chewing

..... And chewing.....

....And chewing.....

....And chewing.....

And chewing some more

And eating

And eating

And eating until the faeries felt sick just WATCHING her

And shredding and barking and running and destroying and doing everything in her power to make the faeries stare out the window and pray for swift death

But they were not going to give up

This dog- as .... troublesome.... as she was- was still the life they had chosen to bring into their home and she deserved only the best and every opportunity to have it

Over the course of a year Isabo gradually began to slow down

She shredded less and didn't bark quite as loudly and rarely destroyed anything, she still ate more in a day than a horse could in a week and she still chewed on a variety of her favorite things (one of the faeries mourned many stuffed animals who had been a victim of having their eyes plucked out and nearly swallowed....) but overall, more or less,

Isabo had started to become the angel the faeries had hoped for

Underneath the exterior of pure, unbridled mayhem on legs, there was a sweet, gentle soul who liked to cuddle and share food and play and be an overall good little dog

Slowly they started to deactivate the many precautions they had set up around the house to give Isabo more freedom

And most of the time she adhered to the rules that she had learned to live by....

.... There were still those few times however that mistakes were made......

For example, letting her downstairs without supervision for the first time may not have been the best move....

For while the faeries were preparing to leave for a few hours they had forgotten the Yorkie was down there

And in that time, she had managed to find her way into the pantry, drag the sack of extra Pixie Dust into the open, open it, stick her head in, and lick up a few spoonfuls

She decided it had a pretty terrible taste after the fourth or fifth lick and finally stopped, but it was too late, the damage was done

For within seconds the energy she was so well known for sky-rocketed

She could outrun a cheetah with ease at this point!

And so she decided to put her newfound speed to the test

Isabo ran around the house in circles, swooping and swishing in and out of rooms like it was her job, narrowly avoiding running into things, being nothing but a black and tan blur as she zoomed to and fro

And when the faeries went downstairs....

.... All they saw was a wrecked house and that black and tan blur going back and forth in circles

One faery was so devastated she fainted

The other just sat down, watched, and reevaluated her life choices

But, as it always did, after a few hours the Pixie Dust flushed out of the Yorkie's system, and the little dog, now down from her dusted high and exhausted from the exercise, lay in bed tiredly, staring at the TV as she tried to resist moving even a single paw

That's how tired she was, even raising a paw was too much for her

"Are you tired? I'm sure you are," one faery said as she came and placed a pillow beneath Isabo's head

The Yorkie whimpered, licking the faery's hand gently

"Yes I know you didn't mean to, have you learned your lesson?" she asked

Isabo stared up at her, sneezing suddenly as a gust of purple sparkly flakes fluttered around them

The faery stuck her hands in the air as an act of giving up and shook her head before reaching down and picking up the little dog

"You torture us you know," she pointed out

Isabo whimpered and nuzzled her cheek

"But we love you Isabo," the faery said softly, sitting down and kissing the little Yorkie before setting her back on the bed

As soon as she was down she wobbled over to the other faery, who was sitting in bed eating yogurt

Isabo sat next to her, stared holes through her, and began to beg

Because when all else is lost, when all hope is gone and life has thrown you for a loop....

There is always food

 Faery Tales, Mermaid Myths, And Other Fantastical Legends

The Zinnia Flowers

Once upon a time

In a land not all that different from this one

There lived two girls

The girls, Lizzie and Lila, were best friends

Better than best friends actually

They insisted that they were sisters

And they kept this friendship for two years, becoming so inseparably close that even hours apart felt like years

It was one day, one seemingly average day actually, however, when everything changed

Lila was in the garden with her mother, planting some more flowers for the beautiful weather of spring, when Lizzie came running towards her from her house across the street, sobbing and stumbling in a panic

"Lizzie? What's wrong?" Lila asked worriedly as she sprinted towards her friend

"We... we.... we're never gonna see each other again..." Lizzie sniffled horrendously, wrapping her arms around Lila tightly

"What? What do you mean?" Lila asked worriedly

"Mommy says we have to leave.... she said we're moving far, far away...."

And unfortunately, as much as Lila didn't want to believe that it was true, they did

On the morning that they were preparing to go she had to listen as Lizzie's mother explained that they didn't yet have a permanent address but that they would send her a letter once they did

"Here," Lila said suddenly, holding a flower out to her friend

Lizzie took it, a little confused, and twirled the pink flower in her fingers

"It's a Zinnia flower... Zinnias mean 'thinking of an absent friend', so ... I'll wear a Zinnia flower every single day until we meet again," she promised

Lizzie smiled at her, holding the flower close

"Then so will I, and when we meet again, we'll wear roses, roses mean all kinds of good things, happiness, friendship, cheerfulness," she mused

"Then it's settled, when we meet again, we'll wear roses,"

That was the last conversation the girls had for fifteen years

For fifteen years they never saw each other or heard from each other again

For fifteen years they had no idea if the other even still remembered them

But for fifteen years they held out hope

And for fifteen years, every single day, the girls both wore Zinnia flowers

Sometimes in their hair, sometimes pinned to their clothes, sometimes as jewelry

Their mothers grew weary of giving them real flowers after only a week and so switched, more often than not, to fake flowers

Fabric flowers or metal flowers or even little beaded flowers

But one thing was for certain, no matter what it was made of or how it had to be worn, they always were Zinnia flowers

It was brought up to them many, many times over the years that they should stop this "silly tradition"

That they shouldn't hold onto something that so clearly was a promise made long ago and that the other girl had likely forgotten by now

That they should both move on

But the girls never moved on

And one day

One fine day

One very, very special day

Lila heard a knock on her door and stopped what she was doing in the kitchen, heading out to open it

"Can I help you?" she asked innocently

"Lila Reyes?" replied a chipper blonde girl with a bright smile and.... a pink Zinnia flower in her hair....

"Lizzie?" she breathed

"Lizzie Thompson?" she asked quietly

"The very one," Lizzie said with a bright smile

Lila didn't wait for anything, the usually quiet girl leaped forward and pulled her long-time friend into the biggest, tightest hug she had ever given

And Lizzie hugged her back with just as much force

"I'm so sorry... I'm so sorry I never found you again... I've been looking for so many years Lila and I just couldn't find you... by the time we had a house in Miami it was already two years later and Mama said that you wouldn't.... probably wouldn't even remember me and that I shouldn't bother you.... I wanted to send that letter, I wanted to so badly... and ... oh just thank GOD your mama still lives in the same place! I had to go through so much trying to remember where you lived and-"

"Lizzie," Lila said immediately, finally pulling away

"It's ok, I promise its ok.... I... I didn't even look for you, I didn't know where to begin... but I never lost faith," she said with a gentle smile, showing Lizzie the silver Zinnia flower pendant around her neck

"I even thought about getting it tattooed but... I hoped we'd find each other and... we said we'd wear roses once we did,"

"And I have not forgotten that," Lizzie smiled, pulling back and handing Lila a beautiful pink rose

Lila smiled brightly, holding it to her heart and ushering her friend inside

"Come on, I think I have some roses in bloom out back,"

"You still garden?"

"Of course, in case you came back, I always knew how much you liked the flowers,"

"And my mama says I'M sentimental," Lizzie teased lightly

The girls spent so long talking that night that they didn't sleep

And within a week Lizzie had her things moved up from Miami and into the room next to Lila's

For the first time in fifteen years, the girls stopped wearing Zinnia flowers

It would have felt weird if they hadn't been replaced with roses

And a month later, they both went to a fine tattoo parlor on the other side of town and had a pair of beautiful red roses tattooed on their wrists

Never again were the girls apart

And never again did they ever wear Zinnia flowers

Lightning Source UK Ltd.
Milton Keynes UK
UKOW06f0152081215

264287UK00003B/54/P